CROW
HOLLOW

CROW HOLLOW

Dorothy Eden

Thorndike Press • Thorndike, Maine

Library of Congress Cataloging in Publication Data:

Eden, Dorothy, 1912-
  Crow hollow.

  1. Large type books. I. Title.
  [PR9639.3.E38C7   1983]   823   83-15924
  ISBN 0-89621-480-X (lg. print)

Large Print edition available through arrangement with Harold
Ober Associates, Inc.

Cover design by Holly Hughes

CROW HOLLOW

I

Cass was late that night. Lois made the salad and set the table, then walked restlessly about, unable to concentrate on anything, least of all her current short story. She stopped to look at herself in the mirror over the fireplace, staring with impersonal curiosity at her slightly hollow-cheeked face with its prominent temples and deep-set dreamy eyes, trying to see it as Rodney would have seen it. Her hair was dark, soft and straight, her whole appearance a little puritan. Cass had told her that, except, she had added when Lois was talking or laughing. "Then," she said, "people sit up and watch."

Rodney must have watched, too. How, otherwise, would he have told her that her face had stayed in his mind every moment since he had first seen her? (Oh, Cass, do come home quickly so I can talk to you!)

There was the sound of the elevator doors banging shut at last, and footsteps coming along the corridor. Cass came in dropping books and bundles. She was a schoolteacher and Lois knew from experience that she left a trail of exercise books in her wake wherever she went. Some day she would write a story about her, she thought. Then quickly came the queer reflection that she might not write any more stories. Writing stories was her profession, and the only way she had been able to earn money since her father had died. Why should she get this idea of giving up her profession because she had met the first man who had made an impression on her?

"My!" Cass sighed, flinging first her things and then herself onto the couch at the window. "What a day! But you wouldn't notice the heat up here. You want to try an East End schoolroom."

"I was in the park," Lois said. She smiled to herself. "I got picked up."

Cass looked at her idly.

"What's that to be so smug about?"

Lois put the bowl of carnations that Rodney had bought for her from a street seller on the table. She thought of the way Rodney had

8

looked at her. His face had been thin and bright and animated, yet for a moment it had had a vulnerable look. She guessed that look didn't show often. She herself wondered afterwards if she had imagined it.

"To be more explicit," she said, "I met him at Jan's party last night. We scarcely even talked, but I knew all the time he was there. You know how everyone else in the room can be practically nonexistent except one person. Apparently Rodney felt the same about me. He telephoned me this morning and we met in the park." She paused to reflect on the warm happiness that filled her. "I think I'm going to marry him," she said.

Then Cass did sit up.

"Marry him! You do believe in legitimizing your chance meetings!" Then she said, "You're pulling my leg."

"I hope not," Lois said. "I hope he asks me."

"How much do you know about him?"

"Practically nothing. But there's something about him — I think he reminds me a little of Daddy. I feel so completely happy with him. And safe."

"Safety isn't the dominating emotion one should have about one's future husband," Cass said dryly. "You could feel safe with the doorman downstairs. But you wouldn't necessarily

9

want to marry him."

Lois laughed. Cass was nothing if not prosaic.

"You think I'm making up fiction. Maybe I am. But I haven't invented Rodney. He's taking me to the ballet tonight."

"Well, find out some more about him," Cass advised. "Don't rush into marriage because you adored your father and haven't been happy since he died. A husband isn't a father."

"I know," Lois said meekly. She loved Cass with her plain face and downright speech. Cass was the person who had stood between her and utter loneliness since Daddy had died and she had come to London. She had said, "Don't put all your affections in one basket. Man is perishable goods, too," and Lois, knowing only too well the truth of that, had kept her emotions well under control, and had allowed no one to touch them. But no amount of advice could alter the kind of person you were. When she loved she loved impulsively and unreservedly. She had been able to live in that state of cool reserve only because she had met no one capable of drawing her out of it. Now she could feel warmth and excitement stirring.

At twelve o'clock that night Lois shook Cass by the shoulder. She stood there in the circle of

10

light from Cass's reading lamp and her face was brilliant with excitement.

"He has, Cass," she said urgently. "He has."

"Has what?" Cass grumbled. "Well, it's no more than you deserve, going out with strange men."

Lois shook her impatiently.

"Cass, don't be low! He's asked me to marry him."

Cass raised herself on an elbow.

"Who and what is this hasty young man?"

"His name's Rodney Armour. He's a doctor and he comes from a village called Finchin about ninety miles from town. He's taken over his grandfather's practice. He's an orphan, incidentally. His grandfather brought him up and educated him. The family place is called Crow Hollow. It's very old, and Rodney's the only successor on the male side. He has three aunts. . . ."

"What else?" Cass asked, for Lois had stopped, her eyes far-off. She had to give herself a little shake and pull her mind back.

"It's funny, Cass, every time I think of Crow Hollow I get a queer feeling. Rodney says one aunt is crazy about zoology. She has a laboratory in the garden where she keeps her specimens. And another is a sort of lady bountiful to the villagers. The third acts as housekeeper. Apparently Crow Hollow has been in the family for generations. The aunts take a great pride in it."

Again Lois paused.

"What on earth made them call it a name like that?" Cass asked.

"Oh yes, I asked Rodney that, too. Once the place was infested with crows. They built their nests in all the trees about. But they've moved away now, or died out, or something."

"I couldn't bear crows squawking all the time," Cass said.

"But they won't be. There aren't any there now." She began to shiver. "I got so cold. Rodney wanted to walk the streets all night talking." The warmth came back to her voice. "You've never asked me what I answered him, Cass."

"I haven't the remotest notion," Cass answered scathingly. "By the look on your face the wedding's tomorrow."

"No, on Thursday," Lois said happily. "I wondered if we could have it here. Rodney says his grandfather couldn't come because he's looking after the practice and his aunts practically never go away from home. And there's nobody I want especially, except you and Alec. Alec would come, wouldn't he?"

"If I tell him to. But he'll probably want to

know what's wrong with the regulation engagement."

"Nothing's wrong with it except that Rodney mightn't get the chance of another break for years. His grandfather's pretty old. And since we're both perfectly sure, we see no point in waiting."

"You are sure?" Cass said gruffly.

Lois's eyes were dreamy.

"You know how sometimes you see a dress in a window and you say, 'That's for me,' and you go and try it on and it looks wonderful and you always love it. That's a poor comparison, but in a way it's how I feel about Rodney. He's for me."

"All right, kid. I guess you're old enough to know. As long as this isn't romantic fiction invented by your fertile mind."

Lois remembered Rodney's lips against hers.

"It isn't fiction, Cass," she said definitely.

As she was getting into bed she said, "I have to call and see Mrs. Marcus tomorrow. She's Rodney's patient and a very old friend of the Armours. She had to come to town for an operation and wanted her own doctor with her. He told her about me this evening and she wants to see me. She's pretty ill. I believe this operation's going to be touch and go." She lay back on the pillows. "I hope she likes me. I want all Rodney's family and friends to like me."

"Why shouldn't they?"

"Oh, well, you read about new brides being usurpers and things like that."

"You see," Cass growled. "Half of this, at least, has its foundations in your confounded literary mind."

Mrs. Marcus was so shrunken that her head, deep in the pillows, made Lois think of a fossilized head, treasure of a Dyak headhunter. Her skin was like a wrinkled yellow leaf. Yet when she saw her visitor, vitality came back to her eyes and she subjected Lois to a long, searching stare.

"How do you do, my dear," she said in a thin old voice. "It was so kind of you to come to see me. I've known the Armours for so long that my curiosity about a new bride was too much for me."

"I'm sorry you're so ill," Lois said.

"Rodney's staying with me until after the operation. One's own doctor is so comforting. I've never had any other doctor but the Armours. First Rodney's grandfather, now Rodney."

"You mustn't make yourself tired," Lois said anxiously.

"Don't worry about that. I haven't talked for

three days. That nurse!" A gleam of mingled anger and humor showed in the old lady's eyes. "I asked Rodney to tell you to come alone so I could talk to you. I wanted to see what kind of girl Rodney had so suddenly decided to marry."

She stopped talking to subject Lois to another stare. Lois was uneasy under the direct gaze.

"Do you think I will do?" she asked nervously.

The old lady moved her hand on the coverlet. Lois understood it was an invitation to come nearer.

"Where did he find you, child?" Her voice was stronger now, and had an accustomed ring of authority. "Will you do? I should think you're exactly what he needs. Exactly. Poor Rodney. Love him a great deal, my dear."

"Why do you say 'poor Rodney'?" Lois asked clearly.

The old lady's eyes flickered. It was almost as if she regretted her outburst.

"Did I say that? He's an orphan, you understand. He's been very much alone."

"But he's had three aunts to look after him. He says they've all spoiled him."

"Yes, three of them," Mrs. Marcus muttered. "And that old house." Suddenly her eyes were fixed on Lois. Their brightness and fierceness gave Lois an odd shock.

"Don't let him take you to Crow Hollow! It's no good for either of you. It's —" Her voice faded. Rapidly all the vitality was leaving her face. Her breath came unevenly. Fascinated, Lois watched her frail hand curving and clenching. Then she came to her senses and hastened to ring the bell at the head of the bed.

In a moment the nurse had come from the adjoining room. She looked at Mrs. Marcus and said accusingly to Lois, "She's been talking too much. You weren't to let her talk."

Mrs. Marcus's dim eyes came back to Lois's face.

"That's how I know, you see," she said, as if she were finishing an explanation. Lois realized that in her own mind she had been making the explanation about Crow Hollow, but she wasn't aware her voice had failed.

She bent forward.

"Tell me how you know," she said urgently.

The nurse took her arm.

"You must leave now. I must call the doctor. Can't you see how ill she is?"

"But there's something important she has to tell me."

"She's beyond telling you at this minute. Go,

please. After the operation perhaps you can see her."

Firmly Lois was guided to the door. She waited in the hospital corridor a little while hoping to see Rodney, hoping to convince herself that Mrs. Marcus's words and her own queer feeling of aversion to that place called Crow Hollow had no connection. It was only the name that gave her the sensation of something sinister. And what Mrs. Marcus had said was a sick old woman's rambling. After the operation she would no doubt give Lois a simple explanation for her warning. Everything must be all right.

But in the night, before an operation could be performed, Mrs. Marcus died.

Rodney said Mrs. Marcus's death was to make no difference to the wedding. The chances of her recovery had been almost non-existent, and she herself would have been the first to wish him to go on with his plans.

Except about going to Crow Hollow, Lois thought. Why had Mrs. Marcus warned her not to go? Now she would never be told. It was something she had to find out from experience. Mixed with her unexplainable apprehension was now the curiosity of her naturally inquiring mind.

II

A telegram from Crow Hollow had come for Rodney. He had shown it to Lois. It read:

YOUR NEWS GREAT SURPRISE JUDITH AND HESTER JOIN WITH ME IN CONGRATULATIONS BRING LOIS TO CROW HOLLOW QUICKLY LOVE OPAL.

Bring Lois to Crow Hollow quickly. . . . Lois, forgetful that time was running short, lay in her bath thinking uneasily that it must be the name that gave her that vague repulsion. It conjured up visions of leafless trees black with crows, and the air strident with their cries. Crow Hollow was probably a charming old-world place, mellow and tranquil. Even if it

18

were not, the place mattered so little compared to being with Rodney. That was the essential thing. Crow Hollow and the aunts would be merely a background. Not that it wasn't probable the aunts were sweet, kindly old things whom she would love. *Bring Lois to Crow Hollow quickly. . . .*

Lois reached for the soap and lathered herself vigorously. She could see the pale, long and slender shape of her body in the water. Rodney was not overly tall. The top of her head reached his eyebrows. He said their heights were well matched. He had said that once when he was kissing her. He didn't have to stoop to do that. Perhaps that was one reason why kissing him was such a sweet thing.

Cass banged on the door.

"Hi! Have you gone to sleep in there? It's nearly two o'clock."

Lois started up guiltily.

"Quit dreaming!" Cass called. "The guests will be here before you've got your slip on."

Lois stood up and dried herself. Cass would marry Alec soon, she thought, so there was no need to worry about leaving her. Cass had been her best friend since Daddy had died, persuading her to come to London and making her stop brooding. She would miss her breeziness and her kindness and unflattering honesty. It

19

had been fun living in the apartment and she was glad she was being married from here. Cass had never thought there would be a wedding reception in the shabby living room with its stained floor, home-dyed rugs and comfortable old furniture. But now she had met Rodney she was cooperating wholeheartedly. She wouldn't have done that if she hadn't liked Rodney. She was too honest. It would have been sad if Cass hadn't liked him, but Lois knew it would have made no difference to her marrying him.

She came out of the bathroom into the bedroom and began putting on her clothes. Her suit, bought with the proceeds of her last successful story, had been her one extravagance. There had been no time to buy any of the usual trousseau things, linen or china or the dozen of everything such as her mother would have had when she got married. Rodney had said there was no need to buy anything. Crow Hollow had all the essential things. The linen cupboards were full; there was enough silver and Worcester plate to set the table for the whole village. After all, you couldn't have things both ways, a hurried, exciting wedding and a complete trousseau. She wouldn't mind eating off Worcester plate.

"Want any help?" Cass asked, poking her

head in at the door.

"Not help," Lois answered. "But if you're not too busy you might come and talk to me."

Cass came in readily. She was dressed for the ceremony, in a neat dark blue suit with gardenias. Alec had sent her the flowers, a thing he didn't often think to do, and she was glowing. Her plain face looked dignified and handsome. It was a good thing, Lois thought, that she was getting married and going away. Now Cass would feel no more responsibility for her and would be free to marry Alec.

"I think I've mixed enough of that cocktail," Cass said. "Though with Alec around one can't tell. Does Rodney drink?"

"We had champagne," Lois said. "It wasn't very good. It was all we could get. Yes, I think he likes a drink."

Cass stared at her thoughtfully.

"Isn't it funny marrying a man when you don't even know his likes and dislikes?"

"It doesn't seem to matter. Yes, I suppose it is funny. A week ago I didn't know Rodney existed. And now here I am marrying him. It must look as if I'm mad. But I'm not. At least, I don't think so."

Bring Lois to Crow Hollow quickly. . . . She stared out of the window, seeing the massed rooftops, black, gray, brown, faded red, dingy

21

and drab like the colors of city sparrows. There was no sun but low clouds and a humid atmosphere. A depressing day on any other day.

"It's my wedding day," she said aloud. "I wish Daddy could have been here. And Mother." Her mother had died when she was a child. She scarcely remembered her. The gap had been so well-filled by her father who had been a scientist, who had been dreamy, forgetful and unfailingly kind, whose cluttered house and timetable-less existence had been a perfect background for his imaginative daughter. But it would have been nice, she thought, to have had a mother on her wedding day, to have had someone as close as that to kiss her and say, "Well, darling, this is your day." But most of all she wanted Daddy, with his kindly eyes crinkling, his smile that showed all his love for her.

In the future there would be Rodney's smile. . . .

"Well, thank goodness," came Cass's voice behind her, "the place won't be cluttered up with sheets of manuscripts any longer."

Lois laughed.

"I hope that isn't what Rodney's aunts will say about me. But I may not do much writing. I may not want to. Your mind has to be empty — for intervals, anyway — to write. In any case, I'd never have set the Thames on fire."

Cass lit a cigarette and looked at Lois with her eyes narrowed against the smoke.

"The queer thing is I'll miss you."

"You'll marry Alec."

"We'll get around to it, maybe. I'd put some rouge on, if I were you. You're awfully pale."

"Yes, I will. I'm not nervous. Just in a dream."

She sat down at the dressing table and began to do her face. She could smell carnations, the ones Rodney had given her the day she had met him in the park. Now they were being married, and the first flowers Rodney had given her were not yet dead. It was as quick as that, quick and yet not quick, as if there had never been a time in her life when she had not known Rodney.

Cass went out. She came back in a minute with two tumblers.

"Brandy," she said, handing one to Lois. "Don't ask me where I got it. I'll get around to having the correct glasses for drinks one day. Drink up. To your marriage. As far as I can see, it's completely crazy. But good luck, anyway."

"Thanks, Cass." Lois sipped the drink. "Thank you for everything. You've been — well, I couldn't have done without you.

That's all I can say."

Cass leaned forward to give her a quick kiss.

"That's all right, child. I've enjoyed it, too. Remember where I live if the phalanx of aunts gets too much for you, or if you want some honest advice."

Bring Lois to Crow Hollow quickly. . . .

"Oh, Cass, I will."

Cass pressed her shoulder.

"That's all right, then."

There was a ring at the door.

"That'll be Rodney and Alec now. Hurry along and let's get this over, and all get back for a drink."

A registrar office wedding. Daddy would have said it was the people who were there, not the place, that mattered. After it was over the registrar, a little man with pince-nez, shook hands with her and Rodney, and then Cass came forward for the regulation kisses, and Lois got her hand lost in Alec's great friendly paw. Then, back at the apartment there were Cass's cocktails to be drunk and the cheese savouries, asparagus rolls and salted nuts to be eaten, and a lot of effervescent chatter to be made to cover the sad feeling of leaving the apartment and Cass.

Cass kissed her again when she was saying goodbye, and said, "Remember what I told you. Alec and I'll be here if you need us."

Rodney didn't hear that. He was taking Lois's luggage downstairs. No doubt he would have wondered why his wife nodded so fiercely. He didn't know what Mrs. Marcus had said, nor was he in the least aware of Lois's own inexplicable shrinking from the very sound of that name – Crow Hollow. . . .

But when they were alone at night in the hotel bedroom and she was taking off her shoes and he came over and kissed the back of her neck, everything became real. There was the bed with its covers drawn back, her suitcase open on the floor, her coat thrown over the back of a chair, and Rodney's hat carelessly on the dressing table. There was Rodney's bathrobe hanging behind the door, and the towel he had used pushed crookedly back on its rail. There was Rodney standing before her, his face thin and receptive. He had curving dark brows and when he spoke his eyes got bright and lively. His nose was long and his skin brown and smooth. With her his face had warmth and gaiety. It was familiar as if she had known it all her life. Familiar, and yet sometimes completely unfamiliar. She had noticed once during the afternoon when Cass had been talking to Alec and her that he had stood apart as if he had, for a moment, for-

25

gotten their existence. His face had had a tired and rather old look, as if he were much more than his twenty-eight years. It was then that she had a sudden frightened feeling that she didn't know him at all. It had only been for a moment. She knew that a person of his imagination and intelligence must have moods and withdrawals. She had them herself. But that unfamiliar side of Rodney seemed to be linked, in some strange way, with her unfounded and foolish apprehension about Crow Hollow.

There was nothing strange about Rodney now. His eyes were sparkling and he was saying, "That was a nice wedding you gave me, darling."

She smiled gratefully.

"Did you think so? I did. I feel a little tight, I think. Cass's drinks aren't all ginger ale."

"Tight, Mrs. Armour! Tut, tut! Then you'll sit right here while I do your unpacking."

She protested, laughing, but he insisted, and she had to sit on the stool at the dressing table while he knelt on the floor and took the necessary things out of her bag — slippers, hair brush, face powder and cream, her new quilted silk robe and the nightgown Cass had given her for a present, white chiffon with yards of material in the skirt. A frivolous thing that only a bride would be bothered with, Cass had said. She watched Rodney shaking it out. His face was turned from her. She could see only the taut line of his cheekbone.

And all at once an unwelcome irresistible tide of uncertainty about him flowed over her. Why did she feel like this now? She had never had any doubts before. She had talked things over with Cass and she had been utterly sure. It was just that with his face turned from her, with his hands on her intimate possessions, he had suddenly seemed to become a stranger.

"Rodney," she said, trying to keep the panic out of her voice, "you don't know any more about me than I know about you."

He didn't turn at once. He was carefully spreading the nightgown on the bed.

"I know all I need to know," he said levelly. Then he turned to face her. There was no lightness left in his eyes. They were guarded and withdrawn. "Are you sorry already?"

"Oh, Rodney, no!"

The very vehemence of her voice was an endeavor to reassure herself. It failed at the end and she was crying. She knew he was staring at her and that it must puzzle and hurt him acutely to see her cry. She made a supreme effort to stop.

"Rodney, I'm not sorry I married you. I'm just tired and excited."

He came towards her. She noticed he still had the nightgown in his hands. But he dropped it as his arms went around her. She had a swift memory of Mrs. Marcus's words, "You're exactly what he needs. Love him a great deal!"

"I'm so ashamed," she murmured. Then she forgot everything in the sweetness of his kiss. No matter how little he knew of her he loved her. Nothing, she told herself fiercely, would convince her otherwise.

But in the night, when she was still awake, he stirred and said, "Willow." He said it twice. His voice was heavy, dull, drugged with sleep. She couldn't tell whether it held longing or dislike. She didn't know who or what Willow was.

In the morning she meant to ask him, but by that time sleep had dulled her own memory and she thought she might have dreamed it. Besides, it was a wonderful day, with bright sunshine and the streets sparkling.

They were to go to Crow Hollow the next day. This was their one remaining day alone, and it had to be exploited to the full.

"We'll ride on buses," Rodney said. "I've never had time to spend a whole day riding on buses — certainly never with my wife. Do you like buses, darling?"

"When you ride on them voluntarily, and not just to get someplace."

She adored everything about that lovely lighthearted day until the very end, when Rodney said suddenly, "By Jove, I nearly forgot. I've got to buy a present for Willow."

"Willow?"

"She always expects one. You mustn't dare to return to Crow Hollow without something for Willow."

So she was a child, obviously. Only a child insisted on presents. Lois wondered idly how she came to be there. Curiously enough, she didn't want to ask questions now. Tomorrow Crow Hollow would occupy all her thoughts. But it mustn't intrude today. So Willow, the child who loved presents, must have no time allotted to her beyond the five minutes it took for Rodney to walk into a jeweler's shop and make a purchase. Lois waited outside the shop. She didn't ask him what he had bought.

III

There had been a fat squat stone lion on either gatepost, but one had been knocked off and lay half overgrown by grass and moss at the foot of the post, and the other had its nose chipped. The massive gates themselves stood quite twelve feet high and there was a stone wall of similar height all the way along the road.

"Your ancestors liked to feel the door was shut against burglars," Lois said.

All the way down in the train she had had to stop herself from a nervous habit of clenching and unclenching her hands. But when they had got out of the train, the brilliant day and the countryside with its heavy sweet summer smell had enchanted her. There was nothing sinister here, nothing, nothing.

30

Rodney had told the elderly and friendly taxi driver to drop them at the gates as he wanted Lois to walk up the drive.

"Right you are, doctor. Might I be adding my congratulations and welcoming your wife here?"

Lois saw the pride and pleasure in Rodney's eyes.

"Thanks a lot, Joe. This is Joe Higgins, Lois. You'll be able to make use of him when I have the car away."

"At your service, Mrs. Doctor," said Joe, touching his cap.

Lois smiled, too. How kind everyone was. The stationmaster had spoken to them; people had seen them coming through the village in the car and waved. Finchin was a charming place with its red brick buildings, its gray steepled church and old old spreading trees. For a village it was comparatively large and the surrounding countryside was thickly populated. Rodney had told her his practice kept him very busy. She might have to be prepared to see very little of him. That wouldn't be too bad if Crow Hollow were as charming as Finchin.

It must be, Lois told herself reassuringly, as they drove out of the village and down a winding road that dipped into a hollow. Her spirits were rising every minute. Her hands

31

now were relaxed in her lap.

Then, at the bottom of the hollow, there was that high gray wall with its outcrop of moss and ivy, and the massive gates and the broken stone lions.

And Rodney was saying, "We're here, darling. . . ."

As the taxi turned and drove away, and Rodney lifted the clanking bolt of the gate, Lois had one last breathless moment of panic.

"Rodney," she said. She tried to laugh as she spoke. "Why did Mrs. Marcus tell me not to come to Crow Hollow?"

"Mrs. Marcus! She told you that!" Rodney's eyes were plainly astonished. "What the devil did she mean?"

"I don't know. She — I suppose she was pretty ill."

"She must have been delirious," Rodney said shortly. Then, all at once, just as the stone wall around Crow Hollow seemed as if it would shut out the brightness of the countryside, the tightness of Rodney's jaw took all the careless happiness out of his face.

"Isn't it a bit late to be thinking of those things now?"

"Oh, Rodney!" Why was he so sensitive, so easily hurt? He seemed to have so little confidence in her love. The desire to reassure him made her forget her nervousness. "Wherever you go I have to go. Don't you know that? But I am a little scared. I can't help that. Supposing your aunts don't like me?"

The tightness of Rodney's face relaxed. He opened the gate and gave her a little push.

"If that's all that's worrying you, get along inside."

There was a short winding drive bordered with very high elms. At the end of it Lois could get a glimpse of a garden and a corner of the house. Excitement began to beat in her. The place looked as if, in spite of her fears, it might be charming.

"Crow Hollow used to be a farm," Rodney was saying. "All the ancestors were farmers. Then Finchin grew, and bits of ground here and there were sold as building sites. Later someone wanted to build a church and there had to be a lot of ground for a cemetery and the Armour then in possession liked lump sums of cash better than land. So he sold enough to successfully ruin the farm. After that no one could make a living here. That's why grandfather took up medicine."

"Where is —" she couldn't prevent her momentary hesitation, and then her substitution of what she had been going to say: "— the church?"

"A quarter of a mile behind the house. We have a private path to it. I'm afraid you'll be expected to follow it now and again. The aunts, particularly Aunt Opal, like to go to church."

"Is the cemetery still used?"

"Of course. People still get buried." Rodney looked at her quizzically. "Don't tell me that you, a writer, have qualms about cemeteries."

"No, of course I haven't." (Only, for a few moments, everything was lovely and bright, but now I think I know what it is that hangs over Crow Hollow. It's not because of the nearness of the cemetery. It's just intuition, premonition. It's probably an absurd fancy. But there it is. Death. . . .)

Lois clung to Rodney's hand. If only Cass were here to say, "It's your writer's imagination."

"You're nervous," Rodney said. The quick gentleness in his voice instantly made her feel better. Whatever happened, Rodney was here, her dear lover, the man she had known instantly was for her. But nothing worse than the aunts disapproving of her could possibly happen. And if they disapproved Rodney and she could live in the village. They could take one of those adorable whitewashed cottages and put in a bathroom. If Rodney would ever consent to leave Crow Hollow. . . .

"In a moment," Rodney was saying, "you'll see the house."

Then, all at once, he pulled her towards him, and said, "Welcome home, my darling."

Under the hoary branches of the elms that once had echoed to the harsh voices of crows he kissed her. She felt the passion in his lips, and the almost fierce tightness of his arms. She responded gladly – but again one corner of her mind was nagging. Why did Rodney do that now and here? It was as if it were their last private caress, as if, from now on, they made love under the eyes of the three spinster aunts.

It couldn't be true, but there was something in the way Rodney ran his fingers through his hair, tidying it, and said formally, "Come along, now. They'll be looking for us," that made her feel at this curve in the drive under the big elms they had lost their lovely private world.

Round the turn the first buildings were the stables. They were built of the same gray stone as the encircling wall, and there was a clock tower.

"The stables are empty except for Aunt Hester's white pony," Rodney said. "The odd-job boy sleeps in the loft. The clock still goes. You'll hear it striking."

A little further on there was a rhododendron bank, and when they came to the end of that there was a stretch of lawn edged with beds of flowers, and beyond that the house.

Inevitably, it too was built of stone. But the bleak gray outline had been softened by creepers, wisteria and ivy. It was quite unpretentious, two lines of long diamond-paned windows forming the lower and upper story, and a porch with gray stone pillars over which the wisteria climbed. Its very simplicity had charm. In the winter, Lois thought, with the wisteria dead and the elms leafless, it must look bitterly cold and bare. But on this bright afternoon, it had a cool inviting look. The wisteria gave it an air of frivolity, like a prim lady in gray with an unexpected frothing of lace at her throat.

"Well?" said Rodney. But there was nothing beyond expectancy in his voice. She could not detect any pride.

"I like it." She was so glad to be able to speak truthfully that her voice at least held plenty of warmth.

As she spoke the hall door opened and an odd little figure came out. She was very short in stature and she was dressed in khaki over-alls. Her large straw hat was tied under her chin with a piece of red checked gingham. She was hurrying across the lawn in the direction of a creeper-hung building with a dormed roof, which evidently was a summer house. She appeared to be quite unconscious of the presence of Lois and Rodney.

"Hi! Aunt Judith!" Rodney called.

The figure stopped, turned and stared. Just that. No welcoming movement towards them. Just that long stare.

"She's shortsighted," Rodney explained.

He took Lois's hand and they went towards Aunt Judith. Lois saw that she wore thick-lensed glasses behind which her eyes were prominent and milky blue. She smiled a large loose amiable smile, but Lois had an instinctive feeling that the amiability was automatic. She didn't think Aunt Judith really saw her. Those milky blue eyes had an unpleasantly blind appearance.

"Back again, Rodney," she said. Her voice was quick and high. "So you've brought her. What a surprise you gave us all. You should have had this holiday years ago, I said."

"Ah, but years ago would have been no use, Aunt Judith. London, this present month, was the best possible time."

Lois felt him press her hand.

"How do you do, Aunt Judith," she said.

"How do you do, my dear. I hope you'll be

very happy at Crow Hollow. Now, you must excuse me. I'm so excited. I've just got a new specimen."

"What's that?" Rodney asked.

"A red-black spider. Otherwise, known as the jockey spider. From Australia. Highly poisonous, its bite can be fatal, but it's such a beautiful creature. Black velvet, with that wonderful crimson stripe down its back."

"That's very interesting," said Rodney. "Lois will like to see your laboratory."

"Of course. Come any time. I'll show you my specimens." She hurried away, her hat flapping on the back of her head.

"You made a good impression," Rodney said.

"I? How? She was much more interested in her horrible spider."

Rodney laughed.

"You'll get used to her. She's a harmless old soul."

Harmless! And she kept poisonous spiders for pets! Lois's lips twitched with the first humorous thought she had had. How interested Cass would be in this. She would say what wonderful material it was for a writer.

Lois tucked her arm in Rodney's.

"I think I'm going to write a story about your Aunt Judith."

"Don't be too hasty, darling. Wait until you

meet Opal and Hester."

They went up the steps to the front door. Rodney opened the door and Lois stepped inside. The hall was lovely, lofty and well-proportioned, with dark paneling and a shallow staircase with carved banisters. A bowl of blue delphiniums stood on a table. The floor, with its mosaic-patterned rugs, was shining and spotless. There was nothing here that wasn't gracious and charming, yet, as Rodney shut the door behind them, Lois, for a brief moment, had the same feeling she had had when the big gates had closed after them. Walled in.

She spoke quickly.

"This is some hall for a farmhouse."

"It's the showpiece. The ancestor who built this place evidently believed in good first impressions."

Lois smoothed her hair.

"I hope the present Armours aren't too fanatical about that. Bring them on, Rodney."

"I can't understand where they are," said Rodney. He cupped his hands to his lips. "Aunt Opal! Aunt Hester!"

There was the quick clipping sound of feet on stone. A door at the bottom of the hall opened and another little person with white hair and flying apron strings came hurrying towards them.

"Rodney! You're here and I never heard you. There was no one to welcome you." She turned to Lois. "My dear, what could you have thought!"

"This is Lois, Aunt Opal."

Bring Lois to Crow Hollow quickly. . . . Lois felt her lips relaxing in a relieved smile. But what a morbid imagination she had. She would have to control it in future for it was entirely false. Aunt Opal with her bright eyes, her pink cheeks, her plump soft body in the starched print dress and apron, was charming. Lois willingly let herself be kissed and patted and then surveyed with curious but kindly interest.

"Rodney, she's lovely!" Aunt Opal clasped her little white plump hands and turned to Lois. "Of course, we expected Rodney to have good taste, but he's shown so little interest in women that we didn't quite know what his taste would be."

"It must have been a shock to you to hear he was married," Lois said.

"Not a shock, dear. Just a very large surprise. Knowing Rodney. . . . But there, you see, when he knows what he wants he just gets it as quickly as possible. I never knew such a boy for going straight at a thing."

She talked about him as if he were still a little boy, Lois thought. But she did it so

40

charmingly, and maybe it was good for him. Having no mother, Aunt Opal had mothered him, the dear sweet old thing.

"Now, Aunt Opal," Rodney said, "Lois knows the story of my childhood."

"She can't know everything, Rodney. But never mind, I'll be able to fill in the gaps when you're out. We'll have such a nice time. Now you'd like to see your room, Lois. I was in the dairy when Rodney called. We still make our own butter, you know, and Clara has to be watched. She never quite gets the knack. You bring the bags, Rodney. Come this way, dear."

Talking all the time, Aunt Opal led the way up the stairs.

"Hester's gone visiting with some of her soup. She should be back any time. She's quite famous for her soup, Lois. Perhaps Rodney has told you. She works out the ingredients and flavors herself. Quite wonderful, really. But you'll be sampling it yourself."

"Lois isn't going to be ill, Aunt Opal," Rodney remarked.

"No, dear, of course not. He means that Hester only makes her soup for sick people," Aunt Opal explained to Lois. "That's true, but I'm sure she'd be delighted to make some for you."

"What's this about Aunt Judith's new

41

spider?" Rodney asked.

Aunt Opal at the head of the stairs turned. Lois was unprepared for the distress and repulsion in her soft pink gentle face.

"Oh, those horrid spiders!" she exclaimed vehemently. "How I hate them. And now a poisonous one! It'll escape and bite us all in our beds, that's what I tell Judith. But I believe she'd like to be bitten. Honestly, Rodney. She's my own sister, but I don't understand her. I sometimes think she's a changeling." Abruptly she turned to Lois. "Do you like spiders?"

Lois saw the tolerant amusement in Rodney's eyes.

"They're not my favorite insect," she admitted. "But I know they're very interesting."

"Well, let me warn you, don't make any rash admissions like that to Judith, or she'll have you living down in her bughouse the way she does herself."

"Bughouse being polite for laboratory," Rodney explained.

Lois laughed. Aunt Opal relaxed too, and gave a resigned sigh.

"Well, there it is. We all have our peculiarities. But I can understand Hester's soup better than Judith's bugs."

"And what is your hobby, Miss Armour?" Lois asked.

"My dear, call me Aunt Opal like Rodney does. I am your aunt now, and so glad to be. So glad." Frequently, Lois noticed Aunt Opal's words ended with a little croon. It was fascinating. One wanted to go on listening.

"Why, my hobby is just Crow Hollow. Keeping the house beautiful. That's enough and to spare for one woman!" She touched the shining stair rail caressingly. (She loves it, Lois thought. The house is her obsession, but in a pleasant way. There's no harm in a woman loving a house. That would be why she had sent that message for Lois to come quickly. She wanted Rodney's wife to be in the house she loved.)

"You keep it beautifully," Lois said.

"With the little help I get," Aunt Opal sighed. "But here I am keeping you talking. Come this way. We've shifted you to the Chinese room, Rodney. There wasn't enough space in your old room for a double bed, and anyway the Chinese room is really the master bedroom. It's where our dear mother died," she crooned.

Lois felt Rodney's eyes on her.

"Quite forty years ago," he said. His eyes were bright and reassuring.

"It's as if it were yesterday," Aunt Opal sighed. She opened a door and led the way into a large high-ceilinged room with windows facing west.

The bed was a four-poster. That much Lois realized with mingled dismay, amusement and reluctant interest. It might be fun sleeping in a four-poster, even if, forty years ago, Rodney's grandmother had died on it. There was a faded but good carpet on the floor, the wardrobe and dressing table were massive pieces of furniture on the same scale as the bed, and the fireplace had fuel in it ready for the lighting. Pictures and ornaments were distinctly mid-Victorian, but the Chinese wallpaper was wonderful. Though cracked here and there and a little faded where the sun had caught it, it still glowed with the beauty of gilt dragons and red roofed pagodas. Lois gazed at it delightedly. It was typical of Crow Hollow, she thought, just as the glimpse of the garden had been on coming through those prisonlike gates, and Aunt Opal's kindness and welcome had been after Aunt Judith's oddness. Here and there you kept finding treasures. It was exciting and absorbing.

"You're admiring the wallpaper," Aunt Opal said. "Our dear mother had it hung. She had set her heart on it. It was dreadfully expensive, of course, and quite unsuitable for a farm-house. But there it was. Our dear mother wanted it, so it came." She smiled her wide ingenuous smile. "Father said there it would stay until it fell off. To justify the cost. But it has worn well, he has to admit that."

"Do you like it, darling?" Lois heard Rodney asking.

"The room? Oh, yes, of course." She didn't, really, apart from the wallpaper and the intriguing look of the four-poster. Otherwise the room seemed chilly and unlived in. She would infinitely have preferred Rodney's room, which would have about it the dear intimacy of Rodney himself. No doubt, with the fire lit and the shutters closed, this one would be cozy, too.

Aunt Opal clasped her hands with her individual ecstatic gesture.

"That's lovely dear. I'm so glad. Clara and I worked hard getting it ready. We loved to, for Rodney's wife."

"Thank you, you're so kind," Lois murmured.

"Now I'll leave you to freshen up. Bring her down to tea in a few minutes, Rodney."

There was the sound of a horse's hoofs coming down the drive.

"And there's Hester, too. I must hurry and make tea. She's always ready for it after delivering her soup. The fresh air gives her an appetite."

"Is grandfather down at the office?" Rodney asked.

"Yes. He said for you not to bother to go down this afternoon, although there were Abel Jackson's peculiar symptoms."

"What are they?"

"Really, Rodney, you know father never gives us clinical information."

"I'd better go down," said Rodney.

"Well, if you must be conscientious. We'll look after Lois. I'll show her the house. There's so much to tell her. Such an old place, such a lot of things happening under its roof."

With her crooning voice still going on, Aunt Opal left the room and Lois heard her pattering down the stairs.

"Must you go?" she said to Rodney.

"I ought to."

She went close to him.

"Are you a very conscientious doctor?"

"I try to be."

"More than you are a conscientious husband?"

"That's below the belt, darling."

Lois made a rueful face.

"It was an awfully short honeymoon."

He caught her close to him. His grip was so fierce it hurt her.

"Try to be happy here, Lois."

She was afraid to look at him, at first. She thought his eyes might have that guarded look again, as if he were hiding secrets he didn't want her to know. But when she raised her eyes she saw that his own were bright and intense. His thin face had a pleading look. She had never seen him like that before. Gay and impulsive; moody and withdrawn; tender; but never like this, like a boy begging to keep something precious to him, but knowing, all the same, that it would be taken from him.

Poor Rodney, Mrs. Marcus had said. Groping to understand, she said, "I'll always be happy where you are, Rodney. I know that." She ran her fingers through his hair. "What's the matter, darling? You act almost as if you're afraid of happiness."

The tenseness began to go out of his face.

"I still can't believe it," he said. "That's all. You remember the story about the children who found the gold and it turned to leaves."

"But I won't, Rodney. I hope I won't."

He kissed her. He was laughing.

"What would you like to be? A big square oak leaf? Or a rhododendron? Or a laurel?"

Would she ever understand him, and the reason for his moods? Better to ignore them at first. Maybe later, when she knew him better. . . . He was her husband, and she scarcely knew him at all.

"I'm frightened of that enormous bed," she said.

"I won't lose you."

"No, don't, please. Or I'll get scared of the ghosts. Your grandmother who wanted the Chinese wallpaper. What was she like?"

He had knelt to open the bags.

"I don't know. I never saw her."

"Of course you didn't if she died forty years ago. But didn't your father talk about her? What was your father like, Rodney? Did he take after any of his sisters?"

"I really don't know. I was too young."

"When he died, you mean. Of course. I shouldn't have asked you. Aunt Opal will tell me. By the time you come home for dinner I shall have the Armour history at my fingertips. Including that unnatural ancestor who wanted a cemetery at his back door. I suppose we ought to go down. There's still Aunt Hester to meet."

"Yes," Rodney agreed. "Come along."

Voices came from the room on the right of the hall. Rodney propelled Lois gently in and she saw a large tall woman move away from the tea-table and come towards her.

"Ah, the new bride!" came a hearty voice. "I'm Hester, as you've no doubt guessed. My, you don't carry much flesh on your bones."

Lois took the square strong hand offered her. She restrained a wince at the grip.

"How do you do, Aunt Hester." She looked into the weather-beaten face with the keen hard blue eyes and long beaky nose. Aunt Hester favored shapeless tweeds and a hair style that drew every hair tightly back from her face.

"How are my patients, Aunt Hester?" Rodney asked. "How many have you killed by persuading them to give up their diets?"

"Diets!" Aunt Hester snorted. "If instead of dieting them you'd give them a course of good meals you'd have no patients left. They'd all be cured. I don't hold with diets. Starvation! Nonsense! Feed 'em, I say. Don't you agree with me?"

Lois realized the stony blue eyes were looking at her. Heavens, she'd frighten any invalid!

"It would depend on the illness," she began tactfully.

"Exactly. That's what I say. You'll be able to do some parish work with me. I go in the pony cart, you know. Room for two. It does a great deal more good than fussing over dirty-minded insects or a house."

"Insects," came Aunt Judith's mild voice (Lois hadn't noticed her in the room), "are not dirty-minded. That's the last thing one could say about them."

"Ho! How about the female spider that consumes her husband if she gets half a chance."

"Not spiders, please!" protested Aunt Opal. "We've had quite enough of that subject with Judith's new specimen today. Lois, dear, your tea. Hester talks so much about the benefit of food, but she isn't giving us a chance to eat any. Rodney, drink up your tea and get away on your call. The moment we've finished this I'm going to show Lois the house."

It was inevitable, of course, that Aunt Opal talked during the entire tour of the house. Lois saw the big old-fashioned rooms to the accompaniment of Aunt Opal's gentle garrulous voice. All the bedrooms except one were on the top floor. Grandfather's faced east. It was the room to which he had moved after his wife's death so that the one with the Chinese wallpaper became the guest room. Its furniture was spartan, a single bed, a shabby leather chair at the window and a well-filled bookcase.

"Father will not keep his books downstairs," Aunt Opal complained. "He likes to read at night and he says he can't be traipsing over the house looking for a book. He sits at the window here. Sometimes he falls asleep, and there he is in the morning, never having gone to bed at all!"

Aunt Opal's own bedroom adjoined grandfather's. It, as Lois had expected, was purely mid-Victorian, crowded with furniture, old photographs, and china ornaments. The bedspread was tasseled, the curtains frilled, the pillows had crocheted slips, and the chair a lace antimacassar.

Aunt Opal's face was beaming with pride.

"So cozy, I think," she said. "So different from Hester's and Judith's. As sisters we're entirely different. It's quite remarkable."

It was true. Hester's room had the spartan simplicity of grandfather's and Judith's, which was little more than an attic with a sloping roof, had a row of jars containing peculiar-looking fungi on the windowsill. Her dressing table, beyond a brush and comb, was bare of all toilet requisites.

Rodney's old room Lois wanted to linger in, because by looking at his things she might have learned more about him. But when she showed interest Aunt Opal said, in a rather repressive voice, "You see, a double bed would have made this room very cramped. Besides, Rodney will be the master of Crow Hollow. He must have the best room."

"I'll shift his pictures," Lois said, looking at the three good etchings that still hung on the walls.

"They won't look anything on the Chinese wallpaper," Aunt Opal said firmly. Surely she wasn't afraid already that Lois would start rearranging the house. Just shifting three pictures wasn't going to make any vital change. She wouldn't dream of interfering otherwise. It wasn't her house. Or was it? Were these women afraid of being ousted?

"No, they wouldn't either," she said quickly.

"I thought we would leave this room exactly as it is. Because one day Rodney's son —"

Aunt Opal looked deliciously embarrassed. Lois laughed and gave her a quick caress.

"Of course, Aunt Opal. You're a little premature, but it's sweet of you."

Aunt Opal drew a deep breath, dismissing emotional subjects.

"Now for downstairs."

There was the drawing room overlooking the entrance and the garden, a large well-proportioned room ruined with too many rug cushions and ornaments, and the faint musty odor of old upholstery. What possibilities it had, if the dark patterned wallpaper were replaced by an ivory one, the fireplace stripped of its ornate carving, the heavy plush drapes removed. . . .

"It's very nice," said Lois politely. (Stifling, she thought.)

52

And the dining room, with its huge sideboard loaded with silver plate, its massive oak table set square in the middle of the room, its heavy window curtains that, as in the drawing room, shut out the light. Then the morning room, Aunt Opal's more particular retreat, Lois divined, by its be-tasseled appearance. And the library, a cold high dark room on the wrong side of the house.

A flagstoned floor led to the kitchen. This was a large old-fashioned room with the good cheer of willow-patterned plates and shining pewter. Aunt Opal introduced Clara, a silent rather dour looking person who apparently reserved her speech for more important occasions.

"She's still worrying over the butter," Aunt Opal observed as they went out. "She hates to be bested by anything. She's a very good cook, but she just hasn't a hand for butter. Do you care to see the dairy? No, we'll leave that today. You must be tired."

"I'm not tired," Lois answered. "What's that room, Aunt Opal?" She pointed to a door down the passage.

"Oh, that's the downstairs bathroom. Clara's room is next to it, and this —"

Aunt Opal seemed to hesitate a moment. Then, with her quick light movements, and with a curious look of pride on her face, she went and opened a door.

The room disclosed was a bedroom. It had a completely modern bedroom suite in light walnut. The bedspread and curtains were gaily patterned chintz, the carpet pale green. There was a chintz-covered stool in front of the dressing table. The dressing table itself held a variety of jars and bottles. Looking at them swiftly Lois saw they bore expensive makes of toilet preparations. There was a cut-glass bottle of perfume with a French name. The drape over the circular mirror was tied back with satin bows.

"What a lovely room," Lois cried. "Whose is it?"

"Willow's," said Aunt Opal softly.

"Willow!"

How could she have forgotten about that mysterious person whose name Rodney had spoken in his sleep, and for whom he had bought a gift. And Willow, she had decided, was a child. But the expensive face creams on the dressing table dismissed the child theory. Whoever Willow was, she had the best room in the whole house.

"Who is Willow?" she asked.

"Willow," said Aunt Opal in her caressing voice, "is my dear companion."

IV

Grandfather and Rodney arrived home just before dinner. Lois had had a bath in the spacious old-fashioned bathroom ("The sort of bath that would be ideal for a wife drowner," she meant to write to Cass), and put on another dress. When she heard the men's voices downstairs she sat a few minutes longer in front of the mirror, studying her face with its false composure. Did she look all right? But why should she be worrying? The aunts had seen her immediately after a long journey and had approved of her. So surely bathed, dressed and perfumed, grandfather could not find her objectionable.

What did Willow's French perfume smell like? she wondered idly. And who would have given it to her, since a companion's salary could not run to expensive perfumes.

"Lois," she heard Rodney calling.

She got up, went out of the room, and walked down the stairs with deliberate calm.

"Well," grandfather said with satisfaction, "she looks healthy, Rodney."

Rodney came to take her hand.

"This is grandfather, Lois."

The old man wore a pepper-and-salt tweed jacket and waistcoat. He had quantities of stiff white hair, and a small pointed white beard which was obviously his conceit. His skin was pink, like Aunt Opal's, and his eyes were bright, shrewd and piercing. His mouth had a slight twist. He could be cruel, Lois thought, if he didn't like you. But probably charming if he did.

"Rodney's wife at last," he said. "This is a great day. I've waited a long time for it, I might say."

"Father, have you washed?" came Aunt Opal's voice. "Dinner's almost ready."

Grandfather flung around. Lois saw the irritable flash in his eye.

"Can't you give me a minute to welcome my new granddaughter. Oh, go and serve the dinner. I'll wash in less time than it takes Clara to carry the joint from the kitchen. You see how it is," he said to Lois, and it now seemed to her that for her sake he was deliberately overlaying his irritability with good humor, "I'm henpecked. All these women in the house."

"And now you have another one."

"Ah, but you have a different role."

Lois looked at Rodney. Rodney said, "You'd better go and get your wash, grandfather."

"Yes. Blast 'em. Always henpecking." The old man shuffled off in the direction of the bathroom.

"Don't let grandfather worry you," Rodney said.

"Worry me? Why would he?"

"Oh, well. Old people get obsessions at times."

"Such as, Rodney?"

Rodney put his hands on her shoulders. His touch was not yet familiar enough to leave her unmoved.

"Miss me?"

She smiled.

"I saw the house and I had a bath in that private swimming pool upstairs, and I unpacked. Your things and mine. Yes, you dope, of course I missed you."

"Come along, you two lovebirds," Aunt Opal called playfully from the dining room.

"Dinner's ready."

There was thick pea soup, a hot joint in rich gravy, cabbage and potatoes, and junket with prunes. Clara took away the empty plates and brought the fresh courses, clattering on clumsy feet and never relaxing the dourness of her face. Rodney and Lois sat on one side of the table facing Aunt Judith and Aunt Hester, Aunt Opal was at one end and grandfather at the other. Lois, eating the heavy meal, had another period of panic. Did this have to happen every night? She was Rodney's wife, she should have planned his meal, they should be sitting at their own table with its flowers and china arranged by her.

"And what did Lois do in London?" Aunt Opal was inquiring. "We know so little about you, dear. We have such a great deal to catch up on."

Lois could feel the eyes of all the aunts on her, Hester's hard inquisitive stare, Judith's mild myopic one.

"I was a writer," she answered.

"Lois made a very good living from writing short stories," Rodney said.

"I wouldn't say very good," Lois demurred. "Adequate."

"But how interesting! How exciting!" Aunt Opal crooned.

"You'll be able to carry on with your stories down here," Aunt Hester boomed.

"So clever," murmured Aunt Judith.

Lois had a distinct feeling that they were all relieved to hear she had what they would term a hobby. It would keep her occupied and amused. She wouldn't be that difficult person, a new wife, wanting to take over the reins too quickly and thoroughly.

"Lois will have other things to do besides write," grandfather put in. "Things I hope she will count more important."

"Father, not now, please!" Aunt Opal implored. "Give him some more vegetables, Hester. Rodney, how did you find your patients?"

"Satisfactory," Rodney said. "Grandfather seems to have done a good job." Then he said suddenly, "Where's Willow?"

Was this the first time he had thought of her? Or had he been waiting to ask that question?

"It's her day off," Aunt Opal answered. "She was going to the pictures."

"Opal, you spoil the girl," grandfather declared, and now the irritability in his voice was unconcealed. "This is her second day off in a week. No wonder Clara's so cross, having no help again tonight."

"Clara's cross because of the butter," Aunt

Opal answered serenely. "Rodney, did you bring Willow a present?"

"And that's another thing," grandfather exclaimed. "This ridiculous nonsense of having to bring the girl something each time someone goes to London. As if she were a child!"

"She was a child when the habit started. You know how she is about presents. It's just impossible to break it off. She'd fret for days. Did you bring something, Rodney?"

Rodney was handing his plate to Clara.

"Yes," he said briefly.

"Ah! How thoughtful you always are, dear boy. Willow will be enchanted."

Had Rodney given Willow the French perfume and the face lotions with the famous names?

"Lois, you haven't nearly finished your vegetables," Aunt Opal exclaimed. "I can see we'll have to find you a country appetite. Won't we, father?"

"She's all right. She's a healthy girl."

"Writing stories, she wants good food." That was Aunt Hester's domineering voice.

"The spider has settled down nicely," said Aunt Judith unexpectedly, as if she hadn't heard a word of the previous conversation. "Tomorrow, Lois, you will come and see my specimens, won't you?"

The meal seemed to last hours. Taken singly the Armours were tolerable, but all together they had an overwhelming effect. Lois hadn't realized how tired she was or how little she wanted to eat. The drawing room, when at last they left the table, seemed like a haven. But there grandfather sat beside her, patted her hand with his dry cool one, and said, "Don't let all those women henpeck you, my dear. This is your home now and we want you to be happy here."

Crow Hollow her home. Up to now she had not been able to rid herself of the impression that she was just visiting. Sleeping in the spare room, being treated like a guest at dinner. . . .

"Thank you," she said politely.

"It's a happy day for me, anyway," grandfather went on. He lit his pipe and his eyes twinkled. He was a nice old man when he wasn't angry or fractious. He had probably been an autocrat in his day, but now he couldn't always get away with it so he suffered a lot from frustration. "Rodney's kept me waiting a damn long time. Plenty of nice girls around here, but he was so deuced selective. At one stage I thought I'd be in my grave before it happened. But I think I'll make the course now."

"But it has happened. Oh!" Abruptly and

very clearly she saw what he had been hinting at all the evening, with his remarks about her health, his glances holding that slightly unpleasant knowledgeable expression on her figure. "You mean," she said slowly, "that you want me to have a baby."

Aunt Opal had hinted at it delicately, but this was completely brazen. Of course she wanted a child, Rodney's child, but not to prove to Rodney's relations that she was a dutiful and satisfactory wife. It was true, she realized with a sense of panic, their private life was vanishing, or had already vanished.

"Make it a boy," grandfather said jovially. "There are too many damn women around here."

Rodney seemed to sleep soundly in the big four-poster but Lois, sunk deep in the billowy mattress, tried not to let her restlessness disturb Rodney. The bed was too soft and stifling, the whole atmosphere of the place was stifling. She felt weighed down with relatives, with curious eyes on her, with incessant voices telling her what was expected of her. If the Armours had been upset by the suddenness and unconventionality of Rodney's marriage their manners were too good to show it. But their good manners stopped short at that. They left no doubt as to what was her duty now. The voices nagged at her consciousness. Aunt Hester, "She hasn't much flesh on her bones. We must feed her up." Aunt Opal, "I thought we would leave this room as it is for Rodney's son." Grandfather, "Make it a boy. Too many damn women. Make it a boy."

It was light very early in the morning. Lois watched the window brightening and heard the country sounds, cows mooing as they were driven from the pasture (the animals, no doubt, who supplied the wherewithal for Aunt Opal's precious butter), a dog barking far away, roosters crowing and the constant background of the birds' twitter. Carefully, so as not to disturb Rodney, she got out of bed and went to the window.

A haze lay over the garden. The summer house with its domed roof looked shut and secret. Beyond the elms there were glimpses of green fields. Beyond them again the church lifted its gray spire against the pale sky.

Peaceful, Lois thought. One could not imagine anything upsetting this little world. No doubt the last event of any magnitude had been grandmother Armour's death. In this room, looking at her Chinese wallpaper. . . . Then Rodney's arrival. Had Rodney been born here? What had his father been? She knew so little. All that had seemed necessary was knowing Rodney as a man and loving him, not learning his past history.

The stable clock struck five. Rodney had said, with a note of affection for it, that she would hear it striking. Hear it! she thought ironically. It had kept her awake all night. To be a successful Armour no doubt you had to grow so fond of the clock that its chimes put you to sleep.

Yawning, Lois realized that she was getting sleepy. Perhaps she was going to be a successful Armour after all and love Crow Hollow. She would go back to bed, snuggle against Rodney's warm back and sleep. Tiptoeing across the floor, however, a sound in the passage arrested her. It was a sniffling sound, like someone stifling sobs. With the utmost caution she crept to the door and opened it a fraction. The weeping became louder then. It came from somewhere down the passage.

Then suddenly someone spoke.

"Hush, child! Hush!" Lois couldn't recognize the voice. It was cold and deliberate and it had a ruthless quality about it that was a little chilling. "It will be all right. I'll make it all right for you."

After that there were footsteps going downstairs and then the sounds ceased.

Puzzled, Lois closed the door and went back to bed. She had a vague idea that the weeper was the mysterious Willow. No doubt she had got into trouble about something and one of the aunts (the voice hadn't been recognizable, but it must have belonged to one of the aunts) was going to use her influence to put things right. The Misses Armour from Crow Hollow would carry a good deal of weight in the village. Willow was a shrewd girl to enlist that influence. Altogether, Lois reflected, Willow knew on which side her bread was buttered. It was going to be interesting meeting her. But the thought of Willow and her cleverness need not keep her awake now when at last she was ready to sleep.

When Lois woke again the stable clock was striking eight. The other half of the bed was empty and a note pinned to the pillow:

Darling: Had to go out on an urgent call. Willow will bring you your breakfast. Have a nice morning. Love, Rodney.

That, of course, was being a doctor's wife and what one necessarily expected. But Lois felt ridiculously disappointed that there was no one there to kiss her good morning. Her first morning in this strange charming place with its undercurrents which she only sensed — or imagined — and she had no husband to support her. She almost felt inclined to weep like that person earlier this morning had done. Or had she dreamed that? She wasn't even sure now that she had got out of bed at five o'clock and looked out at the misty garden. All her recollections were blurred by her subsequent heavy sleep.

A knock on the door roused her from her temporary gloom.

"Come in," she called.

The door opened and a girl, small and slender, came in carrying a tray. She wore the conventional cap and apron of a maid, and a yellow print dress. Her hair, a very pale honey color, was smooth and silky. She wore it parted in the middle, brushed demurely back from her ears and knotted on the nape of her neck. With her downcast eyes, her face also was demure in spite of her full red lips. She looked very young.

"Good morning," said Lois. Aunt Opal had not told her Willow was a maid. She had said she was a companion. In the category of companion surely she would not wear a cap and apron. But Rodney's note had said Willow would bring her breakfast, so who else could this be?

"You must be Willow."

The girl raised her eyelids. Lois experienced a distinct shock then. For her eyes as they caught the light had a curious amber tinge. It was the color of the golden willows in winter, Lois thought. Was that where she got her name? Her eyes were so strange and beautiful that they gave the girl a slightly inhuman look, as if she were feline.

"Yes," she said demurely. "Do you take sugar in your coffee?"

"No, thank you. I'm so glad to meet you, Willow. Rodney's told me about you." He hadn't really. He had let Lois think she was a child. And Aunt Opal had deceived her as to Willow's status in the house. Obviously she was a pet of the aunts. But what a strange creature for three maiden ladies to make a pet of. One would think they would have been more at ease with the dour Clara.

Willow's face had a curious vacancy.

"Has he?" she said without expression.

"Yes, indeed. He's even bought you a gift. Now I wonder where he put it?"

Willow fingered the gold chain around her neck.

"He's given it to me, miss."

"Oh," said Lois. "That looks pretty. Show me."

67

The girl bent forward, displaying the heart-shaped locket. A charming gift for a young girl, the type of girl who liked sentimental things. But was it the kind of thing to give a servant? And should the recipient be as offhand as Willow now was, as if it were her right.

"Very nice," Lois said calmly. She began to pour coffee into her cup. She was very new at being a wife. She mustn't criticize yet, or make decisions about things when she didn't know all the circumstances. "Did you enjoy the picture you saw last evening, Willow?"

"Yes, miss," said Willow in her passionless voice. Lois, with a degree of discomfort, saw the girl's peculiar eyes fixed on her, on her neck, her shoulders, her bosom.

"What is it, Willow? Do you like my nightgown?"

Willow's eyes lighted. Curious. When they were animated they were completely yellow.

"Oh, yes, it's beautiful."

"Do you like clothes?" (And French perfumes and face creams?)

"I love them."

Lois wanted to be friends with the girl. Whoever she was, she seemed to have a certain position in the house, and if even Rodney had to buy her a gold locket, it would be wise to be on the right side of her herself.

68

"You can have a look in the closet if you like. I didn't have time to do a lot of shopping. But the suit I was married in is there, and one or two other things."

Willow went to the closet. Lois noticed that all her movements were deliberate and graceful. She opened the door and began to handle the dresses. The suit with its delicate blue coloring that Lois had thought so beautifully simple and yet festive enough for a wedding she lifted out. Lois felt her clear bright gaze on her.

"Is that considered smart in London, miss?"

"Oh, yes, quite. It was made by a very good designer."

"Oh."

The flatness of Willow's tone told Lois that simplicity in clothes did not appeal to her. She had hoped for something showy and bizarre. But because it was judged smart she would, unwillingly, have to alter her standards.

"It's very nice, miss."

Lois laughed.

"One day, Willow, I'll go shopping and buy something you really approve of."

The encounter interested and intrigued Lois but did little to raise her spirits. Willow, she divined, would seldom give anything away. If she had really shed tears early that morning she

69

showed no sign of it now. She was going to remain an unknown quantity as far as Lois was concerned, for even Rodney, who could have done so, had volunteered no information at all.

The odd thing was that she should find the mystery of Willow so depressing to herself. Surely it should not cause her any concern at all. It must be that the house bred fancies, Lois told herself. She hadn't felt entirely normal since her arrival yesterday. There was a curious oppression that couldn't be completely due to a surfeit of Rodney's family. When she was up and dressed and had explored the grounds she would feel better.

Aunt Opal was in the morning room when Lois went down. She came quickly to the door with her welcoming smile.

"Good morning, dear! Did you have a good night? Rodney said not to disturb you. He was so sorry to have to rush off like that, but there you are, a doctor's wife. Willow just had time to give him a cup of coffee before he went."

Again Willow! Was the gold locket in payment for early morning cups of coffee?

"You all seem to get up very early here," Lois remarked innocently. "I'm sure I heard people moving at five o'clock."

"Dexter brings the cows in at five in the summer," Aunt Opal replied. "Sometimes he shouts a lot at them. I must remind him to be .more quiet."

"Willow brought me my breakfast," Lois remarked. She felt she had to tread delicately here. "As your companion that's hardly her job, is it?"

Aunt Opal gave her charming ingenuous smile.

"Ah, I'm afraid I wasn't quite honest with you there, dear. Willow does help with the housework. Father said it was nonsense that I with two sisters should require a companion. Willow was only allowed to come on condition that she helped with other work, too. But Hester and Judith and I like to give her a higher status than housemaid. For the sake of her own pride. You see, she comes of a good family. Poor child, going into service was very hard for her. We try to make her as happy as possible. You do understand, don't you?"

The pretty bedroom? thought Lois. The expensive toilet set, the cut glass perfume bottle? Suddenly a rush of affection for Aunt Opal with her anxious brows filled her. The dear kind innocent. Willow was the Armour sisters' charity. They were overwhelming her with kindness to make up to her for misfortune in which they were in no way responsible. They lavished pretty things on her and

71

encouraged each other to buy her gifts. They rightly judged that a girl of Willow's kind could most be made contented by possessions. What did it matter if Willow, aloof and unresponsive, felt no gratitude. The performance of this charity was its own reward.

"I understand that you're pampering the girl disgracefully," she said laughingly. She leaned forward and kissed Aunt Opal's smooth brow. "You're so sweet."

"Get away with you," said Aunt Opal. "Now what are you going to do this morning? Some of your writing? So clever of you! And when you want some diversion father's working in the garden. He does all the garden himself, you know. At his age, too, but he has a little idiosyncrasy about gardeners. He thinks they aren't to be trusted. And Judith expects you to visit her in her laboratory. She's working on her moth collection this morning."

"I'll go and see her now," Lois decided.

Grandfather, she perceived, was over the phlox bed. He had his back to her, and with a slight guilty feeling she slipped across the lawn unnoticed by him. Just at this moment she felt she couldn't bear his probing eyes on her, calculating whether, after three days of marriage, she could be pregnant.

She knocked at the rickety door of the

72

summer house, and distantly Aunt Judith's voice called, "Come in."

She opened the door and stepped inside. Light filtering through the creeper-hung windows was green and flickering, like sunlight through water. At a trestle table working over a slide of moths Aunt Judith's figure looked even more quaint and improbable than it had done yesterday. She raised her myopic eyes and looked at Lois.

"You've come to see my specimens," she said. "Just take a look around. They mean very little to the uninformed. Hester and Opal think they should all be destroyed. But I can assure you some of them are quite rare and valuable. I had an article about moths in this part of the country published a few weeks ago."

"How interesting, Aunt Judith! I confess insects do give me goose-flesh, but I realize they must be an absorbing study." She looked at the rows of glass jars neatly arranged on shelves around the circular walls. Some of the jars were filled with liquid and unpleasantly dead bodies floated in the liquid. Others had moving creatures in them. She was reminded a little of the boy who caught tadpoles and tried to keep them alive. Aunt Judith's arrangements were similar, but far more knowledgeable.

"This is an elephant hawk moth," she said in

her absent voice, holding up the moth on a pin. "Dexter caught it for me. He catches a great many of my specimens. I give him a penny or twopence or even threepence if the specimen is a particularly good one."

"How much was that one worth?" Lois asked fascinatedly.

"Threepence. It's not seen much in these parts. Are you going to like Crow Hollow?"

The unexpectedness of the question left her with no time for tact.

"Why, I — I hope so. I think the house is charming."

Aunt Judith's eyes were so vague she couldn't be concentrating on their conversation. She was much more interested in securing the moth on its pin.

"And the inhabitants?"

"I could ask you," Lois burst out (she sounded like Cass then, with Cass's devastating directness), "if you like me."

"Why, of course," Aunt Judith replied amiably. "Before you came, you know, we had a discussion as to whether you would be better looking than Willow."

"Well?" Lois asked rather breathlessly.

"You've met Willow?"

Lois nodded. Apparently the question answered itself.

"Seeing so few young people," Aunt Judith murmured, "we've perhaps made Willow's appearance our standard."

"She is quite remarkably beautiful," Lois admitted. "But she's —" She bit her tongue. It was absurd, but apparently no one here thought of Willow as a servant at all. She was a beautiful girl who did them the privilege of living at Crow Hollow.

"Opal spoils her," Aunt Judith remarked. She behaved as if she hadn't noticed that bitten off remark of Lois's.

"Don't we all?" Lois wanted to say. "Didn't I, after having known her only a few moments, let her handle my clothes this morning?"

Suddenly the subject of Willow was definitely distasteful to her.

"What about the famous spider, Aunt Judith? Aren't I going to be allowed to look at it?"

Aunt Judith's face lit up with distinct pride and pleasure. She looked as smug as if she personally were responsible for the creation of the horrible insect.

"Of course. I didn't know that you'd be interested. It's here. It's come a very long journey. A naturalist correspondent of mine in Australia sent it to me. He didn't know whether it would survive the trip, but spiders are amazing creatures. Practically indestructible."

She pattered across the floor and came back with a roomy glass-topped box. Lois looked inside at the spider. A shiver went over her. She hated spiders at all times, but this one, with its long legs, its black velvety body ornamented with a brilliant crimson stripe, seemed particularly evil.

"You don't like it," said Aunt Judith in her flat voice, her prominent eyes on Lois.

Lois shook her head.

"I just don't like any spiders."

Aunt Judith regarded her thoughtfully. It was impossible to tell whether her myopic eyes held malice or amusement, or any emotion at all. Without another word she replaced the box.

"I must go and talk to grandfather," Lois said. Now the old man in the phlox bed was not to be avoided, but to be sought willingly. "Thank you for letting me see your laboratory."

"Father's in the garden," said Aunt Judith placidly.

It was only when she had closed the door of the summer house behind her that Lois felt she could breathe again. She hoped she hadn't hurt Aunt Judith's feelings by showing too much repugnance, but that evil-looking spider had

76

positively made her flesh crawl. If being nice to Rodney's aunts meant taking an intelligent interest in their hobbies, she could only be glad that Opal and Hester had more simple hobbies.

The relief of being outside was so great that she was able to call, "Good morning, grandfather," with real gaiety.

The old man straightened himself and turned, beaming.

"Ah, the bride at last! Did you sleep well? Did they give you a good breakfast?"

"Yes, thank you, grandfather."

"And what are you planning to do this morning?"

Lois laughed.

"Well, I suppose I'm waiting for Rodney to come home."

"Don't do that, my dear. You can expect him when you see him. He's taken on a real job. Night and day. I know, because I did it myself for forty years."

"You mean Rodney may not be home for lunch."

"He'll have a snack in his office, more than likely. Don't worry. Nurse Baxter sees he doesn't starve."

"But —"

"You're a doctor's wife, now. You've got to expect this sort of thing."

(But most doctors' wives have their own homes to look after while their husbands are away. They haven't three maiden aunts, an exotic servant, and nothing whatever to do.)

"But what am I going to do all day?"

"You could persuade Opal to let you do the flowers," grandfather said vaguely. "And you have your own work. A story about being the wife of a hard-working doctor, eh? Later, of course —"

Yes, later I'll have a baby! Lois thought resentfully.

"Lois! Lois!" That was Aunt Hester's strident voice from the front porch. "Like to come to the village with me? I'm delivering some soup."

"Yes, thank you, I will," Lois called in relief. At least that would be something to do to pass the long hours until Rodney's return.

She turned to see grandfather regarding her with his uncomfortably sharp eyes.

"Don't let the three of them bully you. They will if they can."

"But why should they?"

"They weren't so pleased about Rodney marrying a stranger."

Lois had a peculiar feeling of uneasiness to know that what she had sensed was true.

"Who would they have liked him to marry?"

"Well —" the old man had picked up his hoe and was busy again. "Someone from these parts, I expect. As if it matters where a girl comes from so long as she's a nice girl. I like you, my dear. You come to me if you have any trouble."

Aunt Hester, wearing the shabby tweeds she had had on yesterday and a pair of brogues on her large feet, came across the lawn. She had Lois's coat over her arm.

"Just slip this on," she said. "We aren't going far. There's no need to dress. Dexter's bringing Jewel around, and she doesn't like being kept standing."

Lois put the coat on and accompanied Aunt Hester to the front door where the pony cart was waiting. What trouble would she have about which she had to go to grandfather? she was pondering. So far the aunts hadn't shown any tendency to bully her. They had been very kind. Except, perhaps, Aunt Judith, with her evil spider and her sly sideways glances. Anyway, she could defend herself. As Rodney's wife she surely had sufficient prestige.

"I thought you'd like to get away for a while," Aunt Hester was saying. "We're a bit overwhelming all at once, aren't we?"

"You are all very kind," Lois answered. "Who are you taking your soup to today?"

"To old Mrs. Meacham. Widow of the late postman. A dear old soul and with such a sense of gratitude. She's got stomach ulcers. And do you know," Aunt Hester went on, fixing an intense and somewhat fanatical eye on Lois, "when she was at her worst and could take no other sustenance at all, my soup saved her life. It's true. Even Rodney has to admit it. She could digest nothing else."

"So of course she must be grateful," Lois murmured.

Lois enjoyed driving through the village behind Jewel's broad back, stopping at the picturesque cottage where Mrs. Meacham lived and holding the reins while Aunt Hester went inside. On the way back however, Aunt Hester remembered another call she wanted to make.

"Then drop me at Crow Hollow," Lois suggested. "I'd like to come, but Rodney may be home by now."

"And won't he keep for an hour?" Aunt Hester snorted scornfully.

But she dropped Lois at the big gates and so it happened that Lois walked up the curving drive past the rhododendron bank and into the house. No one seemed to be about. Not having heard the pony cart they wouldn't know she had returned. She was disproportionately glad about that. She would go to her room and write a long letter to Cass.

She was already composing it in her head.

"You couldn't believe what goes on here. The three sisters outdo one another in spoiling their maid, Willow, who looks like a *femme fatale.* Rodney and I sleep in a four-poster, and grandfather has offered me his protection should I need it. It is nice to have an ally, but why do I need one? What is likely to happen to me? Am I going to meet a violent death? No, Cass, that isn't all my writer's imagination. Some of it is true, including Aunt Judith's poisonous spider. . . ."

How Cass would laugh when she read that. She would be writing that she was coming down on the next train. How wonderful it would be to have Cass here. She, an outsider, and not bearing the prejudiced position of a new bride, would be able to sum up the situation.

Smiling a little at the thought of Cass's downright speech clashing with Aunt Hester's, Lois opened the door of her room.

And saw Willow sitting in front of the mirror preening herself in Lois's new suit!

V

The infuriating thing was that Willow did not look at all abashed. There she was in the suit which Lois had so happily worn to her wedding, and which she knew instinctively she would now never wear again, and her face had a vacant look as if she did not realize her offense. Her vacancy, Lois surmised, was cleverly assumed to meet any difficult situation.

"Take it off," she heard herself saying, her voice more controlled than she would have thought possible.

With deliberation Willow unbuttoned the jacket and removed it. Her naked arms and shoulders were milky white. The girl was a beauty. In an evening gown she would look superb. But there was something about her that both repulsed and frightened Lois.

Lois waited until Willow had taken off the skirt, too, and put on her own yellow print frock. Then she said, "Aren't you going to apologize?"

"I'm sorry," Willow answered with perfect composure. "But you said I could look at your things."

"I didn't say you could try them on. And you know that very well. You didn't hear the pony cart returning so you thought I was still safely away."

Willow's long eyes slid towards the discarded suit. They held neither shame nor embarrassment, but perplexity.

"You're telling me the truth, miss, when you say that thing is considered smart? It seems kind of plain to me."

Lois drew an exasperated breath. Was the girl unaware of how she had offended? Then she must really be simple.

"I shall have to tell Miss Armour about this, Willow. Otherwise how can I trust you any more?"

Willow regarded her blankly. She seemed already to know that Lois wouldn't tell, and that even if she did her telling would have no effect.

Lois pressed her hand to her brow.

"Oh, go and leave me!"

Willow smiled. Her smile was entirely without malice.

"Yes, miss," she said obediently.

The humorous gay letter to Cass was now out of the question. Lois could no longer look at things with either humor or philosophy. No doubt she would recover. The sight of Willow wasn't always going to make her burn with anger and indignation. By tomorrow she might even find the episode pathetic. The beautiful country girl eating her heart out for stylish clothes. But now her feelings were too bitter even for tears.

She couldn't tell any of the aunts. Not one of them, she suspected, even sweet Aunt Opal, would take her side against Willow. It was utterly ridiculous, but the fact remained that at present, anyway, a servant counted more at Crow Hollow than its mistress presumptive.

Lost in thought Lois sat at the window. A knock at the door startled her. Was this Willow back again? She hesitated before answering.

"Aren't I allowed in?" came Rodney's voice.

Lois sprang up.

"Oh, darling, of course. I didn't know it was you."

He came in smiling, and instantly her tottering world steadied.

"I was out with Aunt Hester," she said. "I insisted on her dropping me before she went on somewhere else in case you were home. She said 'Nonsense! You won't see him till dinner!' But I knew better."

She was conscious that she was talking quickly to hide her agitation. She didn't want him to know how much Willow's behavior had upset her.

Rodney kissed her. She could feel his hands firm against her back. She stood quite still, wanting him to go on holding her like that.

"Sorry I couldn't say good morning to you," he said. "But these things happen in the life of a doctor. I'm afraid this case is going to use up some time for the next few days. I think it may be infantile paralysis."

"Oh, Rodney! That's bad. Who is it?"

"Johnnie Lumsden. Son of the railway porter. I've had him shifted to the Finchin County Hospital. The damn thing is I don't know enough about this disease."

"You're particularly interested in it?"

He nodded. His eyes were somber, the lines in his face deepened. It was one of the moments when he looked a good deal older than his age.

"I always have been."

Lois pondered. "Then shouldn't you be

doing something about it? I mean — a country practice is hardly the thing."

Rodney let his hands drop to his sides. For a moment it seemed as if he were going to make some eager observation. Then he said with what seemed to Lois deliberate vagueness, "Maybe I will some day."

He felt in his pocket for cigarettes, handed Lois one and struck a match.

"But, Rodney, some day is no good. If you don't start now —"

"Haven't you often said some day you'll write a book?"

"Yes, I have, but —"

"And you've never started it yet?"

"No."

He held the lighted match to her cigarette.

"Then leave me my dream, too."

He flicked the dead match into the fireplace and said in a different voice (if only he wouldn't use that shutting-out voice too often!), "And what have you been doing besides gadding about the countryside in a pony cart? Did Willow bring you your breakfast like I told her to? Tell me, what do you think of Willow?"

Lois hesitated. Indignation was again making her cheeks burn.

"She's very good-looking," she said slowly.

"Much too good-looking. But I completely fail to understand her."

"How's that?"

"Well, I came in just now – mind you, I admit I had given her permission to look at my clothes this morning – and found her sitting in front of the mirror with this on!" She indicated the suit lying on the bed.

"Your suit?" said Rodney. His mildness angered her. Did he think the incident wasn't worth mentioning?

"Of course it's my suit. I married you in it."

"Oh, darling, that's too bad. I hope you told her off."

"Look, Rodney, if I had she'd have taken absolutely no notice. I could tell that well enough. Her attitude wasn't exactly insolent, but it was vague, simple almost. How often does she get away with things by pretending to be simple?"

"I wouldn't know," Rodney said. There was a tolerant look in his eyes. "I should think, with the aunts, she'd find it pretty easy. But I'm not so sure that simple air is put on. She's not much more than a child, really."

"She's not to be allowed to get away with it," Lois insisted. She was growing more vehement as Rodney's tolerance increased. The incident wasn't trivial. It was a serious offense. In any other house the maid would have been dismissed instantly. "I shall have to tell Aunt Opal."

"Really, darling, I shouldn't do that. Willow wouldn't appreciate it."

"*Willow!*"

"Well, you know how difficult it is to get maids. If Willow left, the aunts would consider it an absolute catastrophe."

"So she's to be allowed to pop in and out of my things as she pleases!"

"Now, listen, sweet, I didn't mean that. You'll find as you get to know her that she has a very simple direct mind. She's been pampered here, I grant you, and is used to getting most things she wants. It's an unusual position, but the aunts like it, and if they want to behave like good socialists, then that's their business. Willow's as inquisitive as the devil and she loves pretty things, but she's honest. She wouldn't think she was offending; she wouldn't have meant any harm at all. Look at it that way."

Lois searched his face.

"So you're on her side, too."

"What the devil do you mean by being on any side?"

He was impatient with her. She didn't care. She was angry and bitterly disappointed.

Rodney's anxiety to protect Willow couldn't all be because maids were hard to get.

"It doesn't matter," she said distantly. She picked up the suit, replaced it on its hanger and hung it in the closet. Willow might as well have it now, except that Lois wouldn't give her the satisfaction of receiving it. Repaying insolences with gifts!

"It does matter," said Rodney. "There aren't sides in this house. We aren't an armed camp."

It was terrible. She shouldn't be quarreling with Rodney so soon. But she couldn't be meek at will. There were a lot of things Rodney didn't know about her, as well as the ones she didn't know about him. He would have to learn them, and if he didn't like them he would have to put up with the consequences.

"I'm afraid there will be," she said coldly, "so long as you're all so besotted about Willow's perfections."

VI

Lunch as far as Lois was concerned was a ghastly meal. Rodney and grandfather talked shop all the time, Aunt Opal kept up her running flow of chatter with occasional monosyllabic comments from Hester and Judith, and Willow with light deft movements, and with bland indifference on her lovely face, waited on the table. Immediately after lunch Rodney went away again. He said he had no idea what time he would be home and no one was to wait up for him. So there was an interminable afternoon and evening to be spent brooding over that silly quarrel which seemed so justified on her side and so unjustified on his.

Lois had no intention of letting the vexed question of Willow's liberties drop. She would have the thing out with Rodney once and for all when he came home.

But it was eleven o'clock and she was fighting tears in the big four-poster when he came home. She was so glad to see him that she pushed the thought of Willow right out of her mind.

"How's Johnnie?" she asked.

"Pretty bad."

"Oh, Rodney, I'm so sorry."

He sat on the edge of the bed and his face outside the circle of light from the bedside lamp looked gaunt with weariness.

"I didn't wait up for you," she said. "Everyone else had gone to bed and it was so lonely downstairs I think I was frightened of all your ancestors. I could hear them scraping their boots outside as they came in off the farm." If she talked like this she might be able to take the shadows off his face. "But I did make your coffee, darling, and I brought it up here in a thermos. It'll be piping hot, so drink it straight away."

He roused himself then.

"Are you going to be the perfect wife?"

"Nothing so horrible!" (Don't you remember, we quarreled at lunch time? You expected me to be meek and I wasn't.) It almost seemed as if he had forgotten. Could what caused her so much pain mean nothing to him?

She leaned over to the bedside table.

"I brought two cups. I'm going to join you in this. Will you be likely to be called early in the morning?"

Rodney was beginning to undress.

"I've asked the sister at the hospital to phone me if there's any change. Apart from that I may get another call."

"Then you must wake me," Lois said decisively, "so I can give you your coffee." She poured the two cups full. "That's a wife's duty, you know. You mustn't deprive me of it." That was true, quite apart from the fact that if she didn't make the coffee it would be made by the ravishing enigmatic Willow – perhaps not so enigmatic down in the kitchen in the early morning.

"Let's pray I won't be called," Rodney said wearily. He buttoned his pajamas and climbed into bed.

Lois handed him his cup. In the warm bed, bounded by the circle of light, she suddenly had a childlike faith that everything else was shut out permanently. There were just the two of them, snug and content, ringed by the enchanted light.

"It is true, isn't it?" she whispered. "Us here together."

"I think so," Rodney answered carefully. "I'm half asleep and I'm scared to wake up too much in case it isn't."

"Rodney — if we had our own house —"

Rodney blinked. He drank the remainder of the coffee and handed the empty cup to Lois.

"What did you say, darling?"

"If it could be like this all the time, no one else inquisitively trying to share our lives, making us have misunderstandings. We did quarrel, Rodney, and we still haven't gotten to the bottom of that."

"You mean about Willow," Rodney said sleepily. "Forget it. Willow's a good girl. Doesn't mean any harm."

"Apart from Willow," Lois said carefully, "there are other things. There's nothing for me to do here. I can't play being a lady all the time. I'm in the way — " She stopped. She looked at Rodney. He was sound asleep.

Sighing, she switched the light out. She should have waited for a more opportune time to speak of that idea, a house in the village, anywhere, so long as it was their own home. Where she looked after Rodney herself, where no one pried on them. . . . Dreaming of that enchanting prospect, Lois drifted off into sleep.

When she woke in the morning Rodney's

side of the bed was vacant again. This time there was no note on the pillow. And he hadn't awakened her as she had asked him to. He had completely ignored her request. Was he conspiring with the rest to make her lead a completely useless existence? Or did he think she was usurping Willow! It was clear now that Willow had won that first encounter.

The boy, Johnnie Lumsden, died and within a fortnight there were three more cases of paralysis.

Looking back on that fortnight Lois occasionally marveled as to how she had lived through it. She saw Rodney on an average of once a day, sometimes not that. Frequently he slept down at the hospital if he slept at all. Sometimes she was aware of him crawling in beside her in the early hours of the morning and falling asleep before she could speak to him. Once he was even there when she awoke in the morning and she said unbelievingly, "Are you real? Don't speak too quickly in case I collapse from shock!"

None of the new cases was fatal. Two faced certain but not extensive paralysis, one escaped crippling altogether. There were no more cases. This was largely due to the rigid precautions Rodney had insisted on being taken. He had won this skirmish with the minimum of casualties, but it had left him thin, worn, and extremely quiet. Lois knew he was brooding.

But if he cared so much about solving this disease why didn't he do more about it? The isolated cases Finchin could produce were not going to advance him far along the road. Indeed, most of his energies had had to be expended on fighting with the Council members to get his regulations enforced. He ought to be in one of the big London hospitals.

Lois tried to retain an unbiased opinion. As far as Rodney's future was concerned it was unbiased. But the fortnight that had just elapsed had made her think of London and a house, an apartment or even a room in which she could live alone with Rodney as something approaching paradise.

It wasn't that she disliked Crow Hollow so much as that there was no place for her. She was a guest. Aunt Opal lavished kindness on her, but discouraged any attempt on Lois's part to assist with the work. When she picked a bowl of phlox for the drawing room it was, "Oh, my dear, what will father say? That bed was his special pride. I think perhaps in the future — you see, I know what flowers can be picked without treading on anyone's toes, and what can't." When Aunt Opal found her

helping Clara in the kitchen preparing vegetables for the evening meal she beckoned
agitatedly from the doorway and when Lois
went to her she whispered, "Clara, so
temperamental. She'll think you don't like the
way she does things. Remember how she was
about the butter. Besides, dear, doing the
vegetables is no occupation for you."

"But, Aunt Opal, I must do something!"

"Yes, of course." Aunt Opal was full of lively
concern. "Go and talk to father. He so loves to
chat. He's been such a lot better since you
came. He hasn't had one of his heart turns."

Lois thought of a typical chat with grandfather, a one-sided affair in which he rambled
on interminably about the Armour family and
finished with sly sideways glances at her
figure. Did he think she had been pregnant
before she married Rodney, for how otherwise
would he expect to see any signs of approaching motherhood in less than three weeks?"

"But I mean work, Aunt Opal. A job."

"Ah, yes. Perhaps a place on one of Hester's
committees. That would interest you. I'll speak
to Hester." Then her eyes brightened. "But
your own work, dear. Your stories! I don't
believe you've even attempted one since you
came here. Is the atmosphere wrong?"

It wasn't the atmosphere altogether that had

frozen her brain as far as creative work was concerned. It was her acute uneasiness about the future. Was this state of affairs going on indefinitely? Nothing to do and not seeing her husband alone except on the rare occasions when Rodney went to bed the same time as she did — there to fall instantly asleep. His attendance at meals was irregular. During the last fortnight he had eaten chiefly at his office or at the hospital. When he did eat with them in the big cold dining room he said very little and that little was about his cases and in response to grandfather's questioning. At other times it was Willow who prepared his early breakfast.

Lois would have complained about none of this had it been their own home and she the only one who waited for him and attended to his comfort. As it was, the aunts fussed ridiculously and she was relegated to the merely ornamental.

Perhaps the only way out was to have this baby that was the subject of so much double talk and innuendo. Again, in hers and Rodney's own home she would have viewed the prospect with delight. But here, would the baby even be her own? It would be another little Armour establishing the succession to Crow Hollow, carrying on the line. In thirty years maybe, when the last aunt had been carried down the slope to the cemetery that had once been the bottom pasture, she would be mistress of her own home.

That was exaggerating, of course. When grandfather died she would legally be mistress. Only she knew that Rodney, sensitive and thoughtful, would never oust Aunt Opal. So for thirty odd years, she reflected bitterly, she had to be polite to elderly relatives, undemanding, uncomplaining and accomplice to the pampering of Willow.

Were those the reasons why Mrs. Marcus had told her not to come to Crow Hollow? Whether or not that was so they were sufficient to throw Lois into a panic. But she waited patiently until the danger of an infantile paralysis epidemic was over before approaching Rodney. She was going to choose the right moment this time.

Yet in the end she behaved on impulse. She had come to the village with Aunt Hester in the pony cart. Aunt Hester wanted to make some purchases in the local haberdashery shop, and it was while Lois sat waiting for her to reappear that she saw Rodney's shingle outside a door opposite. It was ridiculous to think that she had never seen Rodney's office. But the village was five miles from Crow Hollow, this was only her second visit and Rodney had not yet had time to drive her in specially. It wasn't Rodney's fault, he had been worked to death, but now was the time when they both escaped for a couple of hours.

She got out of the pony cart, tied the reins to the wheel as she had seen Aunt Hester do, and climbed the stairs that led to Rodney's office.

There were several people in the waiting room. Lois tried not to notice them. They were waiting for the doctor and she was going to take him away. A nurse in a crisp uniform came out and said briskly, "Doctor's busy. Will you wait?"

Lois smiled.

"You're Nurse Baxter, aren't you? I'm Mrs. Armour. Could I see my husband for just a moment?"

Nurse Baxter flushed.

"I'm sorry, I didn't know who you were. I'll tell the doctor you're here."

She vanished and presently came back preceded by a feeble old woman who obviously was a patient.

"Come in, Mrs. Armour," she said.

Lois went into the shabby but comfortable room that was Rodney's consulting room, and he came around his desk to greet her.

"Darling, this is terrible, your finding your way here alone. I should have brought you ages

99

ago. Why didn't you tell me you were coming in today?"

"Because I didn't know. You know how Aunt Hester is. She gives you two and a half minutes to get ready."

"How long is she staying in?"

"At the moment she's shopping. She'll be leaving shortly, I should think. But I'm staying to have lunch with you."

Involuntarily Rodney glanced at his watch. Wasn't he pleased? But he had to be. Surely one could do impulsive things some time.

"If you've got to see all those people out there first I'll wait. I don't mind waiting."

Rodney frowned.

"If you'd told me last night—"

"Darling, didn't I say I didn't know I was coming in?"

"These people will take me an hour. I've got an appointment at the hospital at two."

Lois said slowly, "We haven't eaten a meal together, just the two of us, since we came here. I hardly know whether I have a husband or not. I know it's not your fault, but just once in a while I think your wife should come first."

She saw his mouth tighten.

"Rodney!" she cried inwardly. "We love each other, but we don't know each other. We've got to take time off to do that. Don't you realize how important it is?"

"All right," he said. "We'll go now." He pressed a bell and Nurse Baxter came to the door. "This is my wife, Nurse. Nurse Baxter, Lois. I'm sorry you two haven't been able to meet sooner. Are there any urgent cases waiting, Nurse?"

"No, doctor. I wouldn't think so."

"Then make fresh appointments with everyone for this afternoon or tomorrow. I won't be back till about three. I'll call at the hospital on my way."

"Very well, doctor." Nurse Baxter went out.

"Thank you, Rodney," Lois said.

Rodney had gone to wash his hands in the hand basin by the door.

"Everything you said is absolutely true," he answered without turning.

"After all, you could be called out urgently for a baby and your patients would have to wait."

He rinsed and dried his hands, then he came towards her, and at last he was smiling.

"I'd rather be called out by my wife."

They went to the inn and Lois met Joshua Peabody, the hospitable landlord, his buxom wife and his more buxom and cheerful daughter. They drank Joshua's own brew of light ale and ate roast duck with red currant

101

jelly, and Lois had a second helping of the rich plum pudding.

"You don't eat like that at home," Rodney observed.

Lois shook her head.

"There are too many people watching."

"People! Surely —"

"There are the three aunts wondering if I'm despising their good food; there's grandfather hoping I'll soon develop a healthy appetite so I'll conceive quickly. There's Willow standing behind me wondering if I'll ever give her the dress I'm wearing."

"Lois! What utter nonsense!"

Lois looked up.

"It isn't nonsense, Rodney. It's all absolutely true, just as it's true that I've hardly seen you alone since we came here."

"But, darling! Grandfather, for instance. You don't conceive because you eat good meals. That at least is an exaggeration. In any case, I'm sure grandfather—"

"Don't deny it," said Lois. "It's no secret. Grandfather told me the night I arrived that I was to have a baby as quickly as possible. You see, we have no private life."

Rodney laid his hand over hers.

"Darling, a baby would be wonderful, but as far as I'm concerned you can take all the time you like."

"It's not your decision to make, Rodney. It was taken out of your hands when you brought me to Crow Hollow."

Rodney frowned.

"I know grandfather's inclined to be unbalanced about the succession. It's a bit to him as the thought of everlasting life is to other people. But don't let it upset you."

"I do try not to, but it's unnerving having one's appearance studied assessingly every morning. It shouldn't have to be necessary. The aunts are the same, but not quite so obviously. Aunt Judith would be more interested if I could produce a frog or a spider."

"Lois!"

"That was meant for a joke," Lois added. (Why didn't he laugh? He had had a sense of humor when she had first known him. Did it not exist at Crow Hollow?)

Rodney was staring at her beneath drawn brows. His eyes had a blank cold look.

"What you're trying to tell me," he said, "is that you aren't happy at Crow Hollow."

"I'm sorry, Rodney. It's just that for me it's such a useless existence. I'm not allowed to do anything. Your aunts seem to conspire to keep me unoccupied. I'm still being treated like a guest, as if I'm not going to stay very long.

Apart from that I'm your wife. I want to be making your home for you, getting your meals and waiting for you at nights."

"Yes?"

"Rodney, couldn't we get a house in the village?"

She waited for him to answer. He didn't say anything. His face was still blank and withdrawn.

"It would be much closer to the hospital for you. You could have your consulting room in the house. There wouldn't be the long drive backwards and forwards from Crow Hollow. And it would be ours, Rodney. We could have people to dinner, guests to stay. I could have Cass down. I've been missing her quite a lot. Darling, I didn't want to mention this while you were so worried about the paralysis, but now you have time to think, couldn't we start looking for a house?

"I think," she added thoughtfully, "your aunts might like it. I don't think they can get used to my being there any more than I can. They're very kind and sweet, but they're used to having the house to themselves." (And Willow, she thought. Willow resented her being there. Beneath the girl's noncommittal manner she could tell. Had Rodney's locket been a bribe to persuade her to be pleasant? But this wasn't the time to talk of Willow.)

"I have been neglecting you," Rodney was saying. "That damned paralysis had me worried. But I think the danger's over now. I must introduce you to people. There are one or two girls you might be interested in. Diana Marcus, old Mrs. Marcus's daughter. Brenda Lake from the Hall. You might like to get a horse and go hunting. There's plenty of room in the stables for another horse and Dexter would adore it. He thinks Jewel somewhat beneath his dignity. I tell you what, we'll start by going to the Golf Club ball next week. You'll meet everyone there."

Aunt Opal told her to go and talk to grand-father, Aunt Hester urged her to go riding in the pony cart, Aunt Judith would like her to start catching moths, grandfather wanted the baby. And now Rodney was talking to her about making friends, taking up other hobbies, diverting her from her real job, that of being a complete wife.

"You mean," she said, "that we're not to leave Crow Hollow."

"You don't really dislike it, do you?" Rodney said. His voice was anxious, but still his eyes gave nothing away. "And you are exaggerating about the aunts and grandfather.

Forgive me, darling, but it must be your writer's imagination."

"Oh, no!" Lois exclaimed. "Not you, too. I haven't imagined Aunt Judith's dead frogs and poisonous spiders, or Aunt Hester's fallacy that all poetry lies in the flavor of her soup, or grandfather watching to see if I can eat my breakfast, or Willow trying on my clothes. Rodney, we've got to get away and make our own home. Please, Rodney! I won't be bribed with an outing. Being a grand lady in a big house leaves me cold. I want our own fireside. I want to be able to kiss you without four pairs of eyes watching. I want to preserve our love. Because I'm telling you, if we stay in that house, we'll lose it. It'll die of starvation. And that isn't exaggeration. It's just plain truth." She paused. "I'm not asking you to leave Finchin or your practice here, as you should do. I'm just asking you to leave Crow Hollow."

Watching him, she saw him shake his head slightly but with finality. He didn't need to say, "I'm sorry, Lois. It's quite out of the question." Just as she had failed to get him to take her side against Willow she had failed in her efforts to get her own home. Didn't he love her at all?

She pulled her gloves on and stood up. As

she turned she felt his hand on her shoulder, pleadingly.

"It's two o'clock," she said stiffly. "You ought to be at the hospital."

VII

Rodney promised to be home early the night of the ball, and Aunt Opal had arranged for dinner to be half an hour earlier to give Lois plenty of time to dress. The aunts were tremendously excited. It seemed as if they had never witnessed two people preparing to go dancing before. They all, including grandfather, wanted to see the dress Lois was going to wear. She took it downstairs to show them. It was her moss green taffeta that she had worn the night Rodney had taken her to the ballet, the night he had asked her to marry him. She had a special fondness for the dress for that reason, and she couldn't help the secret hope that seeing her in it tonight he would be again as he had been then, urgent and loving, not jaded and quiet and unreachable as he had been since that lunch they had had together in the village.

She was prepared to give up her dream of their own home and make the best of life at Crow Hollow if only he would meet her halfway.

Aunt Opal thought the dress was beautiful.

"So dignified, so becoming," she crooned. "You must look your best tonight, you'll be meeting everybody."

"I hope you don't catch cold with that bare top," Aunt Hester said bluntly.

Behind his newspaper grandfather cleared his throat.

"Don't dance too late. Don't get overtired."

Lois repressed her irritation. She mustn't get jumpy tonight about grandfather. She and Rodney would come home as the moon was setting; they would be alone, actually alone, in the lovely gentle countryside that she hadn't yet seen by moonlight.

Queer little Aunt Judith had said nothing. She fingered the material with her long thin fingers. She had spidery hands, Lois thought, with a slight shudder. She seemed almost akin to her frogs and lizards and beetles.

"Butterflies' wings," she said in her husky voice. "I must go. I have an article to finish on my observations on the spider. Lois, you haven't been down to see me in my laboratory again. I have a new butterfly Dexter caught. A black and yellow swallow tail. I think you would like it."

"Don't worry Lois today, Judith," Aunt Opal said. "She has too much to think of. Lois, Willow wondered if she could arrange your hair for you tonight. She's too shy to ask you herself, the silly child."

Lois was startled. Beyond a 'Good morning, it's a nice day,' each morning when Willow carried in her breakfast tray, Lois had scarcely spoken to the girl since the episode of the suit. Willow hadn't appeared to deliberately avoid her, but she just never seemed to be about. Was this offer her method of making the peace?

"She's very clever at hairdressing," Aunt Opal went on. "She's often arranged mine quite beautifully."

"Why, of course," Lois said. "She can do my hair."

Before Rodney arrived home a florist's box addressed to Lois arrived. Lois undid the ribbon and lifted the lid off to see the delicate snowy blooms of the gardenias.

Aunt Opal was thrown into another ecstasy of delight.

"Oh, Lois, isn't that romantic! Gardenias! Dear Rodney. So thoughtful of him! Are you going to put them in water?"

"No, I'll leave them in the box." Lois was a little breathless with pleasure herself.

"Then Willow shall take them up to your room."

"Garden full of flowers," Aunt Hester observed, coming into the hall. "Rodney could have saved his money."

Nothing could happen without everyone hearing and seeing. Even her flowers must be discussed. But she wouldn't let herself get irritated tonight. She would live entirely in the present.

True to his word Rodney arrived a good half hour before dinner. He kissed Lois and whispered, "Like my flowers?" his lips brushing her ear. She wanted to say, "I should apologize to you for the other day and you should apologize to me, but let's both of us forget it," only she was afraid even the briefest mention of it would destroy Rodney's gaiety. His moods, she had discovered, were like bubbles to be burst in a moment.

"They're beautiful, Rodney. They'll look wonderful on my dress. Oh, Rodney!"

She clung to him passionately. It was the only way she could show him that she loved him and would stay with him always, no matter where he chose to live.

He kissed her again.

"Happy?" She knew he was really saying, "Are you going to be happy here now?"

She nodded. Well, it was mostly true. Everyone was kind, and if she refused to allow small things to irritate her, if she began to write again and built up her own world, things outside it would lose their power to irritate her.

Aunt Opal called up the stairs in a high voice, "Are you two going to dress before dinner or after?"

"I'm going to start right now," Lois answered.

"Good. Rodney, I thought we'd have a bottle of Madeira. Will you come down later and pull the cork."

"Butler now, you see," Rodney commented good-naturedly.

The aunts were making it a festive occasion for themselves, too, Lois thought. Well, what did it matter? The poor things got so little excitement.

She gave Rodney a slight push.

"You go and get your bath. I've had mine. And don't be too long."

"Lois!" That was Aunt Opal's voice again. "When shall I tell Willow to come up to do your hair?"

"In a few minutes, thank you, Aunt Opal."

Rodney looked at her.

"What? Putting on great lady airs?"

"Oh, no. Willow just wanted to arrange my hair." She saw that Rodney was pleased because he thought she was making a friendly gesture towards Willow. And that was a good thing, too. Perhaps it was entirely her own fault that she hadn't been happy here.

When Lois had the taffeta dress on and was sitting at the mirror Willow came in. Her lovely face had its usual blank secret look, but her eyes glinted as if she, too, were getting what excitement she could out of this occasion.

"I'm entirely in your hands, Willow," Lois said gaily. "You can make what you wish of me."

"Something not too elaborate, miss," Willow said. Lois noticed how she persistently refused to give her her married status. "That wouldn't suit you. An upswept style, perhaps. You might care to wear Mr. Rodney's flowers in your hair."

"Yes, perhaps I will."

Willow picked up the brush and standing behind Lois began to brush with firm even strokes. Lois could see her arm moving in the mirror, and her still demure face.

"Do you ever go to dances, Willow?"

"Sometimes, miss."

"Where? In the village?"

"Yes."

"But you'd like to go to London?"

Willow's downcast eyelids flickered.

"Maybe I would."

"Then why don't you? You could get a job. Oh, I don't mean we want you to go. Indeed, I think it would be a catastrophe here, but you have to think of your own future."

"Yes, miss. I do think of it."

"And yet you're content to stay at Crow Hollow."

Willow nodded.

"Then all I can think," Lois teased, "is that you must have an interest here. Someone in the village." (Who gives you expensive perfumes – none of the village lads would know the name of a French perfume?)

Willow's face retained its sphinx-like secrecy. She lifted Lois's hair and skillfully pinned it in a rich graceful swirl on top of her head. Lois saw her own face with its clear pure modeling accentuated. Her brow seemed higher, her eyes larger and brighter. She began to get excited. This dress with its low-cut shoulders needed an arresting hair style. How clever Willow was!

114

"That's wonderful, Willow. Now I'll try the gardenias."

She took the lid off the box and lifted out the two perfect blooms with their glossy leaves. She put one against her hair. As she did so something dark detached itself from the leaves and ran over her hair. At her ear it paused. Then it dropped onto her shoulder and ran down her arm. She caught a flash of crimson. It was Aunt Judith's red-black spider.

Lois dropped the box and the flowers, sprang off her stool, knocking it backwards, and screamed.

"What is it, miss?" she heard Willow exclaim.

"The spider!" Lois gasped. "It's on me! Get it off! Quickly! Before it bites."

Then Willow screamed too.

"Help! Help, Miss Armour! Mr. Rodney!"

She was no use at all. She just stood at the door wringing her hands and yelling.

Lois, in an ecstasy of horror, shook the full folds of her skirt and when that produced no dark evil object she began tearing the dress off. All the time she could feel those light hairy legs creeping over her, down her back, between her breasts.

Dimly she was aware of Rodney rushing into the room.

"What is it, Lois? What's wrong?" He seized her arms and forced her to be still. "What's wrong? Tell me at once."

"The spider!" Lois choked.

"It's the poisonous spider," Willow said excitedly. "It came out of the flowers." She was still keeping well back by the door. "It ran down her arm. She thinks it's still on her."

Lois was swaying, the room going up and down in waves.

"Stand still!" Rodney ordered. "It's probably just a large harmless spider. But I'll take your clothes off carefully. If it isn't irritated it won't bite." Already he was lifting the dress with the utmost care over her head.

"That's right," he said. "It'll be in the skirt somewhere. Can you hold it while I look?"

Lois nodded speechlessly. If she opened her lips she would begin to scream again and then she would never stop.

Rodney spread the skirt out. Frozen where she stood, Lois was aware of the three aunts and grandfather at the door, all trying to get in, all asking at once what was the matter.

"My spider!" Aunt Judith screeched. "It can't be. It's safely in its box. I looked at it not an hour ago."

"I have an aversion to spiders, too," Aunt Opal was saying breathlessly. "Poor Lois, she's had such a fright."

They thought she was a baby, screaming like that over a spider. But it was the red-black. She could never have mistaken it.

Rodney gave an exclamation.

"Look out!" he yelled. He picked up a shoe and flung it at the dark object that scuttled towards the wardrobe. The shoe found its target. He went and lifted it and stared at the floor and then said in a queer still voice, "Aunt Judith, come here."

Lois took a few uncertain steps backward and sat on the bed. Her lips were still tightly clamped together, her nails biting the palms of her hands.

Aunt Judith, squat and toad-like, crouched over the spider.

"No!" she cried suddenly. "It can't be." Then, "How can it be?"

"That's what I'd like to know," said Rodney.

Everyone pressed in. Lois was aware of them gazing at the dead spider.

"But where was it?" Aunt Opal exclaimed. "In the flowers? But the box had a lid on it."

"Yes," said Rodney. "The box had a lid."

"Then – Judith, for heaven's sake don't weep over the horrible thing! Thank heaven it's dead."

"But it was so valuable," Judith wailed. "It

was my most valuable specimen. How could it have got here?"

Grandfather at the door cleared his throat impatiently. The scene was beginning to bore him and he wanted his dinner.

"It's escaped and found its way up here. Spiders get into all sorts of queer places. The fortunate thing is that it was discovered in time. And nobody has been bitten, I might add."

"Lois might have been bitten, father," Aunt Opal said. "She's had a terrible fright. How do you feel, dear? A bit shaken?"

Lois nodded. She was gradually getting her breath under control. Her heart wasn't thumping quite so violently.

"The lid must have been left off the flowers," Aunt Judith was saying. "But how did the spider get out? I could swear it was safe. Someone must have let it out." Her voice was not so much accusing as perplexed and full of grief.

"Now who would let it out?" Aunt Opal demanded practically. "Who would go near it except you?"

"Well, I didn't let it out," Aunt Judith snapped. "I didn't plan to kill anybody."

"Kill anybody! Judith! What a shocking thing to suggest!" Aunt Opal's eyes were wide open with horror.

"That's what could have happened," Aunt Judith insisted.

"Lois needs a good brandy," Aunt Hester put in. "Go down and get the bottle out of the sideboard, Willow."

"I think Willow needs one, too," Aunt Opal said in her soft sympathetic voice. "She's quite white."

(It was Willow who had suggested she should wear the gardenias in her hair, Lois thought, but her numbed mind wasn't yet registering the significance of that. Nor of the fact that the girl had sprung back and given no assistance when the spider had appeared. It was Willow who had carried the box up to the bedroom. . . .)

"No one was meant to be killed," grandfather said irritably. "That's nonsense. The whole thing has been a silly accident. If Judith has any more dangerous creatures in her laboratory she'd better destroy them at once. And now is that dinner ruined?"

Aunt Opal laughed nervously.

"I'm sure grandfather's quite right, Lois. You remember that box with the flowers was left on the hall table for a few minutes before Willow brought it up. The spider could have got in then."

"If the lid was off," Rodney put in, speaking

the words Lois would have spoken had she been able to.

"The lid must have been off," grandfather said. "You don't seriously suggest that anyone deliberately put the spider there. My daughters are mad, I know, but not mad enough for that."

(One of them is, Lois thought. Which one? Or had it been Willow? Or grandfather, who was pooh-poohing the whole thing on the excuse that he couldn't stand women's hysterics. Or even Rodney. Rodney had sent her the flowers. He hadn't been there when they had arrived, but he had been here since they had been in her room. The lid could have been lifted off. Surely she wasn't crazy enough to suspect Rodney, her husband, the man who loved her. . . .)

"Lois, you remember you did have the lid off the box when it arrived," Aunt Opal was saying. "Perhaps you left it off. Anyway, the box was on the hall table for quite ten minutes, and anyone could have looked in it and left the lid off. Or even since it's been in your room."

"The spider," said Rodney grimly, "has still got to escape from the laboratory and make what seems to have been a bee-line for the house."

Aunt Judith had been on her knees on the floor, brushing the remains of the spider onto a

120

shovel. Now she looked up and said precisely, "I ought to clear that point up for you. The spider wasn't in the laboratory. It was in my room. I had had it there all the afternoon. I was completing my article and I was watching it. But it was safe in its box, I'm sure of that."

"Are you quite sure?" grandfather demanded. "How about when you feed it? And don't you prod it sometimes? Of course you do. I've seen you. Are you positive you closed the box completely?"

"Of course that's what happened," Aunt Opal exclaimed in a relieved voice. "But really, Judith, in the future, like father, I must ask you not to keep dangerous pets. This might have been a nasty accident."

"And here's the brandy," declared Aunt Hester, taking the bottle from Willow. "Dash it all, but I think we could all do with a nip. Let's go downstairs. Lois, get your dress on and come down."

Lois saw Rodney pick up the taffeta dress from the floor. Did he really think she could wear that dress now? Her lips were quivering. She put up her hands to hide them. Everyone would think she was a complete baby, behaving like this because of a mere accident. Even Rodney was convinced now that it was an accident. She could tell by his face.

"Come along now," said Aunt Opal briskly. "Get your dress on or you'll be late for the ball. Come downstairs, everyone else. Lois will be dressed in a few minutes."

Rodney was trying to turn the dress right side out. Willow came forward and with a deft movement straightened the dress. With it in her hands she approached Lois.

"Don't touch me!" Lois gasped. She backed against the bed. She saw Willow's eyes yellow and lambent as she stopped, the dress in her hands, and stared. She saw Rodney's lips forming the words, "Darling, what's the matter?" and Aunt Opal coming forward, her soft face puckered, her shocked voice saying, "Lois! Willow isn't going to hurt you! Pull yourself together."

"It wasn't an accident!" Lois declared, her voice sounding strong and clear. "It couldn't have been. The spider was meant to crawl on me. I might have pinned the flowers here." She indicated her bosom. "It would have been crushed and bitten me!"

She felt Rodney's hand closing around her arm. He turned to the others.

"Would you all go, please. We'll be down presently." He took the dress out of Willow's hands. "Lois will be all right in a moment."

"She's saying extraordinary things, Rodney,"

grandfather remarked. "Is she —"

"She's suffering from shock," Rodney said shortly.

"What I meant was, is it her condition?"

"He means am I starting a baby," Lois explained harshly. "Well, I'm not, and thank God I'm not."

Then she began to cry.

Dimly she was aware that everyone had gone and she was in the room alone with Rodney. He was holding her close and she could feel her body shaking against his. Gradually his very quietness quieted her, too. Her sobs grew less. She felt exhausted. The whole thing seemed to have happened hours ago. She had been watching the Armours and struggling for self-control for an interminable time. But now she was alone with Rodney and his arms were comforting and reassuring.

"That's better," he said. "Aunt Hester left some brandy for you. Swallow it quickly." He held the glass to her lips. She gulped and swallowed. She almost felt safe again. Almost.

Rodney left her to go to the bathroom for a wet cloth. He came back and sponged her face gently, wiping away the tears that still ran over her eyelids.

"It was no accident," she whispered.

He dried her face with a soft towel. The feel

of his hands was wonderful. They were so firm, gentle and expert.

"I shouldn't have behaved so badly," she went on. "I wouldn't have if I had known it was an accident."

"But, darling, how could it have been anything else?"

"Someone put the spider there. It may have been meant just to frighten me. Or it may have been. . . ."

"Lois!" He was shocked as Aunt Opal had been, staring at her with his dark hurt eyes. "What possible reason can you have for thinking such a thing?"

"No reason," she said. "Just intuition. They don't want me here. I've always known it. They won't let me be a real part of anything. I'm treated like a guest because they know I won't be here long. Or it might not be the aunts, it might be Willow. She's jealous of my clothes, hates having to wait on me, perhaps she's jealous of my being your wife. You never know what goes on in her head."

"Darling, you are hysterical now. You don't know what you're saying."

"You think it was an accident, too, don't you?"

"Because it couldn't conceivably have been anything else. Honestly, Lois. You've got to believe that. Who would be fooling around with a deadly poisonous spider for a joke?"

Lois looked at his serious and distressed face. She realized, with a sensation of utter hopelessness, that he was accepting the accident theory because any other was too impossible to contemplate. His precious family couldn't be placed under suspicion like that. He thought he had an hysterical wife who had shown up badly in a crisis. That was all.

"All right, Rodney," she said flatly. "The joke seems to be on the spider."

"Then put your dress on, dear."

"Do we have to go to the ball?"

"It would be much the best thing for you to do."

"I don't feel like dancing now."

"After you've had some dinner you'll be all right."

"Will I?" Her voice was hopeless. What had she come into here? A household that showed its dislike of her by effusiveness on the surface and mean dangerous jokes underneath? And a husband who thought she was an hysterical schoolgirl. "Not that dress, Rodney. I couldn't wear it now." (That was two perfectly good articles of clothing she had had to discard — the suit Willow had tried on and now the taffeta dress.) "Give me my black one out of the closet. But I really don't feel like dancing."

Rodney kissed the back of her neck.

"Silly one. You'll be all right in a couple of hours."

Did one recover from the malady of premeditated murder as quickly as that?

VIII

Ordinarily she would have enjoyed the ball. As young Doctor Armour's wife she was the center of attention. She was introduced to a great many people, listened to their names and talked politely to them. She danced with the husbands of the women whom she chatted to, and talked about golf, the country, Rodney and Crow Hollow. She knew that the women were saying, "She's good-looking, but how quiet she is!" and the men, "She dances well, but she hasn't a spark in her." It wasn't fair to Rodney that she should be so lacking in vivacity. He had wanted her to make a good impression. But she couldn't help it. She was still clinging desperately to her self-control. Every time she allowed herself to think she felt the light hairy touch of the spider on her skin, she saw the circle of relatives dressed for their festive little dinner, staring, talking, dismissing her accusations, always talking.

The spider couldn't have got into the flowers by accident. It was almost an impossibility. Rodney must realize that. He was defending his precious relatives at the expense of his wife! He was valuing their integrity above her life!

She could see Rodney across the room dancing with a tall fair girl. He was laughing as she talked. He could laugh, she thought bitterly. He had already dismissed the affair from his mind. The spider hadn't crawled on his flesh.

"Good gracious, Mrs. Armour, did you shiver?" her partner exclaimed. "You couldn't be so cold. It's deuced hot in here."

"I'm not cold. I — perhaps I'm a little tired. Would you like to get me a drink?"

"By all means. Name it."

"Oh, a whisky, I think."

She had been introduced to this man, but his name, too, she had forgotten because there was no room for anything in her mind but the nightmare. He was a nice pink-cheeked boy and he was going to say that Mrs. Armour drank. "She stopped me in the middle of a dance to make me get her a whisky!"

But the moment he had walked away she had forgotten him or anything he might say. She was seeing the aunts around the table at dinner. Aunt Opal was wearing a large cameo brooch that pinned the modest ruching of lace at her neck. Aunt Hester looked massive and important in black velvet. Aunt Judith had on a dark red silk, queer and old-fashioned but yet with the status of a dinner dress. Grandfather was eating heartily and looking up now and then to say, "Eat your food, Lois. You can't dance all night on an empty stomach." And they were all thinking what a pity it was she wouldn't wear the pretty green dress, and what a baby she was to be so frightened. Every time Willow stood by her to put a plate down she had to repress an instinctive wincing away.

She sat down while her partner went to get the drink. The fair girl dancing with Rodney saw her and said something to him and they both came over.

"Lois, this is Diana Marcus," Rodney said. "I was telling her you met her mother before she died."

"How do you do," said Lois politely. But this girl's was one name that sank into her consciousness. Marcus. The old lady who had warned her not to come to Crow Hollow.

Diana sat down beside her.

"Go away, Rodney," she said. "We want to talk."

Rodney grinned. He looked very youthful and handsome. He was having a good time, conveniently forgetting the earlier episode.

"All right, I'll give you ten minutes."

"My partner, I've forgotten his name, is getting me a drink," Lois said.

"Do you want it badly?"

"No, of course not."

"Then let's go and powder our noses." Diana got up and led the way, saying over her shoulder, "I've been so wanting to meet you, but Rodney's a bit of a hermit, I know. He must have fallen terribly in love to get married so quickly. I've never known him do an impulsive thing before."

In the washroom they sat on stools in front of the mirror. Lois looked at her own reflection. She had had to use makeup to put some color in her cheeks. Her eyes were still large, bright and slightly dilated. She wondered if Diana had noticed her tenseness.

"It was pretty sudden for both of us," she said. "We just knew." (But was Rodney so sure now, or had he made a mistake?)

"How lucky you are," Diana murmured.

Lois turned impulsively.

"Miss Marcus, can you tell me why your

mother warned me not to come to Crow Hollow? It sounded quite melodramatic." Lois tried to laugh.

"Mother loved to be melodramatic, poor darling. No, I'm afraid I don't know why she should say that. Did she scare you?"

"I was pretty nervous, anyway. Rodney's got so many aunts."

Diana laughed.

"I don't know why mother should say that. She thought such a lot of Rodney. She always hoped he would marry a nice girl. I should think you're just the kind of girl she had in mind. So why should she tell you not to come to Crow Hollow? There's only one reason I can think of and that's a pretty feeble one for a person of my mother's intellect."

"Rodney says she was wandering that night."

"Yes, that might explain it. You see, she wasn't too pleased with Rodney's aunts. They'd more or less stolen her maid."

"Not Willow?"

"Yes. The beautiful Willow. Not that I ever had much affection for her myself. But mother had trained her from a little scrap of a thing, and you know what it is getting a good maid nowadays. She wasn't a bit pleased when the Miss Armours bribed her to go to Crow Hollow."

"Bribed her?"

"Mother says they did. Behind her back. Willow said she was to get all kinds of wonderful things. Tell me, did she?"

Lois thought of the pretty bedroom, of the doting way the aunts spoke of Willow, of Clara's jealousy. Did this explain the perfume and lotions? Had Willow a weakness for them and they had comprised her bribe?

"She certainly isn't treated like the average maid," Lois admitted.

"And do you like her?"

"I really can't sum her up. I can't decide whether she's simple or very deep." Deep and secret, never giving anything away, going her own way about getting the things she wanted.

"That's exactly how I felt about her. But she's decorative. Mother used to say the Miss Armours had better watch out, next thing Rodney would be —" Diana stopped abruptly, realizing she was talking to Rodney's wife. "But he wasn't that sort," she finished rather lamely.

Wasn't he? He had bought Willow a gold locket, a sentimental gift. Was it for someone he looked on as a child or — Angrily Lois dismissed her thoughts. How low she was to have any suspicions at all about Rodney. He hadn't found out he had made a mistake in marrying her so recklessly. He hadn't conspired with

Willow about the spider — Willow had thought of that herself. She had done it, perhaps not to kill, but to frighten Lois, to warn her away.

No, the spider had been an accident. It had! It had!

"Let's go back — and get that drink," she said unsteadily.

Now Diana would think by her agitated manner that she was jealous of Willow. Jealousy wasn't the emotion she felt. Or was it? Or was it fear and hatred?

The dancing came to an end at last. In spite of several drinks Lois felt nothing but utter weariness. She climbed into the car beside Rodney and thought that she was too tired to care where he took her, back to Crow Hollow or anywhere else in the world.

It was two o'clock in the morning when they drove up to the house, and there was still a light in grandfather's window.

"When he can't sleep he reads late," Rodney said in explanation.

But when they went inside Aunt Opal in her dressing gown, with her hair in two plaits so that she looked like a pink innocent child, came down the stairs.

"I heard the car," she said. "Rodney, father's had another turn, but he's all right now."

"A bad one?" Rodney asked.

"No, quite slight. I happened to be awake and I heard him. He will sit up late in his chair by the window," she explained to Lois. "He gets overtired and then he has a turn."

"I'll go up and see him," Rodney said. "You go to bed, darling. I won't be long."

He ran up the stairs and disappeared along the landing. Aunt Opal looked at Lois.

"Don't worry, dear. Father often has these turns. It's his heart. No doubt the excitement tonight upset him."

"Are they serious?" Lois asked.

"Well, of course, at his age anything is comparatively serious, isn't it? But Rodney says we're not to worry. Father is really very strong. Now, what about some hot milk before you go to bed? I was just going to have some myself. And you do look very tired."

"Yes, I am tired," Lois admitted. Indeed, she was on the verge of tears. Aunt Opal's kindness was undermining her self-control. Suddenly her suspicions and fears seemed grossly exaggerated and unfair. Crow Hollow was a haven. Everyone loved and cherished her. "I would like the milk, Aunt Opal."

"Good girl. Come to the kitchen and we'll heat it. Did you enjoy the ball? I do hope so after the very bad start you made. So unfortunate. But we've quite decided it was entirely owing to Judith's carelessness. She's simply devastated with remorse."

"It's been upsetting for you, too," Lois said, realizing suddenly that she wasn't the only one concerned. It must have been a bad shock for a gentle nervous little creature like Aunt Opal.

"Well, of course, we didn't like it a bit. But let's not talk about it any more. Tell me everyone who was at the ball."

Rodney found them in the kitchen sipping their milk, and Lois saw the tiredness leave his eyes. He was thankful that she was being herself again.

"I'll have a glass, too," he said. "Grandfather's all right now. He's sleeping, in fact. It's what we should all be doing. Any calls for me, Aunt Opal?"

"Not one, thank goodness. Lois says she met Diana Marcus."

"Oh, yes, Diana admired her tremendously. In fact, everyone admired you, my sweet."

"Thank you, Rodney," Lois whispered. She had to put her glass down and get up before they saw the tears in her eyes. "I'll go up now. Don't be long." She kissed Aunt Opal and went up the stairs. She was so tired now that she was almost convincing herself that that monstrous thing had never happened at all. In the morning it would prove to be no more than a nightmare.

But in her room she saw the gardenias lying on her dressing table, their petals turning faintly brown, and the spider running off them onto her hair and down her arm was as clear and terrifying and horrible as ever.

IX

Grandfather had recovered by the morning, indeed so much so as to have one of his familiar spats with Aunt Opal. On her way to the bathroom Lois heard their voices coming from grandfather's room, his low stubborn rumble and Aunt Opal's unexpectedly sharp treble. Lois fancied she caught Willow's name. She couldn't be sure, but in spite of her curiosity her aversion to eavesdropping prevented her from stopping. No doubt Willow had taken grandfather's morning tea to him cold again. She wasn't very sympathetic with his tantrums this morning. He could make a fuss about some trifle such as cold tea and yet expect her to be unruffled by escaping death by a mere chance. He was a self-centered and egotistical old man whose sole thoughts were for food and a great-grandchild. It was difficult to understand Rodney's fondness for and loyalty to him. But Rodney had known him when he was much younger and probably a great deal more likable. And Rodney was an Armour. That was the key to the whole thing. If you were an Armour you either understood or were tolerant about each other's idiosyncrasies. If you weren't, Lois told herself wearily, you couldn't be expected either to understand or tolerate.

She was so tired she could scarcely stand. She had a hangover, she told Rodney ruefully. But it was a mental, not a physical hangover. A cold shower couldn't cure it, although the invigorating water took some of the lassitude out of her body. Breakfast was an hour later on Sunday mornings and everyone was expected to be down for it. This morning it would be even more difficult than usual, for in addition to making conversation in the ordinary way there would be all the questions about the ball. But at least Rodney was home and could make the necessary answers.

The altercation with grandfather had apparently been more serious than usual, for Aunt Opal had not regained her placidity by the time they sat down to breakfast. Her color was high and her eyes very bright. She looked like a ruffled dove. It wasn't fair of grandfather to be so difficult. Or if he must be difficult he should be to someone less tender and sensitive than Aunt Opal. Aunt Hester now, who sat eating her porridge with her usual hearty appetite, and who laughed to scorn any criticism of her behavior. Or Aunt Judith, who was so much in a dream that tantrums had no effect on her. Anyway, if it were because the tea had been cold Willow should be blamed.

Apparently, however, Willow had been blamed, for when she brought in Lois's and Rodney's porridge Lois noticed instantly that she had been crying.

"Well, you two," said Aunt Hester, finishing the last minute speck of porridge off her plate and finding time to speak. "I suppose you're pretty tired. Lois looks as if she hasn't had a wink of sleep. I'll have two eggs, Willow, thank you." She looked up at Willow, stared, and as the girl went out exclaimed, "Opal!"

Aunt Opal looked up.

"What's wrong with Willow now?"

"Wrong with her?"

"Don't tell me you haven't noticed. She's been crying again."

"Crying!" said Aunt Judith vaguely. "It wasn't her spider."

"Oh, bother your precious spider!" Aunt

Hester exclaimed. "What a one track mind you've got. As if Willow would shed tears over that. What's wrong with her, Opal?"

"Oh, it's father!" Aunt Opal said distractedly. "He's in such a mood. First it was Willow and then it was me. He's been so much worse after he's had a turn. Couldn't something be done about it, Rodney?"

"I gave him a sedative last night," said Rodney. "There's nothing you can do but let him rest."

"Rest! And he works himself into a temper over tea that was perfectly hot. I think he must be much worse than we guess."

"Oh, I don't think so," said Rodney easily. "Actually the attack he had last night was very slight. I'm afraid he just likes to be contrary. You shouldn't let it upset you."

Aunt Opal dabbed at her eyes.

"He was so angry! I don't blame Willow for crying. Poor child! As if she hasn't enough to do carrying tea all over the house."

"Poor Willow," Aunt Judith echoed vaguely. She was gazing out of the window at the blue sky. "I wish it would rain. Such a long dry spell we've had. I haven't been able to get any worms. Did you know that the common earthworm is invaluable to gardeners? It digs, drains and ventilates the ground."

Lois looked at her hypnotically. Was she quite mad?

"Lois isn't eating anything!" Aunt Hester boomed. "Look after her, Rodney."

Rodney lifted her porridge plate away. Porridge after dancing all night! Anywhere else one would have asked for grapefruit or thin toast. But here one was smothered, had no individuality left, forced lumps of porridge down because the Armours liked porridge for breakfast and that was that.

"Some toast?" Rodney suggested.

"Rodney, she hasn't touched her porridge. She ought to be hungry after all that exercise last night."

Lois looked up.

"I have a hangover," she said clearly.

"Lois, what nonsense!" Aunt Opal exclaimed. "You were perfectly sober when you came in last night. Wasn't she, Rodney?"

"I think she just may be pulling your leg," Rodney said.

So she wasn't even allowed to shock the aunts. One day she would. She would stand up and say, "Which of you doesn't want me here? Which of you tried to murder me?"

"What I have feels like one," she said defiantly. She caught the quick look that passed between Aunt Hester and Aunt Opal. Heavens;

now they would think it was something much more interesting than a hangover; they would be rushing upstairs to placate grandfather with the news. "I'm just tired," she said hopelessly.

"Then some breakfast, surely, is the best thing in the world," Aunt Hester said.

"A little toast?" Rodney said again.

The telephone in the hall rang. Willow answered it and presently came to the door, standing there with her reddened eyelids clearly visible.

"It's for Mr. Rodney."

Rodney stood up.

"Rodney, not this morning. You won't have to go out this morning," Lois pleaded. "It's Sunday," she added lamely.

Rodney gave her arm a quick press and went out of the room. In a few moments he was back.

"Sorry," he said. "But babies have no respect for the sabbath." He leaned over to kiss Lois on the cheek. She sat still and unresponsive, fighting her dismay that Rodney was leaving her, her dislike of the aunts witnessing his caress, her strong disinclination to be left alone in the house with them.

"Rodney, you haven't nearly finished your breakfast," Aunt Hester said.

"The earthworm, like plants, has a system of

cross-fertilization," Aunt Judith observed dreamily. "How much simpler it is to lay eggs than to have babies."

"Lois shall come to church with me," Aunt Opal declared decisively. "That will fill the morning for you nicely, dear, and you haven't seen our church yet. We just walk through the woods and across the cemetery. Our own private path. So convenient."

"Show her our mother's grave," put in Aunt Hester. "We're not all in that cemetery, you know, Lois. It's comparatively new. Most of us are in the older one the other side of the village. Some day we'll take you there, too."

"A nice cheerful morning," Rodney observed, trying to make her smile at him, to join in his lighthearted attitude towards the aunts.

When she wouldn't he said, "I'll be back as soon as I can. Don't let grandfather do too much, Aunt Opal."

"And how can I stop him, the mood he's in?" Aunt Opal demanded. But her voice was philosophic again. The thought of the walk to church through the cemetery with Lois had cheered her up.

Lost in her own thoughts Lois didn't absorb much of Aunt Opal's chatter on the walk through the green cool woods where Dexter looked for Aunt Judith's specimens, nor did she take in the sermon the vicar preached, nor the curious heads that bobbed over pews trying to catch a glimpse of her. It was only in the cemetery afterwards, as Aunt Opal led the way to an ornate marble headstone, that her mind began to function again.

"Our mother," she heard Aunt Opal saying reverently.

Lois read the words, "Ellen Hester Armour, aged 57 years." Ellen Hester Armour didn't belong here, of course. She belonged in the room with the Chinese wallpaper, with the four-poster bed and the high carved ceiling. She hadn't been born an Armour. How had she felt coming to Crow Hollow as a bride, sleeping in the big bed with grandfather? Had she been an alien? Had she been made welcome and yet divined she wasn't wanted? Had anything ever frightened her so badly that she had wanted to run away? At least she hadn't run away, for she had stayed and borne four children, the three aunts and Rodney's father. Rodney's father, Douglas, whom no one ever seemed to talk about. All she knew of him was that he had died when Rodney was too young to remember him. Losing an only son must have been a great grief to grandfather.

"Is Rodney's father's grave here, Aunt Opal?" she asked.

Aunt Opal's soft face had a repressive look.

"No, dear. He didn't die at Crow Hollow. He died in South America. Of some obscure tropical disease. It wasn't the shock it might have been to us. He had left home very young, entirely against father's wish. He was a great disappointment to father."

"And his mother?"

"She came to Crow Hollow. Father insisted that she should. He went to the boat to meet her. Rodney was little more than a baby. They stayed in London for a while. Father made her buy a complete new wardrobe. He was most generous. She got some beautiful things. She was very good-looking." (There's been some jealousy there, Lois thought, looking at Aunt Opal's tightening mouth. The strange daughter-in-law coming home and getting things the daughters were denied. But she had the baby, that would be the reason. Grandfather, with his passion for male successors, would be able to deny her nothing.)

"Did she like Crow Hollow?" Lois asked.

"No, she didn't," Aunt Opal said flatly. "She wasn't one of us."

Lois's head spun.

"But — but, Aunt Opal, I'm not one of you, either."

"Oh, my dear," Aunt Opal exclaimed

145

warmly, "you're Rodney's wife."

"But this girl was your brother's wife."

"An entirely different thing. You see, Douglas was quite a scamp, really. Quite a black sheep. So difficult to understand with the upbringing he had had. Having alienated himself as he did we naturally didn't feel compelled to take his wife. Except for the ridiculous fuss father made."

What had they done to her at Crow Hollow? It wouldn't be a poisonous spider they had frightened her with, but something would have happened.

"She – died?"

Aunt Opal pointed to another headstone, a modest cross in a plot behind Ellen Hester Armour. Lois read the name Marguerite, loved wife of Douglas Armour. In her thirty-second year.

Not very much older than she herself was. Much too young to die.

"What did she die of, Aunt Opal?"

"We didn't quite know," Aunt Opal replied smoothly. "Some kind of low fever. It even had father baffled. He said she had probably picked it up in the tropics. Very sad. We kept Rodney, of course. Fortunately he was too young to grieve for long. We – or I, at least – tried to be a mother to him."

Marguerite, thought Lois. Such a pretty name. Marguerite, the stranger, the unwanted sister-in-law hating Crow Hollow, compelled now to sleep in the ground that had been the bottom pasture.

A bird, black and swift, flew overhead. Its shadow glanced over the grass. It gave a harsh croak as it alighted in a nearby tree.

"What's that?" Lois gasped.

"Only a crow, dear. You're getting jumpy."

"A crow!"

"Why not? After all, this is Crow Hollow. There used to be thousands of crows. One hardly sees one nowadays, though lately I've sometimes fancied there are more about. They may be coming back. My dear child, you can't be shivering in this warm sunshine!"

"I think — I'm a little cold."

"Then you must have caught a chill at the ball last night. Come, we'll hurry home. We can't have you getting ill."

No, she mustn't get ill as Marguerite had. She mustn't catch a fever that no one, not even Rodney, could diagnose. Following Aunt Opal's sprightly little figure across the field and into the wood she fancied she could still hear that crow squawking. She didn't know why its sound made her shiver. She longed to get home and find Rodney waiting. She had to get out of this morbid imaginative state. Everything was all right. Marguerite had died from natural causes and the spider last night had been an accident. It was a lovely day and Rodney would be waiting for her.

Rodney wasn't home when they arrived, but lunch was ready. Willow, with all traces of tears gone, was carrying in the salad. Grandfather, looking much as usual, was in his place, and Aunt Judith in her khaki slacks was scurrying upstairs to wash her hands. Aunt Hester came to the door to say, "Did you inquire if Eliza Jenkins is still in bed? She is. Then I must make her some soup."

Rodney wasn't home, but Crow Hollow was as normal as it would ever be.

During lunch, however, another minor crisis arose when grandfather suddenly announced, "Judith, in the future you will be so good as to keep no live specimens, poisonous or non-poisonous, in your laboratory."

For the first time Lois was aware that a subject had Aunt Judith's complete attention. Her mouth fell slightly open. Her round short-sighted eyes stared at grandfather. She looked like a flabbergasted child.

"Would you kindly explain, father?" she asked in a trembling voice.

"There's nothing to explain," grandfather

said irritably. "I'm just asking you either to release or destroy whatever live specimens you have. Lois had a bad fright last night with that unpleasant spider and I won't have a repetition of that."

"But, father, I had only one spider and it's dead. I have nothing else that could be of any harm whatever. The lizards and beetles are completely harmless."

"Even a lizard or a beetle crawling on one could give one a nasty start. I don't want it to happen. So get rid of them, will you. Today."

Grandfather returned to his salad. The subject, as far as he was concerned, was closed. He was accustomed, Lois sensed, to implicit obedience, just as his daughters were accustomed to obeying him. But why this sudden concern about poor Aunt Judith's specimens? Last night he had been inclined to dismiss the matter lightly enough. What had made him take it so seriously as to place a death sentence on the remaining creatures in the laboratory? Had he discovered something of significance? Lois felt a chill creeping of her flesh. Then, catching the sideways glance grandfather gave at her half-empty plate, enlightenment came to her. He was alarmed lest another fright might prove dangerous to her because she might be pregnant. He was taking no chances at all. He was quite fanatical on that subject.

Almost inclined to laugh hysterically, Lois caught the dumb grief on Aunt Judith's face and she was instantly moved to sympathy. Poor little Aunt Judith. She couldn't have meant any harm with the spider. Could she?

Late in the afternoon Rodney came home. He drove the car up to the front door and blew the horn until Lois, followed by the inevitable trio of aunts, came out.

"Get in," he said to Lois. "We're going for a drive."

"When will you be back, Rodney?" Aunt Opal asked.

"Not for dinner. Not till late. Don't wait up for us."

The outing was so unexpected as to be enchanting. With a deliberate effort of will Lois shut out of her mind everything concerning Crow Hollow and absorbed the peace of the evening and the quiet complete delight that came with Rodney's company. They had dinner at the inn with Joshua Peabody waiting on them himself. Rodney bribed him to bring out a hoarded bottle of Napoleon brandy that, as he said, practically no one except himself and his Maker knew about. All the things Lois had wanted to talk about (I saw your mother's grave. Why did she die so young? There was a crow in the cemetery. Grandfather has told Aunt Judith she has to destroy all her live specimens. Willow has quite recovered from the scolding she had this morning. She must have a versatile temperament.) faded out of her mind. She sipped the wine and smiled at the light in Rodney's eyes.

"It was a boy," said Rodney. "A bouncing boy. He took a lot longer than he should have to come. I spanked his bottom for keeping me away from you."

"On the sabbath," Lois murmured. "He'll probably be a parson."

"Darling, do you like this evening? This Sunday evening drinking Josh Peabody's Napoleon brandy."

"I like it very very much."

"Wouldn't it be a good time to do something about this baby —" Lois controlled her desire to wince. It had been very faint, practically nonexistent. "This is nothing whatever to do with grandfather or anything that will please my family. It's entirely between ourselves, as if you and I were completely alone in the world. Let's pretend we are and I'm saying to you, 'Wouldn't it be nice if we had a baby?' " His long bright eyes were on her compellingly. "Wouldn't it be nice?"

She picked up her glass and felt the cool liquid run down her throat.

"I think it would be nice, Rodney. Let's have a baby."

The stable clock was striking eleven as they parked the car in the garage that had been built next to Jewel's stall. They could hear Jewel stirring and champing at her hay. Footsteps went past as they came out at the door. They belonged to the shy and uncommunicative Dexter from whom Lois could rarely extract a word.

"Hello, why aren't you in bed?" Rodney asked.

"Mild night, thought I might get a moth or two for Miss Judith," the boy answered in his deep embarrassed voice. "Thought I'd go into the woods."

"You ought to get some sleep," Rodney said. "You won't make your fortune at this game."

"Good luck, anyway," Lois said. "It ought to be wonderful in the woods tonight."

"Yes, miss. Thank you, miss."

The boy shuffled away. The house was in darkness except for the one familiar light in grandfather's window. Lois crept upstairs followed by Rodney, trying to make no sound, praying no door would open and an inquisitive head be thrust out.

"Are you going in to grandfather?" she whispered.

Rodney shook his head. His eyes were bright and impatient. Lois gave a little sigh of happiness. Grandfather and the aunts did not exist tonight.

In the bedroom the dragons on the wall glowed golden and beautiful. When the light was out Lois thought she could still see them shining. Or perhaps it was that she had drunk too much of the Napoleon brandy. Or that loving Rodney so much made a radiance even in the dark. . . .

Out of a deep sleep in the morning she was roused by Aunt Opal's urgent rapping at the door.

"Rodney! Wake up! It's father. Come quickly!"

X

"He had been sitting at the window reading," Aunt Opal explained to Lois later when Lois, hurriedly dressed, had come down to the morning room. She was very pale, and she kept dabbing at her eyes with her handkerchief, although she wasn't crying. "He so often did that. He must have had one of his turns, a bad one, and he fell sideways into the cushions on the chair. His face was quite hidden. Rodney isn't sure yet whether he died of the heart attack or from suffocation. He says it looks like suffocation, but the distress of trying to get his breath may have caused his heart to fail."

"How dreadful!" Lois whispered. "Poor grandfather!"

She could feel almost fond of the queer,

proud, stubborn old man now he was dead. And genuinely sorry that after all he hadn't lived to see a great-grandchild.

"We mustn't fret," Aunt Opal said tearfully. "He was over eighty and he had had a good and full life. His son disappointed him, but dear Rodney came to fill the place of a son. He had great happiness out of Rodney, and lately out of you, my dear. And now he has gone to join our dead mother."

Lois had a vision of the arrogant headstone in the cemetery, Ellen Hester Armour, and of the modest one beyond it. Only yesterday Aunt Hester had said, "There aren't many of us in the new cemetery." Now, as soon as this, there would be one more. Whose would be the next? Lois, dearly loved wife of Rodney Armour. . . .

"Don't be so upset, dear," Aunt Opal entreated. "It's sweet of you. Funny old father. Such a bear at times. Only yesterday, the way he made poor Willow cry, and the way he upset Judith over her specimens."

Now Judith would be able to keep her specimens. If, as Lois suspected, they meant more to her than any living person, she surely must be relieved at what was grandfather's timely death.

"His light was on when Rodney and I came in last night," she said thoughtfully. "Rodney said he would be reading. He said he wouldn't go in to see him. If he had, he might have saved him."

Suddenly the knowledge that she and Rodney had been making love while grandfather, possibly, was dying or already dead, was terrible to bear. So even last night, when she had thought she had escaped from the family, she hadn't, after all. They existed to destroy the beauty she and Rodney created.

"Now you mustn't worry about that," Aunt Opal was saying firmly. "You and Rodney couldn't have known. Death is meant to come."

"His light must have still been burning this morning when you found him," Lois said irrelevantly.

"Yes," said Aunt Opal. "Yes, it was. Burning there in broad daylight." She was breathing a little quickly, as if she were reliving that frightening scene. "I was only thankful I went in before Willow did. Such a shock it would have been to the child."

Aunt Hester came in at that moment. She, also, had not been shedding tears, but her handsome face had a high congested color and she looked mildly indignant, as if grandfather had done something completely unconventional, something no Armour would ever have done.

"Now we must all keep busy today," she said in her autocratic voice. "There's nothing like occupations to keep one's mind off tragedy. Opal, I hope Clara is cooking the meals as usual."

"I should think so," said Aunt Opal faintly. "I haven't spoken to her."

"We must eat if we're to keep our spirits up. Don't look so squeamish, Opal. A good meal is the very thing you need. Then I suggest we all arrange what we must individually do. Rodney, of course, is seeing the undertaker and the vicar. He says an inquest will not be necessary."

Lois heard a long sigh escape Aunt Opal. Poor thing. No doubt she would have thought an inquest a shameful thing to have happen to one of the family.

"I have told Dexter to have Jewel ready for me immediately after breakfast," Aunt Hester went on. "I propose to call personally, on our more intimate friends, with the news. Lois, I think you might be clever at doing flowers. There are so many in the garden. If you could make some sprays which could be from the servants — the florists, of course, will be sending the more important wreaths. Some of the phlox, perhaps. Father was so fond of phlox."

Lois had a vivid memory of her first morning at Crow Hollow when grandfather had stopped work in the phlox bed and told her to come to him if she had any trouble. He had kept his word about helping her, too, because although he had pooh-poohed the spider incident, he had issued that edict about Aunt Judith's specimens. Now he was dead, and there would be no one to go to if more trouble came.

"And Opal, I think you ought to arrange with Clara about doing some extra baking. We're bound to have a large number of callers. I shall make some soup tonight, but we'll want a great many more substantial things than that. Then there's the telephone. Someone will have to be handy to answer that all day. We certainly can't trust Judith. She's growing more absentminded every day."

"Willow, perhaps," Aunt Opal suggested. "She's very intelligent."

So she was supposed to be intelligent, Lois reflected. Then either the aunts were too dazzled by her perfection to realize the truth, or else that dumb look was a pose.

Willow was called and instructed in her duties. Standing meekly before the aunts in her neat cap and apron she looked obedient and submissive. But Lois fancied there was a gleam in her eyes, almost of triumph. What would she be triumphant about? Some affairs of her own, no doubt. Or perhaps just this new duty of being in charge of all telephone messages. If her intellect were low any responsibility would be a triumph to her.

Then Rodney came in. He looked drawn and rather grim. Lois wanted to go to him and comfort him. After all, he had been very fond of grandfather, probably he was the only one in the house who had genuinely cared about the old man. But the aunts were beginning to fuss. Aunt Hester insisting on some sustenance being taken and Aunt Opal patting the couch for him to sit beside her.

"Poor Rodney," she was murmuring. "Such a shock. Willow's making you some tea, if I'm not mistaken."

Lois sat stiffly on her chair saying nothing. Rodney didn't need a wife. He was surrounded with, smothered by, women. Did he really enjoy it? She thought he must. And why should Willow be making him tea, as if she were used to doing little thoughtful things for him?

"Can I see grandfather?" she asked.

Rodney looked across at her.

"I think not, darling."

That was worse, of course, than seeing him. Now one lived with one's imagined vision of

159

the way a person looked after death by suffocation. Momentarily she forgot the aunts.

"Rodney, you're worrying because you didn't go in to see him last night. If I hadn't been with you you would have."

"Forget it," Rodney said briefly. "As far as I can decide death occurred in the early hours of the morning. About one o'clock. Quite two hours after we came home. If I had gone in to him then I would have found him alive and well."

"Father frequently sat up until one or two o'clock," Aunt Opal put in. "You mustn't blame yourself, Lois."

She hadn't been blaming herself, but now the words were in Aunt Opal's mouth. Was everyone thinking it might indirectly have been her fault because she had so completely distracted Rodney's attention from grandfather?

"His light was on when we came in," Rodney said. "Was it still burning when you found him, Aunt Opal?"

Aunt Opal began to cry, hiding her face in her handkerchief.

"Yes, it was. So strange, burning there in daylight. I knew at once something was wrong. And then there was father on the couch, face downwards, the way he must have fallen."

Willow came in then and sure enough she

was carrying a teatray. She must have listened until she heard Rodney come downstairs so that it would look as if the tea were for him particularly. As it probably was.

"Ah, good!" exclaimed Aunt Hester. "Now we'll all feel better."

Rodney took the cups from Willow's tray and passed them around. He said something to Willow which Lois didn't hear. She smiled in her secret way, her yellow eyes lighting. Was she in love with Rodney? Lois wondered for the hundredth time. Or was she just vain and spoiled, pleased for any kind of attention.

"Where's Judith?" Aunt Opal asked. "I've scarcely seen her since she was in father's room this morning."

"Well, she won't be expiring from grief," Aunt Hester declared in her forthright way. "She's got a reprieve for all her bugs. She was frightfully upset last night, but that's all over now."

"Hester, what a dreadful thing to say!"

"Come, Opal, don't be such a hypocrite. You must admit father's been a bit of a tyrant lately. To you, too. Always bickering and nagging."

"Dear father, he was just growing old. One must be patient with the old."

"You weren't so patient yesterday when he had Willow in tears."

A slow flush spread up Aunt Opal's face. Her cup clinked gently against the saucer as if her hand were trembling.

"None of us liked that," she said. "So unfair, too. Because the tea was quite hot."

"That's what I'm saying," Aunt Hester pointed out. "Father was getting too overbearing altogether. Exaggerating trifles and making people suffer. He even had me on the block yesterday. Said I had to give up this childish business of making soup for the sick. Said I was making myself a laughing-stock, with my lady bountiful complex! Me! A laughing-stock! I never heard such nonsense."

"He's had these tyrannical moods before," Aunt Opal said gently. "Poor dear! I think he missed our mother more than we realized."

"Who missed our mother?" asked Aunt Judith, at that moment coming in. She was wearing her usual overalls, and her short stiff gray hair was mussed. "Father? Oh yes, perhaps."

Absently she took the cup Rodney offered her.

"Did Dexter catch you any moths last night, Aunt Judith?" he asked.

"No, but he got me a lizard this morning, just after the sun was up. A beauty." Her face had a curious exalted look.

"So you'll be able to keep it," Aunt Hester said slowly.

"Yes, I'll be able to keep it. And perhaps," her voice was childishly eager, "I could get that new microscope I want. If there's enough money. Will there be much money, Rodney?"

"I'm going down to see Greaves presently," Rodney said. "I don't know what's in the will. But you can have your new microscope."

Aunt Judith turned her glowing face to Lois.

"Father was so particular about us spending money wisely," she explained. "It will be so strange. . . ." She broke off, entranced with her dreams. She was too simple, Lois thought, and Aunt Hester too forthright to hide her feelings that practically amounted to relief that grandfather's reign of petty tyranny was over. Aunt Opal was more gentle and sensitive, more earnestly conscious that the three of them should feel filial affection. But she, too, probably had a sensation of unaccustomed freedom.

"It's funny to think," Aunt Judith said dreamily, "how father never would listen to what I told him about the habits of earthworms."

Lois, struggling with her sensation of horror, felt Rodney touching her arm.

"I'm going to see grandfather's solicitor," he

said. "Come for a ride to the village."

It was wonderful to escape from the house, and to have Rodney to herself with neither aunts nor Willow hovering about him.

"I'm so sorry, Rodney," she said. "It's been such a shock for you."

"Grandfather was very good to me," Rodney answered. "I owe him everything." He paused, and then said again, "Everything."

Lois thought of that long-ago day when grandfather had met the boat from South America, had bought pretty clothes for Marguerite to help her over her grief, had insisted on her and her baby making Crow Hollow their home. He must have been thoughtful and kind then. He could have ignored the wife of the son who had spurned him. But he had lavished kindness on her, although she had died in the end. . . .

"But you were his grandson," Lois pointed out. "And his only male heir. And he was so frightfully keen on heirs. I think he owed you something, too, for taking over his practice and living at Crow Hollow. That's what he made you promise, isn't it?"

Rodney gave her a startled look.

"Oh, I only guessed," she said. "When you turned me down flat on my suggestion about living somewhere else."

164

"Darling, I should have explained. But I thought you were unhappy at Crow Hollow and I — when I get worried I get a bit inarticulate."

She looked at him consideringly. So slowly she was beginning to know him. With three aunts and a possessive grandfather constantly prying on his thoughts he had lived within himself. In London, away from Crow Hollow, he had relaxed, but here the habit of reserve was too strong on him. Even this confession of inarticulateness had been difficult for him to make. But she was beginnng to understand. Warmth and hope were beginning to flow through her. Give her time and she would break down this reserve, she would have him free and happy and unrestrained as he had been when she had first met him.

"I do understand, Rodney. Really I do. But now grandfather's dead —" Was she, too, like the aunts aware of relief and freedom?

"We will stay," Rodney said. "That was my promise. To give a home to the aunts and live at Crow Hollow myself. After all, it will be different now. You're the new mistress. You can do exactly as you like."

"It won't be different, Rodney. I mean, I can't take over from Aunt Opal. It wouldn't be fair or kind. It will be exactly the same, except that now I'm allowed to pick a few flowers to make sprays for the servants."

She caught the taut anxious look on his face. Abruptly she realized his dilemma, his desire to make her happy and to keep faith with a dead man. She couldn't worry him now. Later, when he had got over the shock of grandfather's death. Later. . . .

Rodney was leaning forward to kiss her. His eyes, wide open, were looking deep into hers. She knew if she returned his kiss it was a tacit submission to his wishes, a consent to spend the next thirty-odd years at Crow Hollow, obeying the aunts' wishes. Unless, like Marguerite, she died young, unless she preceded Opal, Hester and Judith to the Armour plot in the new cemetery. . . .

Rodney's face with his appealing eyes filled her vision. He was her husband. She loved him. Temporarily all else faded and there was just her desire and his lips against hers.

XI

The fine weather broke at last. Dark clouds rolled up and the wind in the elms was wild and desolate. The rain rapped sharp fingernails on the window of Lois's bedroom, and the dragons on the wall glowed and seemed to writhe in the gloom. Between one shower and the next grandfather was laid in the plot adjoining Ellen Hester Armour. The soil was black and rich. Once it must have grown fine crops for the Armour farmers. Now it was receiving their bones.

All the village and a great many people from the adjoining counties had come to say their farewells to the old doctor. The church had been filled, and now the cemetery seemed to be moving with people. They couldn't all get near enough to hear what the vicar was saying. But the aunts were close. The three of them, clad in black, stood in a half circle at the grave's edge. Aunt Opal had been weeping a little. Her soft flushed face was tearstained and pathetic. Aunt Hester's large nose protruded aggressively. Aunt Judith's pale myopic eyes were on the dark wet soil. They moved and watched intently. She was searching for something. Lois held her breath. She didn't know whether she would laugh hysterically or faint if the youngest Armour sister pounced triumphantly on a worm.

But everything passed off with decorum, and the next day the sun struggled to shine again. With grandfather's coffin out of the house Aunt Opal became her brisk cheerful self. She decided on a complete spring cleaning, then belatedly said to Lois, "That's if you'd like it, dear."

"Of course," said Lois. She realized abruptly what Aunt Opal was inferring, and said quickly, "Please go on doing just what you would if I weren't here. You're used to running this house. And you do it a great deal better than I would. Please, Aunt Opal, I mean that."

Aunt Opal's lips quivered. Her eyes filled with tears.

"You're such a dear girl, Lois. We're so fond

168

of you. I'm sure Rodney couldn't have found a nicer wife."

"Don't flatter me so much," Lois laughed. "I'm just lazy, that's all."

But it was rather sweet making Aunt Opal happy. She was a dear and it was crazy to think that she, with Judith and Hester, had ever wanted to keep Lois an outsider. Like Marguerite. . . . The spider incident seemed very far away.

Now she could pick flowers out of the garden without fear of stealing grandfather's most prized blooms. Dexter had had the lawns added to his duties until another gardener could be found, and he was there with the lawnmower about a week after grandfather's death when Lois went out to cut roses. Lois liked the inarticulate boy with his shambling walk. He was so earnest, and so anxious to please, as proof the way he would spend half the night in the woods looking for moths for Aunt Judith.

She called, "Good afternoon, Dexter," and added, more to please him than for any other reason, "what roses would you suggest I cut for the drawing room?"

Dexter, enormously flattered, became unexpectedly talkative.

"How about them yellow ones, miss? They'm

good. I remember the old doctor saying when he planted the bushes. He said how hard it was to get a good yellow rose."

"You got on well with the doctor, didn't you, Dexter?"

"Yes'm. He used to say I was a good boy. It's kind of funny coming home nights without seeing his light in the window. And that makes me think of a queer thing."

"What queer thing, Dexter?"

The boy looked embarrassed and half afraid.

"You know, miss, how Aunt Opal said the light was still burning in the morning when she found the old doctor."

"Yes, Dexter."

"Well, that couldn't be so, miss."

"Go on," said Lois in a tense voice.

"Because that night I went looking for moths. You and the young doctor saw me. I got home near one o'clock and the old doctor's light was out then."

"But, Dexter," Lois stammered, "are you sure you were looking at the right window?"

The boy's eyes were scornful.

"I been here four years, miss. I always knew which was the old doctor's room."

"And — the light was out."

"Yes, miss. The light was out."

At random Lois cut a rose.

"Then he must have wanted to sit at the window in the dark. And died there."

"Yes, miss. But it seemed kind of queer Miss Opal saying the light was on in the morning."

"She was so flabbergasted, poor thing — there'll be some simple explanation." She cut half a dozen roses, trying to concentrate on what she was saying. "I wouldn't go around talking about this, Dexter."

"No, miss. I haven't mentioned it to anyone else."

Dexter went back to his lawnmower and Lois walked away with her basket of roses. But as soon as she was out of sight she had to find a seat and sit down. Her legs felt peculiarly shaky. One part of her mind wanted to think and the other shied away from what would be unsatisfying and intensely disturbing conclusions.

Why had Aunt Opal lied about the light? If she had done it only once it might have been absentmindedness, but she had done it twice, the second time with emphasis. If grandfather had died sitting at the window in the dark, why not say so? But why would he switch off the light and go back to the window? Normally he wouldn't put it off until he got into bed. Even if he had been undressed, on the point of getting into bed, he may have wandered across the room in the dark. But he had been fully dressed.

There was only one sound explanation Lois could find, and that one horrified her, filled her with as deep a chill as the spider episode had done.

Someone had gone in to grandfather and whoever it was had found him in one of his attacks. But instead of staying to render assistance he had switched off the light. He had left him to die. Or else. . . . No, that thought was too terrible to contemplate — that anyone had assisted him to die. . . .

Who benefited by grandfather's death? No one in any particular mercenary form for, as Rodney had told her, Crow Hollow was left to him with the provision that a home be provided for the three aunts during their lifetime. Each aunt received an annuity. After sufficient capital for that purpose had been reserved there was not a large estate remaining. No, the consideration could not have been monetary.

Lois pressed her hands to her temples. She felt that she was living in a nightmare. This was all utterly fantastic. No one could have caused poor old grandfather's death. There must be a simple explanation. She must see Rodney — and at once. Tonight wouldn't do. She couldn't carry that knowledge all afternoon alone.

Half an hour later she was sitting in Rodney's waiting room. Nurse Baxter had given her a surprised look and then said, "I'll tell the doctor you're here, Mrs. Armour."

A few moments later Rodney himself came out. He crossed over to her quickly.

"Is there anything wrong? Nurse Baxter said you were here and you looked ill."

"Do I?" said Lois vaguely. "I'm perfectly all right. But I must see you alone, Rodney."

"Of course. Come in. How did you get into the village? Aunt Hester?"

"No. Joe Higgins. I telephoned for him."

"But —"

"Yes, I know. While I waited for him I had to answer a thousand questions as to why I wanted to come to the village, why I wanted to see you when I'd be seeing you at dinner tonight, why I couldn't let Aunt Hester drive me in the pony cart, why the matter was so urgent."

She was clenching and unclenching her hands as she talked. She was aware that Rodney had made her sit in the chair facing him, and had motioned Nurse Baxter out. Then he was sitting facing her, watching her with his grave steady eyes.

"Take it easy, darling. You're excited about something."

173

"Indeed I am," said Lois vehemently. "There's something funny going on at Crow Hollow and you'll have to believe me because I've got proof."

Then, drawing a deep breath to steady herself, she told him what she knew.

"Why should Aunt Opal lie about the light?" she said. "Why should grandfather sit in the dark fully clothed?" She watched Rodney's taut face. "Oh, I don't mean someone actually held a pillow over his face —"

"Lois, stop that!"

She leaned forward.

"No, you've got to face facts. Something odd happened in grandfather's room that night."

"There could be various explanations about the light."

"Explanations! Suppositions! No proof."

"No," said Rodney impatiently, "and there'll be no proof about anything else. Really, darling, your tendency towards the melo-dramatic —"

"You don't intend to do anything?"

"Certainly. We'll get to the bottom of this light business."

"Rodney, supposing you find out something — distressing."

"I wish you'd believe there's no remote possibility of that."

"Don't you realize all your aunts disliked grandfather? In fact, I think they hated him. He was pretty difficult and unreasonable."

Rodney came around to her. His eyes were rueful.

"I'm just beginning to wonder what you think of my family. First someone was trying to murder you with a poisonous spider and now it's poor old grandfather who's had it."

"You think I'm neurotic."

"You are a bit overwrought."

"You don't take either incident seriously."

"Dearest, it's all so farfetched. My family just isn't like that."

"Why did your mother die so young?"

Rodney made a helpless gesture.

"I was eight years old when she died. I just wouldn't know. And what possible connection has my mother's death with you or grandfather?"

"That's what I'd like to know."

Rodney bent over her.

"Really, sweet — I'll come home with you right away. We'll get to the bottom of this. But the aunts are going to think it darned funny, us rushing home to know why Dexter didn't see grandfather's light at midnight. Why, the boy practically walks in his sleep."

"I can bear their amusement," Lois said stiffly.

They weren't amused, of course. They were puzzled and inclined to be hurt that Lois had rushed to Rodney with some information she hadn't told them.

"Grandfather's light," said Aunt Opal. "Why, of course it was on, just as I said. In fact, it was Willow who told me. She had knocked at grandfather's door and got no answer. It's dark in the passage at that end, as you know, and she could see the light under the door. She got scared and came to me. Isn't that so, Hester? You heard her come to my room."

Aunt Hester nodded. "That's right. I wouldn't place too much faith in what Dexter says, Lois. The boy's not completely —" She tapped her head. "He's all right to look after Jewel and do odd jobs, but you couldn't trust him with anything important."

"He's clever at catching moths," Aunt Judith said.

"That's it," Aunt Hester nodded. "If a boy goes around mooning after moths —"

"Anyway," put in Aunt Opal, "it's quite possible father did put his light off to sit in the dark. He frequently sat in the dark, when there was a good moon and he wanted to look at the garden. Flowers looked different by moonlight, he used to say. Then he probably switched it on again later when he felt ill. Isn't that likely, Rodney?"

"I should think that's the answer," Rodney said. He glanced at Lois. His eyes were kind and tolerant of what he considered her foolish hysteria.

She had wanted an explanation, and now she had one. Aunt Opal hadn't lied about the light because there was Willow to corroborate her story. But wouldn't there be another explanation — that whoever had been in the room had automatically switched off the light, and later, remembering her mistake, had gone back and switched it on again? Sometime before morning, after Dexter was asleep.

Grandfather had upset all the aunts the day preceding his death, but surely none of them seriously enough to endanger his own life. Unless it were Aunt Judith, who valued her specimens above everything.

No, no, it was all fantastic. Rodney was right. Nothing like that would happen here. Her dramatic discovery was useless. Of course no one would see it in the light she had. Even she herself was beginning to think she really had behaved with foolish impetuosity. Why hadn't she gone to the aunts with the story before getting a taxi and rushing to Rodney? She hadn't done that because she had known there would be some plausible explanation forthcoming – just as there had been. And now she was made to look silly and childish, and there was a certain amount of hostility in Aunt Hester's eyes, at least. Who was she to rush about making insinuations about the family's integrity?

Well, she thought hopelessly, she had done her best for grandfather. But even he would have resented her criticism of the actions of any member of the Armour family, even though those actions had hastened his death!

Rodney had to go out and make a call – he was already an hour late – and she was left there with the three aunts. For the first time she was embarrassed and uncomfortable with them. She felt like a traitress, and she deserved their hostility.

But unexpectedly they were kind.

"Willow's going to make us all a nice cup of tea," Aunt Opal declared cozily. She rang the bell and in a few moments Willow, secret and beautiful, appeared.

"Tea, please, Willow. I know it's an odd time, but Lois is a little out of sorts. And see if you can beg some of those lemon honey tarts I saw Clara making from her."

"Yes, miss," Willow said obediently. Lois saw the girl flick her a glance. Her face was sulky now. She resented having to make tea at an odd time because Lois needed it. The girl *was* jealous but was it because she had to wait on Lois or because Lois was Rodney's wife?

She started to go out, and then remembering something, returned.

"This is my night to go to Dalchester," she said directly to Aunt Opal. "Is it all right?"

"Oh, yes," said Aunt Opal. It seemed to Lois that her voice had changed in some indefinable way — or was that imagination, too? "Lois, once a month Willow goes to spend the night with her parents. She returns the following night. Rodney has always driven her to the station and met her again. Do you think he will be able to tonight?"

"Why, of course," said Lois. "If someone isn't having a baby or something awkward like that."

"That's all right, then, Willow."

"Yes. Thank you, miss." Who was she thanking? Aunt Opal? Or Lois for her generosity in lending her husband? Lois thought she would never be able to decide whether Willow's remarks were made in all innocence or whether they were deep and double-edged.

What did she and Rodney talk about on those drives — with Willow out of uniform and her strange eyes shining?

"Rodney's always been so good to Willow," Aunt Opal observed complacently when the girl had withdrawn. "He looks on her more as a friend than a servant. Such a nice attitude."

"Rodney never was a snob," Aunt Hester said. "But then Willow's no ordinary servant."

"You don't let her be an ordinary servant," Lois wanted to burst out. "You make her think the house would collapse without her."

How much had Willow had to do with that spider episode? And Willow was the one who had found grandfather's light burning in daylight.

"She walks like a cat," Aunt Judith said suddenly. "Have you ever noticed? That rhythmic grace. She's a very sensuous creature."

"Don't use those queer adjectives, Judith," Aunt Opal said snappily. "She's a very good-looking girl. I just can't think what we would do without her."

Rodney was home in time to drive Willow to the station. He invited Lois to go, too, but suddenly she couldn't face coping with Willow's enigmatic conversation or the way Willow would look in the moonlight. Her problems were too numerous already. She said she had a headache and would go to bed early. She noticed Willow was wearing Rodney's

180

locket when she left.

Rodney came straight upstairs when he returned. Lois was in bed, and he sat on the edge of the bed and looked at her in a thoughtful probing way. She probably looked pale and washed-out in comparison with Willow's radiant beauty, but she couldn't help that. At the moment she didn't even care.

"Did Willow catch her train?" she asked.

"Yes."

"How often have you been driving her in like this?"

"Once a month for the last couple of years."

"I suppose she likes it."

"She finds it convenient."

(What does she talk about when she's out of this house? Does she use all the enchanting feminine tricks which she must possess under that secretive exterior?)

"Rodney, why do the aunts pamper her so much?"

"I expect it's because they're three childless women who want someone to spoil. They spoiled me, too, and they'd spoil you if you'd let them." (Would they? Lois wondered.) "Besides, Willow's such a pretty thing, and anyone's instinct is to cherish something pretty."

"Who buys her all those things in her bedroom?"

"What things, darling?"

"The expensive face creams and things. I've never been able to afford them."

"I wouldn't know about that," Rodney answered. His voice was completely honest. "She's a vain little piece and the aunts pay her well. She probably buys them herself. Or she may have a boyfriend in Finchin. She doesn't tell much, you know."

"Rodney, a boyfriend in Finchin wouldn't even know the name of a French perfume. Can you imagine?"

Rodney laughed.

"That was a bad guess. All right, I don't know where she gets her stuff from. But don't let's worry about her. How's your head?"

"Not terribly good."

"You worry too much about things that don't even exist."

"After all, Rodney, grandfather did die of suffocation. You said so yourself."

Rodney frowned. His jaw tightened.

"Look, darling, if you fell unconscious on a soft pillow you'd smother, too. Honestly, sweet, you'll have to stop thinking these things. As a matter of fact, I'm worrying about you. I think you'll have to have a change."

"A change?"

"Yes. Get right away from Crow Hollow for

two or three weeks. God knows how I'm going to do without you, but you are in a nervous state and it'll be the best thing for you."

A change — an escape from Crow Hollow even if only for a couple of weeks. She would be able to breathe again.

"Would you like it, darling? Is there anywhere in particular you'd like to go?"

"Oh, Rodney, I'd adore seeing Cass again. I've neglected her badly. I've put so little in letters." (Because things seemed so monstrous and unlikely in writing.) "I really do think she'd do me good. But couldn't you come, too?"

"Afraid not. I haven't even grandfather to keep an eye on things now. Anyway, I think a complete change from all of us is the wisest thing. The Armours have been a little overwhelming. Eh, dearest?"

Lois held up her arms. She loved Rodney more than she had ever thought she would love anybody. She hated to be parted from him. But this escape to London, to the apartment and Cass with her humor and her practical common sense, was like a reprieve.

XII

Cass, a familiar figure in her crumpled pajamas and brilliantly floral housecoat, stood at Lois's bedside with a tray.

"You needn't think," she said, "that I'm your blooming maid. I'm just breaking it gently that you'll have to turn to yourself."

Lois laughed.

"It will be wonderful even peeling potatoes. You've no idea."

Cass sat on the edge of the bed. Her round shrewd blue eyes were affectionate.

"So you don't take to being a lady."

"It isn't being a lady, Cass. It's being a nonentity. As if, by being kept useless, my existence will be forgotten."

"You had your chance when the old man died."

"That's what Rodney said. He thought he meant it, but he didn't really. Even he couldn't see the aunts ousted. Besides —"

"Besides what?"

Lois's eyes got dark and introspective.

"Nothing, Cass. I mustn't dwell on it. I've come here to recover from my silly suspicions."

"So you think if you became too obstreperous the next incident would be something less chancy than a poisonous spider or a pillow over your face."

Lois looked up wildly.

"Cass, you don't believe that, too."

Cass slapped her gently through the bedclothes.

"I side with Rodney. He has all my sympathy for marrying a writer. They don't see things the way they are; they see them the way they'd be most effective in a book. You set to work and write a book about Crow Hollow. Seems to me you've got material there that's crying out to be used. And it would keep you occupied and happy."

"I wonder," said Lois slowly, "if that's been partly the trouble. I've felt I couldn't write down there, but I've been writing since I was sixteen, and stopping suddenly like this — perhaps that's why I've felt so lost."

"It could be," Cass agreed. "Why, you

haven't even written me a decent letter. 'It's been nice weather here. Grandfather's phlox bed looks wonderful.' That's the sort of thing I was starved on."

Lois laughed, then stopped laughing as again she remembered.

"The first letter I wrote to you was going to be really good. But that was the day I found Willow trying on my suit. Something dried up in me then. I couldn't seem to write naturally about anything."

"This Willow," said Cass thoughtfully. "Everything else probably exists in your imagination, but she's real. She seems to be the heroine — or the villain — of the piece. You ought to try to find out more about her."

"Yes," Lois answered reluctantly.

"You said she goes to Dalchester to see her parents."

"Yes, she does."

"Then couldn't you make some inquiries of somebody in Dalchester?"

"Willow's just a maid working for the Armours. That's all I would find out. And no matter what I discovered nothing would change the aunts' attitude towards her."

"Extraordinary," Cass muttered. "But never mind. If she's so beautiful it's inevitable she'll get married soon, and that will be the end of

Willow as far as you're concerned."

At Crow Hollow Lois would have given full rein to her morbid conviction that she would never be rid of Willow, that the girl would be there like a shadow to the end of her life. But here, already, she felt sane and imbued with some of Cass's common sense.

"Yes, I expect she will," she said with relief. "And talking of weddings, haven't you and Alec fixed the day yet?"

"We're waiting for our house to be finished. It's such a doll's house. I expect you could put the whole thing in your drawing room. But we like it. Hey, what's wrong?"

Lois hastily flicked away a tear.

"Nothing. I mean − do you know how lucky you are, having your own home?"

Cass squeezed her shoulder.

"Two months of marriage to a doctor and you're worn out. Wait till I tell that Rodney of yours what I think of him. Never mind, good old Cassandra, the mug, will build you up again. How about starting by drinking that coffee?"

Lois sipped the coffee. She felt better all the time. Being with Cass and free entirely of shadows was wonderful. She would like to stay for months. Would Rodney mind very much?

She wrote a new story and got Cass's meals

and shopped. She wrote to Rodney several times and once, dutifully, to Aunt Opal. Rodney's answers she looked forward to eagerly, but they gave her no nostalgia for Crow Hollow, although it must be beautiful now with the leaves of the trees and creeper flushing deeper and deeper, and dahlias out in the garden. Winter was coming. Could she endure the desolation of a winter there? She would rather stay here with Cass. She was a person with a profession. She should be able to choose her place of abode for at least six months of the year. Would Rodney mind if she stayed here until the spring?

Then, walking towards her favorite park one day, she passed a flower seller with late carnations on his tray. Abruptly and intolerably the perfume brought her to life. For a month she had been in a dream, but now, now, her senses were alive again, she had to go back to Rodney. How could she have stayed away so long?

She sent a telegram RETURNING TOMORROW and hurried back to the apartment to pack.

When Cass came home and saw the suitcase she said dryly, "So you love the guy, after all."

Lois nodded, her cheeks glowing.

"I needed the rest, you've been marvelous to me, Cass, but now I feel wonderful again."

"So I'm relegated to the status of a tonic."

Cass gave her cheerful grin. "Well, if I've given you courage to cope with the ravishing Willow I seem to have performed some use in life." Then she said with the rare seriousness that made her words so much more impressive, "Don't let things get you down, kid. You don't need to. You've got the stuff it takes. But don't keep me in the dark this time. I want to know everything. Everything. See?"

Lois knew that this, in Cass's cryptic way, was just as much an offer of help as grandfather's had been. There was little that Cass, so far away, could do about any event that happened at Crow Hollow, but her offer was comforting, nonetheless. Cass might scoff at her fears, but she wouldn't ignore them as even Rodney did.

But nothing disturbing was going to happen. Everything from now on was going to be simple, placid and beautiful.

There was another reason, not told even to Cass, why she had wanted to return. She wasn't sure whether she would tell Rodney yet or not. When she saw him waiting on the station, however, saw his slender upright figure with his shoulders squared with that peculiar tenseness she knew so well, she realized she could keep nothing from him. She stepped off the train and walked sedately towards him.

189

"Hello," she said.

Never demonstrative in public, Rodney leaned to give her a brief kiss. But his eyes were shining.

"Hello, darling, had a good time?"

"Wonderful, thanks. I've been cooking meals and writing stories and shopping and going to theaters and walking in the park. Our park, Rodney. I sat on the same bench. When that bench is worn out we'll have to raise a monument there to mark the spot."

"You enjoy London, don't you?"

"Yes, I do. But there are other things I enjoy, too." She took his arm. "Let's drive home very slowly."

He smiled. He looked young and happy.

"The beauty about a car is that there's no telephone in it. We'll crawl."

Joe Higgins, waiting with his taxi, tipped his hat to them as they went out.

"No fare today, Joe," Rodney called.

"That's all right, doc. Glad to see you back, Mrs. Doc."

"Thank you, Joe. I'm glad to be back." She was glad, too. The countryside with its yellowing trees and stubble fields looked warm, placid and restful. It had a fulfilled look, and that fitted in with her mood perfectly.

"How are the aunts?" she asked as they drove

slowly down the narrow road.

"Oh, very well. Aunt Opal's up to her eyes in preserves. Aunt Hester has taken over the garden, since it seems difficult to get a reliable man. By the way, remind me to stop in the village to get some strychnine. Aunt Hester complains that rabbits are getting in the garden and nibbling the small plants and she wants to kill them. Aunt Judith is the same as usual. She hasn't acquired any more specimens of particular interest, thank the Lord."

"And Willow?"

"Oh, Willow's all right."

No details about Willow. Well, that was all right, too. Why should there be?

"Rodney, it was nice of you not to ask me to come back, to let me take my time."

"I wanted you to have the break. I wanted you to come back exactly when you were ready. But it's been a hell of a time. Last night when I got your telegram I could have jumped over the moon."

Lois laughed, leaning her head against his arm.

"What did you do?"

"I went down to Josh Peabody's and booked the rest of his Napoleon brandy."

She was so happy he was glad to have her back. How could she really have enjoyed being away? She let her fingers run down his arm.

"Rodney, we're going to have a baby."

Instantly she was aware of his tensing.

"Are you sure?"

"Do I have to answer in medical terms? I haven't been to a doctor. I only know by myself, and — and instinct. But I'm practically certain."

Something wasn't quite right. He wasn't as jubilant as he should be. But Rodney seldom showed jubilation.

"Rodney, stop the car and kiss me."

Obediently he stopped the car. He turned to look at her, and although his mouth was kind there was that withdrawn look about him again.

"So that's why you came back," he said. It wasn't a question, but a statement.

"Yes, of course it is partly. I wanted to tell you at once. I didn't even tell Cass. But that wasn't the only reason —" She wanted to tell him about smelling the carnations and the irresistible longing that had swept over her. She wanted to explain that for a month she had been in a peculiar dormant state, recovering from the strain of the events at Crow Hollow, and thinking of nothing, then how suddenly she had come to life. But the closed look on his face dried up her spontaneity, as always. She

192

could only say lamely, "I wanted to come back. Truly."

"Did you?"

"After all, the baby didn't need to bring me back. I could have had it in London. Rodney, you hurt yourself by being so — so critical of emotions."

He gave a little sigh.

"I'm sorry, Lois. I wanted to think it was just for me —"

"But it was for you, Rodney. Please believe me."

He bent his head to kiss her. She could feel the controlled hunger in his lips. She longed to comfort him, to convince him she was entirely his. But it was impossible while he deliberately held himself away so much.

"Rodney, are you pleased about the baby?"

"Of course, darling. Delighted. You're very clever. As for what the aunts are going to say, there'll be no holding them."

The aunts! This was Rodney's and her baby, not the aunts'. But they would have to know.

In the meantime everything was all right. Rodney was pleased, she knew. She had just chosen the wrong time to tell him.

There was an enormous bowl of red and yellow dahlias on the table beside Lois's bed. Aunt Opal, who had followed Lois upstairs, said indulgently, "That's Hester. She insisted on putting them there. Hester's gone quite crazy on gardening. Well, it's a hobby for her. We women without men have to have hobbies." She smiled her sweet patient smile, and Lois wondered, as she had done other times, why Aunt Opal never married.

"The dahlias are lovely," she said, taking off her hat. "I'm sure you, at least, never needed to be a woman without a man, Aunt Opal."

Aunt Opal bridled satisfactorily, but there was something else besides pleasure at the back of her eyes. What was it? Sadness over a long-ago romance? Poor Aunt Opal with her soft feminine body which was made for love and babies, having to direct her affections to other people's children. Rodney, Willow, the baby that was coming.

"That's as may be," she said enigmatically. "But I did use to have pretty hair. Quite golden. Can you be ready for dinner in half an hour?"

"Yes, of course."

"Clara's a little touchy today. I've had to help her with the apple jelly. Butter and preserves are Clara's failings. Otherwise she's a good cook. But she can't bear correction. This afternoon she quite lost her temper, all over the silly old jelly. So I don't want to make matters worse by having her keep dinner. Really, one needs to be a diplomat to manage servants nowadays."

"I'm sure you are one, Aunt Opal."

Aunt Opal patted Lois's hand gently.

"You say such nice things, dear. It's so nice having you back. We've all missed you. Rodney's been quite a bear. So unlike him. Willow's been the only person who could get a smile out of him."

Lois was conscious of that familiar trickle of distaste, distaste only, not fear. Why did Aunt Opal have to spoil things when she was feeling so happy to be back by mentioning Willow's name in that way? Of course, on Aunt Opal's part, it was entirely innocent. Rodney's response to Willow, also, would be innocent and natural, the way a man responded to a pretty girl. But how innocent were Willow's motives?

Lois, who had been brushing her hair, put down the brush with a bang. She wasn't going to start her silly and groundless imaginings the moment she had arrived back. They were over and done with. From now on she accepted and enjoyed Willow's charm as did everyone else.

"I'll just change my dress and then I'll be down, Aunt Opal," she said briskly.

Aunt Opal moved forward eagerly.

"Oh, did you buy some new clothes in London?"

"Yes, one or two things."

"Do show them to Willow, dear. The naughty child does so love new things."

Yes, thought Lois grimly, she does. Willow would look at the clothes whether she were shown them or not, that was definite.

She wasn't going to get suspicious and impatient so easily!

"Of course, Aunt Opal. Tomorrow I will."

Rodney came in while she was changing.

"Darling, I'll get Foster to have a look at you tomorrow. It may be a little early for anything definite, but I'd like you to have a checkup. And I suggest we say nothing to the aunts until it is definite."

"That's exactly what I think," Lois said gratefully. "It would be awful if we had to disappoint them in the end."

She hadn't realized how she had dreaded their fussing. A postponement of that made her feel lighthearted and gay.

She went down to dinner cheerfully, calling a friendly greeting to Willow whom she saw in the hall.

Willow answered, "Good evening, miss," in her expressionless voice, without giving any sign that she was pleased or displeased to see

Lois back. But the girl's beauty shone like a star in the dark hall.

There was a fire in the dining room, and the room with its drawn curtains and dark shining furniture looked almost cheerful. Aunt Hester, looking highly colored and handsome in a dark red dress, came forward to kiss Lois decisively on one cheek.

"Well, child, I heard you were back. I hope your holiday did you good."

"I feel very well, thank you, Aunt Hester."

"You look a bit peaked. City food, I expect. There's nothing like a good country meal. Well, we're glad you came back."

Had they thought she might not come back? Had they hoped she wouldn't and were now putting as good a face as possible on her return? But Aunt Hester's welcome seemed genuine enough, even if it hadn't been as affectionate as Aunt Opal's. Aunt Hester wasn't very good at showing emotions. She covered her feelings with her brisk domineering manner.

"Did Rodney remember that strychnine for me?" she went on. "I'm doing the garden for a bit, as he's probably told you, and those naughty rabbits keep getting in."

"Yes, he did remember it, Aunt Hester."

"Good. I'll try it out."

Aunt Judith came in with her soundless sidling walk (like a spider, Lois thought) and fixed her blank gaze on Lois.

"Ah, Lois. Back again."

"Yes, Aunt Judith. How are you?"

"Very busy as usual."

"What on earth at?" Aunt Hester demanded. "I have the garden on my hands now, it occupies practically all my time. I've had to neglect some of my invalids. And Opal's been preserving. But you escape all these jobs."

"I've been cataloging my specimens," Aunt Judith replied stiffly. "It's quite a task, as I am sure Lois would understand."

"Have you got any new specimens?" Lois asked.

"Nothing important. But you must ask Dexter to show you where the toadstools grow in the woods. He's brought me some beauties. Crimson, with golden spots."

"Deadly poison," Aunt Hester said. "How you do like poisonous things, Judith! Ah, here's Opal. Now perhaps we can have dinner."

Aunt Opal, followed by Rodney, came in and they all sat down. Lois could hear a rising wind beating against the windows. It had a cold sound. It gave her her first apprehension of winter here, stormbound in the house with all these women. But it was cheerful tonight with the snapping fire. She wouldn't allow herself to look ahead.

"So nice to be all together again," Aunt Opal said in her cozy voice. Willow carried in the soup and passed the plates around.

"You'll be ready for a hot meal, Lois. Indeed, we all are. It's getting positively wintry at nights."

As Willow went out Aunt Judith leaned across the table. There was a queer sly look in her eyes.

"You didn't ask Lois if she brought a present for Willow, Opal. Did you, Lois?"

A present for Willow! Why on earth should she? If everyone else treated Willow like a spoiled child she at least was not going to do so.

"I'm afraid I didn't," she answered clearly.

"That's nonsense, Aunt Judith," Rodney said. "Willow wouldn't expect Lois to bring her a present."

"But everyone else does," Aunt Judith insisted.

"And how often do you go to town and buy presents for anyone?" Aunt Opal said sharply. "Never! Besides, no one is compelled to buy gifts here. A gift is made spontaneously or not at all. Isn't that so, Rodney?"

"I'm afraid it's a bad habit as far as Willow is concerned," Rodney said evasively. "She gets so intoxicated with possessions. She ought to be broken of it."

"Oh no, it gives the child such pleasure," Aunt Opal protested softly. "It would be unkind never to think of her."

"Opal!" Aunt Hester exclaimed indignantly. "This soup is burned."

Aunt Opal sipped tentatively.

"I believe you're right. Oh, that Clara! She's getting so temperamental. Just because I corrected her about the apple jelly. I do hope she hasn't ruined the roast."

But the meat was charred, the potatoes and cabbage soggy, and the apple pie undercooked. Aunt Opal was nearly in tears.

"Really! I did want this to be a good meal for Lois's first night back. I'm almost afraid Clara is getting more than I can handle."

Aunt Hester pushed her plate away.

"Poisonous mess," she muttered. "I'll speak to Clara."

Aunt Opal started up.

"No, please don't, Hester. Please don't. You're so blunt. You'll make matters worse."

"Leave Clara alone," Rodney suggested mildly. "Anyone can have his off-moments."

"I'm sure she's done it deliberately," Aunt

Opal wailed. "But I suppose Rodney's right. We must overlook it for this once."

"Perhaps she's in love," Aunt Judith suggested.

"Oh, no, no, not Clara. Now if it had been Willow there would be some reason to think that. But not staid old Clara."

"It's a puzzle to me that Willow doesn't fall in love," Aunt Hester observed. "A nice looking girl like that. What do you think, Rodney?"

"She's only a kid," said Rodney indulgently.

Lois looked at him sideways. Did he really think that? Couldn't he see through Willow's pose — she behaved like a sweet and precocious child because it got her what she wanted. But she wouldn't always behave that way.

"Willow's not a child," Aunt Opal said. "She's over twenty. Ah well, I expect some day we must lose her to some young man. I only hope he'll be worthy of her. Now, let us sit by the fire, and in a little while Willow shall make us some sandwiches to compensate for that dreadful dinner."

It was as Lois was going to her room that Clara, darting along the passage leading to the kitchen, waylaid her and said, "Could I have a word with you, ma'am?"

"Of course," said Lois. "I'll come to the kitchen."

"No, not there, ma'am. That Willow listens at doors."

It was intolerable to think that there was no room in the house in which she could be private except her own bedroom. Not stopping to reflect on that then Lois led the way upstairs.

"We'll be quite undisturbed in my room," she said.

Clara followed her into the bedroom and shut the door behind her. Fixing her smoldering gaze on Lois she said, "I want to give notice, ma'am."

"Oh, Clara, I'm sorry. But if there's something wrong shouldn't you go to Miss Opal?"

"I won't have no truck with Miss Opal, ma'am. You're the rightful mistress here, and I'll give you my notice."

A little taken aback Lois said again, "I am sorry you want to go, Clara. What is the trouble? Was it the dinner tonight?"

"No, it wasn't the dinner, though I couldn't fix my mind on it the way I was feeling. Nor was it the apple jelly. I can make apple jelly every bit as good as Miss Opal's, and butter, too, if it comes to that. She only makes up those things about my preserves so's to explain my bad temper."

"Oh," said Lois slowly. "Then what is the reason for your bad temper?"

"I thought you'd have guessed that, ma'am. There's only one reason it could be." She paused and her face was full of resentment. "It's that Willow. I can't work with her any longer."

"What's wrong with her, Clara?"

"Wrong! I'd say just about everything. She's lazy and impertinent. She doesn't do half her work. She spends hours in that fancy room of hers preening herself, and then when I goes off about the work not done she runs to Miss Opal or one of your aunts and complains that I bully her. Bully her! You can't bully that kind. They haven't any natural feelings."

So Clara had reached that conclusion, too, that Willow was strange and secret and impervious to a great deal.

"But Clara, this must have been going on for a long time. What particularly has happened now to make you give notice?"

"I been thinking of it for some time, but today put the lid on when I had to do all that apple jelly, and baking and cleaning, too, and Miss Opal comes to me and says, 'Clara, I hope you can manage today. I've given Willow the day off until this evening.'"

"But why?" Lois asked. "Didn't she have her usual day off this week?"

"That she did. Why'd she get another one? Well, as you can guess, it would be no use asking Willow. But I know well enough. It's because she didn't like the idea of you coming back. She never did like you being here. It's put her nose out of joint, so to speak. That sounds crazy, her just being a maid, but the Miss Armours have spoiled her something shocking, ma'am, and she thought she mightn't get so many little presents and things. Anyway, she must have had a tantrum after your telegram came, and Miss Opal had to pacify her."

"Clara, this is all fantastic."

"It does sound that way, ma'am, but that's how I see it. And I don't care to be put upon any longer. Now, if there was just you and Mr. Rodney—"

"All right, Clara," Lois interjected quickly. "I appreciate your loyalty and I'm very sorry you're going. But I think you ought to tell Miss Opal yourself."

Clara shook her head stubbornly.

"I'll just go, if you don't mind. Miss Opal might try bribing me with Fleur de lis perfume, or something like that," her voice was scathing, "and it wouldn't work with plain old Clara."

Lois debated telling the aunts, and decided against it. Clara might have changed her mind by morning. If she hadn't they would find out soon enough that she had gone. But the ever-present problem of Willow nagged at her all the evening. It wasn't pleasant having her own guess that Willow resented her presence substantiated. All at once all her old doubts and fears were back. She kept seeing the spider run down her arm and hearing Willow scream as she jumped back out of danger. Willow had known to keep her distance, so she must have known it was no ordinary spider. And the next morning grandfather had made her cry. Why? Because the tea was cold, or because he suspected she had had something to do with the spider? Had he let her see he knew the truth — and so he had died?

It was Willow who had seen the light under his door in the morning. Had she known it would be shining there? Was she the one who had run back to the room to switch it on?

In bed later Lois moved restlessly and said, "Rodney, why didn't Willow like me coming back?"

Rodney moved over to press his face against her neck.

"Darling, it's your first night back. Don't let's talk of Willow."

"Everyone else was pleased to see me," Lois said doggedly. "Why did Willow have to be bribed with a day off?"

"Did she?"

"Yes. Clara told me. Clara's leaving because she resents the way the aunts spoil Willow."

"Honey, are you in a conspiracy with Clara?"

"Rodney, must Willow stay? It's utterly ridiculous, but I don't think we'll ever have peace in this house while she's here. She's too disturbing."

"She is disturbing," Rodney admitted lazily. "She's too damn good-looking. But you have no need to be jealous."

Lois sat upright.

"Jealous! Rodney, how perfectly absurd!"

Rodney's arm around her pulled her down again.

"That's the effect one derives from your arguments," he said good-naturedly.

Then he kissed her and the laziness went out of his body. She could feel his tense hunger.

"Have you missed me?"

"Of course."

"Why didn't you come back sooner?"

"You didn't ask me to."

"I couldn't. You had to stay as long as you wanted." His voice was jerky, tight with emotion. "I could have come to London to see you. I wouldn't do that. It had to be you yourself wanting to come back. Uninfluenced." Imperceptibly his grip lessened. He had been trying to convince himself, but he couldn't entirely. "It was because of the baby, wasn't it?"

Lois could hear the wind against the house again. She could hear a branch rasping on the roof somewhere, and downstairs a window was banging. The momentary warmth and comfort of Rodney's embrace left her. As she grew aware of his doubts she felt tired and flat and empty. He wouldn't believe anything she said, so why should she struggle to convince him about her love for him?

"It would be untrue to say the baby wasn't partly the reason," she said wearily. "Have you made an appointment with Doctor Foster?"

"Yes, for tomorrow morning. You'd better come in with me. It will raise less comment here."

But when Doctor Foster confirmed her own knowledge, the aunts would be told and Willow would hear. Lying in the dark Lois suddenly had a clear vision of Willow, lovely and secret, bending over her child's perambulator. . . .

She began to shiver uncontrollably.

Rodney was instantly professional.

"Darling, what's wrong? Have you caught cold?"

Lois tried to bite her trembling lips. The wind seemed to be in the room, billowing the curtains and touching her with icy fingers. "I think — I must have. I feel shivery all at once."

"Willow won't have gone to bed yet. I'll get her to make you a hot drink."

Lois clutched him.

"No!" She couldn't keep the panic out of her voice. She was at once ashamed of it and tried to speak lightly. "Don't disturb Willow. If I must have a drink you make it, please!"

XIII

The surprising thing was that it was a cold Lois had, and that had surely enough been the reason for her shivering the night before. She had thought it was her foolish and uncontrolled nervousness, and it was a relief to attribute the whole thing to a cold. She felt dull and headachy, but not too ill to keep her appointment with Doctor Foster.

Rodney had to go out early to a pneumonia case. He told Lois to be sure to stay in bed until Willow brought her breakfast, and he would call back for her later. Absorbed in his work, he had forgotten about Clara and the turmoil into which the house would be thrown. Lois hadn't. She didn't wait for Willow to bring her breakfast because she shrewdly guessed that Willow wasn't capable of cooking a breakfast. She got up and dressed. Being on her feet made her feel worse. She had her first sensation of nausea — that was the baby, bless him — and everything seemed unreal. In a moment she would wake up and find herself back at the apartment with Cass, or at home with Daddy, trying to make him leave his work and come for a meal. Dear Daddy with his kindness, his little jokes and his preoccupation. She wished he could have known Rodney. If she had had some family it might have counterbalanced Rodney's family and made them seem less overwhelming.

As she was finishing dressing Aunt Opal tapped at the door, and then, without waiting for Lois to speak, burst in.

"Oh, you're up," she said. "Perhaps that's just as well, because dear knows when breakfast will be ready. Clara's gone! Without a word to anybody she's just up and gone."

For some curious reason Aunt Opal's voice, usually so soothing, made the pain beat in Lois's head. Her indignation with Clara had given it a sharp penetrating timbre.

"Willow came to me this morning saying there was no sign of Clara and her bed hadn't been slept in. I couldn't believe she had really gone until I saw she had taken all her things.

Why couldn't she tell me instead of creeping away like a thief? If she had a grievance I could have done something about it. If it was just that silly apple jelly —"

"It wasn't the apple jelly, Aunt Opal," Lois interrupted. She hadn't meant to disclose any knowledge of the miserable business, but standing there listening to Aunt Opal's tirade some loyalty to Clara, or just some peculiar perversity of her own, made her speak.

"It wasn't — but how do you know, Lois?" Aunt Opal's voice suddenly sharpened. "Did Clara speak to you?"

"Yes. She told me last night she wanted to leave."

"But, Lois! Why didn't you tell me?" Aunt Opal's face puckered perplexedly. "I'm not saying Clara should have come to me. She's got some peculiar notions, and if it was I who upset her she would do this to annoy me. But really, dear, if only you'd said."

"I don't know why I didn't," Lois said vaguely. Her headache was knocking against her temples, making her feel sick and dazed. "I wasn't very well last night. I've caught a cold, I think. I still feel a little queer."

"Then you should stay in bed."

"No, I'll be all right. I'm going out with Rodney this morning. I'm sorry about Clara,

Aunt Opal, but nothing could have been done, anyway. It was no use persuading her to stay, the way she feels about Willow."

"About Willow!"

"Oh yes, of course, I didn't tell you. Clara resented Willow's privileges."

"Willow's privileges! What utter nonsense! Willow gets no privileges but those she earns. Clara, I would point out, earned none. Clara, with her sulks and her temperaments!"

Lois suddenly realized she felt too tired to argue with Aunt Opal. To give her her due she was so biased in Willow's favor that no doubt she didn't realize she pampered the girl beyond all reason. Anyway, no arguments would convince her otherwise.

"Willow," Aunt Opal went on, "is the sweetest natured and most satisfactory maid we have ever had here. Both my sisters agree on this. We treat her well because we don't want to lose her. One has to do that with maids nowadays."

"Then what about Clara?"

"Clara was treated well, too, but she was such a prickly person one couldn't do much for her. Really, now I'm getting over the shock of finding her gone. I'm beginning to realize it may be a very good thing. She was getting beyond me to manage, as I told you last night.

We'll get another cook. In the meantime Hester and I will cope somehow. But another time, Lois dear, if one of the maids comes to you with any grievance perhaps it might be wise to let me know."

"I'm afraid, Aunt Opal, if you go on treating Willow the way you do no other maid is going to stay." What had given her the courage to say that? Her indignation about Clara's injustices, or the unreality of everything this morning?

Aunt Opal gave her pretty placid smile. The sharpness had gone out of her voice. It had its old crooning note.

"Now, foolish child, you're getting as bad as Clara. Willow holds a superior position. She is really my companion. It was only because father insisted that she had other duties. Naturally she is entitled to advantages. You leave this servant problem to me, dear. Don't you worry your head about it. Now I must hurry down and see about the breakfast. I must say I'm glad that at least we don't have to wonder if Clara has walked off with the silver!"

Aunt Hester, however, had taken charge in the kitchen and breakfast was not above half an hour late. Willow, her serenity unchanged, carried in the porridge and everyone sat down.

Faced with the steaming porridge, Lois found she could not eat. She swallowed a mouthful, then sat back trying to dispel her dizziness.

"What's wrong with my porridge, Lois?" Aunt Hester demanded.

"Nothing's wrong with it, Aunt Hester. It's me, I'm afraid."

"Lois has caught a cold," Aunt Opal explained gently. "I told her she should have stayed in bed. You really should have, dear."

"I'll be all right," Lois said stubbornly. She couldn't be going to be ill. The very thought of having to stay in bed here filled her with sheer panic. And the panic was probably caused by the way she was feeling. She was in a vicious circle.

"I'll bring you your coffee, miss," she heard Willow saying unexpectedly behind her.

"Thank you, Willow," she managed to say. She nearly laughed at the irony of feeling gratitude to Willow. That was the last emotion she thought she would have had in connection with Willow.

After the coffee she felt better. When Rodney came in she was quite ready to go with him.

"Lois hasn't eaten any breakfast," Aunt Hester told him. "She shouldn't be going out."

"We really think she should spend the day in bed, Rodney," Aunt Opal added.

Rodney looked at her. She could see the understanding in his eyes. For the first time he understood that she hated the aunts fussing. Her jubilation over that made her feel almost normal again.

"The drive will do her good," she heard him saying. "We'll get some morning tea in the village."

Alone with her in the car he said, "What's wrong? Why aren't you eating?"

"I just feel rotten with this cold. And porridge, Rodney!"

"Never mind. If Foster tells us what we want to hear you'll have a good excuse not to eat it for the next few months."

She had known she wasn't wrong, but it gave her a feeling of excited joy to hear Doctor Foster confirm her opinion.

"Mind you, we can't be absolutely sure for a few days," he said. "But I think there's no doubt. Now you're to go home and go to bed."

"To bed!" Lois echoed. She liked this elderly doctor with his lined face and mild perceptive eyes, but she didn't like his prescription.

"Yes, you're running a slight temperature. You've caught a chill. Nothing in the least serious, but you don't want to take risks now. Your husband can prescribe for this particular ailment. Come and see me again in a month."

He stood up and held out his hand. "And congratulations, Mrs. Armour. This is grand news. It's a pity my old friend, Doctor Armour, couldn't have lived to hear it."

"Yes," said Lois warily. "He was very anxious to have a great-grandson."

"He certainly was. He made no secret of it. Well, let's go and congratulate the young man's father instead."

Lois didn't hear very clearly what Doctor Foster said to Rodney because her dizziness had come back. She caught the words, "Two or three days in bed," and then Rodney took her arm and led her out, and she was in the car again, and all the joy she had felt had drained out of her at the thought of having to stay in bed with the aunts looking after her.

When they arrived back and Rodney helped her out of the car she clutched his arm.

"Rodney, if I have to go to bed you stay with me. Please!"

"Of course, darling. As long as I can."

"Until the telephone rings, I suppose."

"You'll be sleepy by then. Come and we'll tell the aunts."

"Must we? They fuss so."

"But they will take particularly good care of you, and that's what I want. Think how hurt they'd be if we kept them in the dark."

"Yes, I suppose so. Well, let's get it over."

Perhaps it was the way her head ached, but the resultant scene was a great deal worse than she had imagined it would be. Aunt Opal wept softly, holding her lacy handkerchief to her eyes. Aunt Hester clasped her large hands over her stomach and said, "She must be built up! She's too thin!" (How long did she think a pregnant woman stayed thin!) And Aunt Judith had a peculiar dreamy look in her eyes as she visualized, Lois guessed, the beautiful new specimen the baby would be.

"So a new life replaces the old," Aunt Opal crooned tearfully. "How wonderful it all is."

"Homo sapiens," Aunt Judith murmured.

"What?" barked Aunt Hester.

"Homo sapiens. The classification."

"In the meantime," said Rodney practically, "Lois's cold is worse and she has to go to bed."

"We said you shouldn't have taken her out. Ah, but of course, you were going to the doctor. You two naughty conspiring children." Aunt Opal shook her finger playfully. Then she stood up. "I'll get Willow to fill a hot bottle at once."

"I'll make you some soup, Lois," Aunt Hester announced. "You'll find that perfectly easy to eat."

"Thank you," Lois murmured. "You're all so

217

kind." Her glance as she left the room rested last on Aunt Judith who sat dreaming over the little new *Homo sapiens* that she would like to put in a bottle and catalogue.

After all, the day went quickly. She slept a good deal, and twice Rodney was there when she woke. Towards evening when she woke again her head felt better, and her spirits began to revive. She looked around for Rodney, but the chair where he had been sitting was empty. She tinkled the little bell which Aunt Opal had thoughtfully placed at her bedside, and in a few moments Aunt Opal came bustling in.

"What is it, dear? Do you want something?"

"No, thank you, Aunt Opal. I just wondered if Rodney were in."

"Oh, dear, he had to go out. He was dreadfully sorry, but he got word that that pneumonia case was worse. He said he might be some time, but you weren't to worry."

Lois's newly revived spirits instantly flagged. It was stupid of her to be so affected by Rodney's absence, but today she couldn't help it. Whenever he wasn't near she was filled with the oddest sensation of panic.

"Are you feeling a little better, dear?"

She moved her head tiredly.

"I thought I was, but—"

"I know what the trouble is exactly. You

need something to eat. After all, you've had nothing all day. You must be quite starved."

"I'm not in the least hungry, Aunt Opal."

"That's what you think, but when you've eaten a little you'll feel a great deal better. Just wait while I run and tell Hester."

While she was gone Lois idly counted the dragons on the wall. It was getting dark and they were beginning to shine and wink in the gloom. She could see eight on the left-hand wall and six and the tail of the seventh jutting out from the closet on the right-hand one. If she kept concentrating on them she could control her panic. When would Rodney be home? He couldn't stay away very long when she was ill. But she wasn't seriously ill and his pneumonia case was.

Aunt Hester's footsteps up the stairs were accompanied by the clinking of china. She came in carrying a tray.

"Well," she boomed, "the invalid feeling a little better?" She set the tray down and put an extra pillow at Lois's back. "Just sit up a little. There! That's right. Now I'll put the tray here and you can just eat that soup up, every drop."

"Thank you, Aunt Hester. It looks delicious."

Lois eyed the bowl of steaming soup with fragments of vegetables floating in it without enthusiasm.

"It is delicious. There are eight different vegetables in it. I've experimented a great deal with different blends to get just the right flavor."

Lois took a spoonful and tasted it. It was easy to swallow, but the flavor wasn't quite what Aunt Hester had claimed it to be. It had a curiously bitter taste. That probably would be her own palate affected by her illness. Perhaps she would feel better if she had the soup.

"I'll just leave you to eat it at your leisure," Aunt Hester said kindly. "I'll come back later."

There seemed to be a great deal of the soup and the taste didn't improve as she went on. But she manfully swallowed it all and lifted the tray onto the bedside table.

It hadn't made her feel better. She felt queer and uncomfortable with that bitter taste still in her mouth. A little later her symptoms began to resolve themselves into actual nausea. She struggled out of bed and pulled on her dressing gown. This baby, she thought. Was he never going to let her eat anything?

Abruptly the room swung. Darkness filled her eyes. She clutched at the bed for support. As the darkness momentarily cleared violent cramp seized her in the stomach. Somehow she staggered out of the room and along the passage to the bathroom.

She thought she would die there. Dimly she wondered if anyone would come. She didn't care. She would rather die than experience more of that agonizing sickness.

But gradually the spasm passed. She began to think of her bed as an elysium. Slowly she dragged herself to the door and got out into the passage.

Aunt Opal was just coming up the stairs. At the sight of Lois she began to run.

"Lois! Whatever is wrong? Are you ill?"

Lois nodded speechlessly.

"My dear child! Let me help you back to bed. Whatever made you so ill?"

"The soup," Lois enunciated clearly, then darkness came in front of her eyes and she fell forward.

The light was on, the blinds drawn and she was back in bed when she came back to consciousness. Aunt Opal was sitting at one side of the bed and Aunt Hester at the other. They were watching her intently. She had a scarcely formed desire to slip down under the bedclothes out of their sight. But her weakness was too great either to think of or care greatly whether they watched her die or not. She was quite sure she was going to die.

"Are you feeling better?" Aunt Hester asked.

Lois tried to speak. She tried to shake her

head. Both attempts failed.

"She'll feel better in a little," Aunt Opal said soothingly. "She's just coming around. I think that brandy now would be a good idea, Hester."

Why wasn't Rodney there looking after her? Why hadn't they sent for him?

She saw Aunt Hester lift a glass from the bedside table. The thought of swallowing anything brought back the feeling of sickness, but not violently. She was too tired now.

Aunt Hester slipped an arm under the pillows and raised Lois, holding the glass to her lips. The brandy trickled into her mouth. Some spilled, but some ran down her throat, leaving a trail of warmth. In a few minutes she began to feel stronger. She realized that the pains had gone from her stomach, and it was only her back that ached now, throbbing every little while with peculiar intensity.

"Better now?" came Aunt Opal's gentle anxious voice.

"Yes, thank you."

"That's a good girl. You gave us such a fright. You've certainly caught a real chill. Or I'm more inclined to think it was a germ. Don't you agree, Hester?"

"It was definitely some gastric trouble," Aunt Hester said. "The idea of blaming my soup!"

Her booming voice was good-naturedly indignant.

But it had been the soup. For immediately after eating it she had become ill.

"The soup being the first food you took all day," Aunt Hester went on, "that was the unfortunate effect it had. Anything else would have been the same. Of course, catching a germ like this your – ah – condition would probably accentuate it."

Lois felt too ill to argue with them. She was worried about the pain in her back.

"Where's Rodney?" she asked.

"If only we knew!" Aunt Opal exclaimed. "We've been trying to get him since six o'clock. But the Haydocks', where Abe Haydock is ill, haven't got a telephone and the nearest farm with a telephone is three miles away. We've phoned there and asked them to take a message, but it apparently hasn't got through to Rodney yet."

Lois had a sensation of utter despair.

"Then get Doctor Foster."

Aunt Hester leaned forward.

"Do you think that's really necessary, Lois? For a stomach upset? It's after ten and he's not young and it's a bad night to bring him out."

For the first time Lois realized rain was beating against the windows. Outside it was dark and wet and the dahlias would be being beaten to the ground and the leaves blown from the elms. Everything was dying. Aunt Opal and Aunt Hester had sat there watching their mother dying and watching pretty Marguerite dying. Now once more they were there, on either side of the four-poster, waiting and watching.

"I want Rodney," she whispered, tears creeping out beneath her closed eyelids.

"He'll be here soon, dear. He must be here soon. Try to rest."

When Rodney came at last she was hardly aware of his arrival. The people about her were shadows and the shadows on the wall people. The dragons had come alive, they were writhing and turning, pursuing the shadows that moved across them. Their glittering shapes hurt her eyes. She had to close them and even then sparks of light kept flashing across the darkness. One of the dragons even got on the bed. It slid down the bedpost and writhed across the eiderdown towards her. She could feel the heat from it through the bed-clothes, and its long nails clawing at her. She felt herself shrinking instinctively from the sight of its face, but when the head showed itself the face was Willow's, serene and beauti-ful.

She screamed then, and she heard Rodney's voice from a long way off. "Steady, darling. You'll be all right."

Later she felt her head lifted and something, not brandy, poured down her throat. Almost immediately after that she went to sleep.

When she awoke again it was growing daylight and it was still raining. She could hear the water running down gutters, and see the gray blur on the windows. The dragons on the wall were lackluster, the room perfectly normal. She herself felt better, very weak and unreal but almost free of pain, and vaguely astonished to find herself still alive. Was she alone? She turned her head slightly and saw Rodney sitting in the chair where Aunt Opal had been the previous night. He didn't know she was awake. His eyes were closed and in the dim light his face looked thin and shadowy. She didn't think he was asleep. He didn't look relaxed enough for that.

"Rodney," she whispered tentatively. Then, when he didn't stir she said louder, "Rodney."

Instantly he was awake and bending over her. He felt her forehead, then her pulse. She waited without speaking for him to satisfy himself.

Then he said in a relieved voice, "Good girl."

"Am I better?"

"Much better." After a little pause he said under his breath, "Thank God."

He sat on the edge of the bed.

"Feel pain anywhere?"

"Not exactly. I'm just a little tender here and there."

He nodded.

"But I feel so weak."

"You will for a few days."

"Rodney, have you been up all night?"

"That's nothing. I often sit up all night."

She frowned, trying to get form out of the chaos of the night.

"I wanted you so much. The aunts couldn't get in touch with you. They — they did try."

"They should have gotten Foster."

"They didn't think I was ill enough." (Or did they? Had their refusal to get Doctor Foster been deliberate?)

"No, I don't think they did. It was my fault — I should have anticipated that that chill might have upset your stomach."

"But you couldn't know, Rodney."

"Why not?"

"You couldn't know I was going to be poisoned."

Rodney's face seemed to narrow and sharpen.

"Now, darling —"

"It was the soup," Lois said. "Immediately after I had eaten it —"

Rodney pushed back her hair caressingly.

"Look, darling, you mustn't talk any more now. I'm going down to heat some milk for you. When you've had that you might sleep again."

"Rodney, it was the soup!" Her voice rose in weak hysteria.

"All right, darling, we'll talk about that when you're stronger. I won't be five minutes."

So he was humoring her because she was ill. If she had been well he would have said straight out, "More of your ridiculous imagination!" But he couldn't now because it might upset her too much. He would give her hot milk and send her to sleep so she would forget what had happened. Or think she had dreamed it. He wouldn't listen to her because he would rather risk her being poisoned than believe that one of his aunts, or Willow, Willow who had hated her coming back to Crow Hollow, was guilty.

Lois lay tense, waiting for his return. She listened to the rain and thought of the long day ahead, lying here, tired and ill, wondering who cared for her and who hated her. She closed her eyes and thought she counted the minutes until Rodney's return, but when she reopened them Rodney was sitting by the bed and her milk was cooling in the tumbler.

"You went to sleep," he said. "I'll heat this again if it's cold."

"I must be getting old," Lois murmured. Her feeling of unreality, as if her mind and her body did not belong, was not unpleasant. "Rodney, am I going to be all right now?"

He took her hand between his. His face was gentle, grave, the face she loved. Of course she was going to be all right with him to reassure her.

"You're going to be perfectly all right," she heard him saying. "But not the baby. Not this time, darling."

She gazed at him blankly, trying to take in his words. That pain in her back, the pains in her stomach, the dragon with Willow's face clawing at her. . . .

"Even if Doctor Foster or I had been here all the time I doubt if we could have prevented it. You were so ill. Being such a little way along it isn't so serious a matter. You'll be well again in a few days."

He looked at her wide shocked eyes.

"Don't be too disappointed, darling. We'll start again."

"My little baby," Lois whispered. "They killed it."

"Now, Lois."

"But they did! You won't believe me, but they tried to kill me. Instead they killed my baby. Rodney, take me away from here! Please take me away!"

She was sobbing violently, the sobs tearing at her aching body.

"Rodney, if you love me – if you want me to live – if you want children . . . Oh, my little baby!"

"Just a moment, darling. Keep your arm still."

His voice, calm and unhurried, reached her even through her hysteria. She felt the sharp prick in her arm. She felt him raise her and the warm milk against her lips. She was trembling so much that her teeth clattered against the glass.

"Drink it," said Rodney's voice hypnotically. "Drink it!"

She swallowed convulsively. She wanted to go on sobbing, but she was too tired. Everything was becoming unreal again and very far off. . . .

XIV

She awoke to the sensation of light in her eyes and realized that it had stopped raining and the sun was shining. It must have been late afternoon for the slanting sunlight shone across her face.

"Is that sun worrying you?" came an unfamiliar voice. "I'll pull the curtain across."

Lois saw a figure in a nurse's cap and apron cross over to the window.

"Who are you?" she asked weakly.

The girl turned.

"Don't you remember me, Mrs. Armour? I'm Nurse Baxter."

Lois gave a sigh of purest relief. So Rodney had listened to her at last, and wasn't going to let his aunts look after her. How good of him to send Nurse Baxter, that girl with the nice frank face whom she had liked from the beginning.

"Of course I remember you," she said. "I didn't see your face."

Nurse Baxter came across to the bed.

"Feeling better after that nice long sleep? Doctor said you were to take some food as soon as you woke. I'll just see how your temperature is."

Before Lois could speak she had popped the thermometer in her mouth. In a little while she took it out, looked at it and shook it.

"We're doing nicely," she said cheerfully. "Now I'm just going to slip down and make you some nice thin toast."

"Nurse," Lois called.

"Yes, Mrs. Armour?"

"Make the toast yourself."

"Why, of course I will. I never trust any maids to do cooking for my patients."

"Thank you," Lois whispered, hearing the intended reassurance in Nurse Baxter's voice.

Everything would be all right now. Rodney was seeing that she was safely looked after, and when she was well enough to get up he would take her away. Everything was all right!

But when Nurse Baxter came back with the toast and a pot of tea the tears were slipping down Lois's cheek again.

"Now what's this?" Nurse Baxter demanded. "The moment I turn my back you cry."

"I lost my baby, nurse. Did Rodney tell you? They made me lose my baby."

Nurse Baxter spread a table napkin on the bed and brought another pillow for Lois's back.

"That was bad luck, Mrs. Armour, but there's no use crying about it. You'll have another one."

"Not here, nurse. They won't let me. They pretend they want me to have a baby but they don't really. They'd like Rodney to have one, but not with me. I'm not the right woman."

"And who's all this 'they'?" Nurse Baxter asked good-naturedly.

Lois reflected. Was it all three of the aunts, or just one of them? But it was only indirectly the aunts. Instinct told her that. The person at the bottom of it all, whom no doubt the aunts shielded and encouraged, was Willow. Willow hated her to be there, but she would have doubly hated her to be there and have a baby, too. Willow hadn't stopped at the deadly spider, so she wouldn't stop at a little poison in soup that she knew was being made for Lois.

One of them would have to leave Crow Hollow, either she or Willow. Since she didn't answer immediately Nurse Baxter went on briskly. "Stop worrying your head about all this. Have a sip of this nice hot tea and you'll feel better."

Obediently Lois sipped the tea. But it was useless to tell her to stop thinking.

"Did Rodney find out about the soup, nurse?"

"The soup you ate before you were ill?"

"Yes."

"Well, you see, the trouble was it was made in a little dish. Just enough for one. And you ate it all. The dish had been washed when the doctor came home and of course, you being so ill, it was too late for him to analyze anything."

"Then there's no proof?"

"Doctor says not. And your aunt isn't half indignant either, I might say, at aspersions being cast on her soup. She prides herself on it, doesn't she?"

Lois nodded wearily.

"Do you think I was poisoned, nurse?"

"Well, now, if I were you, being sick like that so quickly would save any serious consequences. But doctor says it could be the result of your chill. And the Miss Armours say how you couldn't eat any breakfast long before you had the soup. So it must have been coming on then."

"It was an experiment," Lois said slowly. "Someone who didn't know what poison to use or how much. She didn't know whether it would be fatal or not. She just risked it."

"Well, you're still alive and doing nicely," Nurse Baxter said practically. "Do try that nice toast. It'll make you feel fine."

Later Aunt Hester, carrying a bowl of autumn crocuses and walking with unfamiliar softness, came in.

She said, "These are almost the only flowers not spoiled by the rain. I thought you would like them. How are you feeling now?" Her voice, like her tread, had an unfamiliar hushed quality. Lois wondered if it were her feeling of guilt that had subdued her. After all, if you had attempted to murder a person and had failed it must be a peculiar thing facing your would-be victim.

"Mrs. Armour is doing nicely, thank you," Nurse Baxter answered for Lois.

"That's fine! That's fine!" Aunt Hester said heartily. "I'll make you —" Her automatic offer was cut off abruptly. Her face with its bold strong features wore a look of almost pathetic uncertainty. "It wouldn't have been the soup, you know, Lois. If anything was wrong with it all I can think is it must have happened after I left it to simmer."

Yes, that could have happened. Lois had long ago thought of that. And the person who would have most access to it in the kitchen was of course, Willow. Had anybody questioned Willow? But they would get nothing out of her. She would be as secret and unreadable as the sphinx.

"If you don't mind, Miss Armour," Lois heard Nurse Baxter saying firmly, "doctor said the patient wasn't to have visitors."

Aunt Hester looked annoyed, then apologetic.

"I'll come and talk to you some other time, Lois. Take good care of yourself. See she eats well, nurse."

"Thank you for the flowers, Aunt Hester," Lois said politely.

The fragile autumn crocuses could have been on her grave. Instead she could look at them in a bowl on her bedside table and wonder if Aunt Hester (or whoever it was) was cursing herself for blundering with the quantity of poison. There would be no opportunity to make another attempt while Nurse Baxter was here, but after that –

"Now what are you worrying about?" Nurse Baxter asked, coming to straighten Lois's pillow.

Lois drew her brows together.

"I keep hearing a noise outside, a harsh sort of noise."

"Oh, that's those crows. There have been a lot of them about today since the rain." Nurse Baxter went to the window and looked out. "You can see them in the elms now. This place used to be infested with crows, you know. Before my time, though. It almost looks as if they're coming back."

Lois gave a little shiver.

"Oh, no," she whispered. "I hope not."

When Rodney came in again it was dark and the crows had, apparently, gone to roost, as the night was completely silent. He sat beside her without speaking and for the first time since her illness Lois was conscious of a feeling of relaxation and peace. For a few precious moments she was able to forget the past and her fears about the future. But her forgetfulness could not last long.

"Had a busy day, darling?" she asked.

"Pretty hectic."

"How's the pneumonia case?"

"He'll pull through now."

"I'm glad. Thank you for sending Nurse Baxter, Rodney."

"You needed a nurse. I thought you'd like someone you knew. Feeling more comfortable now?"

"I'm feeling fine." She sighed a little. "If only this could go on without interruption."

"What could go on?"

"You being here with me and no one else. How long can Nurse Baxter stay?"

"Until you're well, of course."

"Promise me, Rodney. Promise to have her stay until I can look after myself again."

"Of course, darling."

"Rodney, I—I'd rather not see the aunts for a little while. They might talk about the baby and I'd rather not. Just yet, anyway."

"All right, sweet. I've told them they're not to come in here chattering."

"Rodney, are you very disappointed about the baby?"

Rodney's voice held caution.

"Very disappointed. But thankful it was too early to be serious for you."

Lois's hand clenched and unclenched on the blankets.

"We shouldn't be too sorry about that baby," she said slowly. "It was conceived the night your grandfather was killed. I would always remember that."

She didn't realize she had made the direct accusation of murder until she saw his face tighten. But she had to go on.

"Rodney, that soup —"

"There's absolutely no proof about the soup. The dishes had been washed and there was nothing to be analyzed."

"I know there's no proof," Lois said hopelessly. "You've only got me to believe, and you don't seem to find that easy. I'm not hysterical any more, Rodney. I'm trying to be sensible. But you'll know some day I was right — if it's not too late."

Rodney went to say something, then checked himself.

"Stop worrying," he said gently. "It's bad for you."

"I don't worry so long as Nurse Baxter cooks my meals. Rodney, when can I get up?"

"In a day or two. Don't be in a hurry."

"How many crows are there in the elms now?"

"I don't know. Quite a lot. It's extraordinary the way they've come back. Aunt Judith's greatly intrigued. I think she plans doing an article on them."

"Lying here listening to them," Lois said, with desperate calm, "I think I'll go mad."

Rodney bent over her in concern.

"Darling, they're not as bad as all that."

"It's not the noise they make. It's what they mean."

"Now you're just being plain superstitious.

That's a result of being in a weakened state."

"I keep thinking of your mother," she whispered. "What made her die?"

"Nothing remotely connected with what's wrong with you."

"But how do you know? You were only a child. Rodney, I promised not to worry you any more, but couldn't we go away from here? There's something about this house — and now the crows have come back. . . ." Her voice trailed off. She knew her argument was weak and unsubstantial, and that it wouldn't have any effect.

"You concentrate on getting well first," Rodney said. "That has to be uppermost in your mind."

The next day when he came to see her he said, "Darling, the aunts are getting hurt about your not wanting to see them. You take as much time as you want to, but think of them as three rather lonely women who are very fond of you."

The aunts may just possibly be entirely innocent of the events that had happened. Lois was essentially fair, and she had to admit that.

"How are they?" she asked reluctantly.

"Oh, very well. Though Aunt Judith is inclined to be a little sulky. She says someone has taken the toadstool Dexter brought her the other day, a particularly fine specimen apparently, and no one will admit to any knowledge of it."

Lois's eyes darkened.

"Poisonous?" she asked.

"I should think so. Most toadstools are. What anyone else would want with it —" He broke off, looking at Lois's set face.

"I remember Aunt Hester saying," she said on a high breathless note, "how Aunt Judith liked poisonous things. Don't you see, Rodney, a little of the flesh of that toadstool crushed and put in the soup. . . . That way there would be no proof. You see how simple it is, and yet how clever. So much surer than the spider. But the trouble was they didn't know how much toadstool would be fatal."

She gazed at him intensely, willing him to believe her.

He walked across the room quickly.

"That's absolutely conjecture. Why, Aunt Judith —"

"But it might not have been Aunt Judith," she interrupted feverishly. "It was Aunt Judith's spider, too, but she need not have been guilty. It could be someone who doesn't want me here — like Willow."

Then Rodney, who really had seemed momentarily to be interested in her theory, shook his head decisively.

"Darling, Willow loves her pretty neck far too well to risk it for the sake of a little jealousy. Always providing she is jealous. No, I think you're letting your imagination run away with you again."

So it was no use. Lois began to feel a cold and deliberate anger. Why should she stay here in danger because Rodney wouldn't believe or refused to believe any danger existed? She had tried to do what he wanted, but this was too much. Apart from the danger, if he loved her he would not willingly let her stay where she was unhappy. The conclusion was that he did not love her enough. So she would have to leave him. She couldn't live any longer in a place where someone hated her enough to kill her. As soon as she was well enough she would go. The thing was to keep Nurse Baxter until the last possible moment — nobody would dare to make any attempt on her life while the nurse was there — and then she would be strong enough to go alone.

Buoyed up by her plans, from then on her strength returned rapidly. She would not let herself feel grief at leaving Rodney. She forced herself to retain her anger and indignation. If Rodney wanted her enough he knew where to find her. From now on she made the rules. Cass would understand. She would say, "Of course you can't live in a place where they have killed your baby."

With that decision made it was easier to be natural and friendly with the aunts. In a few days everyone would be happy – they at having Rodney's unwanted wife out of the house and she at being miles away from Crow Hollow. Rodney? He had brought this on himself. She wouldn't tell him she was going. She couldn't bear another scene that got them nowhere. The solution lay in his own hands.

On her second day up, Nurse Baxter prepared to leave.

"I'm sorry to be going," she said, "but the doctor can't do without me any longer. And you're doing fine now, dear."

"Yes, I'm doing fine," Lois said. She didn't really feel strong enough to leave tonight, but if Nurse Baxter was going she wouldn't stay in the house any longer.

"There's a new cook downstairs," Nurse Baxter went on. "Doctor's engaged her himself. So if you've been feeling nervous you just stop right away. Doctor wouldn't engage anyone who would start any funny business. Anyway, dear, it was all pretty farfetched, don't you think? Poison in the soup. That sounds more like the Middle Ages."

Lois said nothing. Nurse Baxter's common sense and lack of imagination was too much for her to swallow that sort of story. So was everyone's. The point was that no one else had been a victim as she had been. One couldn't expect other people to see it entirely her way.

She went downstairs that last afternoon and had tea with the three aunts. Willow served the tea. Lois watched the four cups being filled from the same teapot and forced herself to be calm and unafraid. The aunts fussed, of course, seeing that she had the most comfortable chair and plenty of cushions.

"So nice to be all together again," Aunt Opal crooned. "Such a worrying time we had with you, Lois."

"She needs to put some flesh on her bones," Aunt Hester inevitably remarked. "This cook Rodney has found for us seems to be all right. I'll have a word with her about nourishing meals. The trouble is, she's so fussy. Doesn't like anyone coming near the kitchen. Haven't you found that, Opal?"

Aunt Opal nodded, frowning, obviously disliking being dictated to in her own house. Then she said resolutely, "But since Rodney went to the trouble of getting her we must give her a fair trial."

Willow silently poured tea and handed it

around. Whether or not she liked the new cook one would never know. She had her wonderful light colored hair done differently today, piled on top of her head into smooth shining rolls. Her perfectly shaped face did not need that ornate style, but she looked remarkably well, nevertheless.

"A sandwich, miss?" Lois heard her asking in her polite indifferent voice.

"Thank you," said Lois. A sudden impulse that she was at a loss to explain made her add, "I never showed you the new clothes I bought while I was away, Willow. There was no time before I got ill. If you come up in a little while you can see them."

There was a gleam of interest in Willow's eyes. The only time she ever looked interested, Lois realized, was when somebody mentioned clothes or possessions.

"Thank you, miss. I'd like to."

"That *is* nice of you, Lois," Aunt Opal said in a pleased voice. "Willow does like to see the latest fashions."

A crow flew, squawking past the window. Aunt Judith put her cup down and went to look out.

"Extraordinary," she said. "They really are coming back. I wonder what brings them. In the old days, of course, it was supposed to be an ill omen. But there must be a scientific reason for it."

"Dirty brutes," Aunt Hester said. "And so noisy. They frightened Jewel this morning, nearly threw me out of the pony cart."

"Here's Dexter coming," Aunt Judith observed. "He's got me some more toadstools. They don't look the equal of that one that disappeared. Such a perfect specimen it was, Lois. You would have admired its beauty."

"Judith, stop being so childish about a toadstool," Aunt Hester snapped. "Who was going to steal it? You've put it somewhere yourself in your absentminded way."

Lois watched Willow. The girl had put the plate of sandwiches down and was standing with her hands behind her back. Was it because they trembled?

"Yes, Judith, we've had enough of that subject," Aunt Opal said in her soft voice. "I'm sure Lois doesn't want to have to listen to it."

Aunt Judith turned to regard them with her pale prominent eyes.

"You weren't all so contemptuous when my spider got loose. After all, that particular species of toadstool contains almost as high a percentage of poison."

For one moment there was complete silence, everyone staring at Aunt Judith. Almost as if, for a split second, they were petrified.

Then Aunt Opal said with a note of sharpness:

"But a toadstool can't bite. Don't be so utterly ridiculous, Judith," and the moment passed.

The problem had been how to get away unnoticed. At first Lois had thought she would slip away, taking the short cut that led past the church and the cemetery, and walk the five miles to the station. But with Nurse Baxter leaving earlier than she had expected her to do she realized she was still much too weak for a long walk. She had pondered the question all day, and knew that the only solution was to have Joe Higgins call for her in his taxi. But what errand could she invent for the benefit of the aunts? The ideal thing would be to have Joe wait out of sight at the main gates. If she could use the telephone unobserved she would phone him. But that was another problem. It was absurd that it should be so difficult to leave one's husband. At least the difficulties absorbed all her mind and left no room for grief at what she was doing.

Then another brilliant idea occurred to her. When Willow came to her room to see the new clothes she would take the girl into her confidence. There was no doubt that Willow would cooperate, for there was nothing she wanted more than to get Lois out of the house. In addition, it would ensure her safety from any attack during the short time she remained. Provided Willow was the attacker. . . .

As she was putting a few things into an overnight bag – Rodney could pack and send the rest of her things later – Willow tapped at the door. Without bothering to conceal the bag Lois called to her to come in.

Willow's eyes instantly went to the folded articles of clothing and the open bag.

Lois answered her unspoken question.

"I'm going away, Willow."

There was no mistaking the interest in the girl's face now. What a superbly lovely creature she was when she showed animation.

"For long, miss?"

"Quite a long time, I think. I've decided to tell you because I want you to do one small thing for me."

"Certainly, miss."

"When there's no one about, telephone Joe Higgins to wait for me at the main gates at half past four. The train goes at five, so that will give me plenty of time."

"Yes, miss. I can do that easily enough. I can watch my chance. But aren't you telling anyone you're going?"

"Not at the moment. I don't want a fuss."

Willow nodded understandingly.

"They do fuss, don't they. Especially Miss Opal. She nearly drives you batty."

Lois concealed her surprise. Was Willow, the unfathomable, going to make confidences? She must go carefully so as not to make her withdraw into her silence again.

"Miss Opal is very kind, Willow. And generous, too."

"Oh, she's generous enough. But fight! You should hear how those three women fight about me." Willow smiled a smug, superior, thoroughly irritating smile. "Being a maid in a house you can't help overhearing things quite often."

What did they fight about? The privilege of spoiling Willow? On the point of asking, Lois stopped herself. It was bad enough Willow listening at doors, as Clara had declared she did, but worse to cross-examine the girl about what she heard.

"Then why do you stay here, Willow, if you don't like the Miss Armours?"

But that was the wrong question. For Willow's face instantly became secret again.

"It suits me, miss."

She was a cheap little creature, Lois decided, out for all she could get, but not hesitating to discuss her employers behind their backs.

She went to the closet and took out the new evening dress she had bought. It was oyster colored crepe and she guessed it wouldn't appeal to Willow, whose preference was for showy colors.

Willow looked at it, her eyes narrowed critically. Then she said, "I like the green best, miss. The one you wore the night the spider got on you."

"Do you, Willow? I'm afraid I've never been able to like that dress since. If it's any use to you you can have it."

Willow's eyes glinted. Her full red lips curved in a delighted smile.

"Can I really, miss? Thanks ever so much."

Lois took the taffeta dress out. Even handling it and hearing it rustle brought back vividly that dreadful night. She had to get away from here quickly. Rodney would have to understand.

"I'm just taking a few things with me. I'll send for others later, if I need them." There was no necessity for Willow to know that she wasn't coming back, ever.

But the girl knew that already, Lois could tell by her knowing air. Was she thinking that now Rodney was deserted she would be able to comfort him — successfully? If Rodney

preferred Willow's ministrations, as he sometimes appeared to, all the more reason for her
to go.

She picked up a hat that had fallen off its peg
when she had taken the taffeta dress out.

"What's that, miss?" Willow asked inter-
estedly.

Lois displayed the gay little confection of
flowers that she had bought on an impulse,
forgetting that it was unlikely she would be
going to a cocktail party or any occasion
suitable for such a hat in Finchin.

"It's a cocktail hat. Quite useless, really."

"It's pretty," Willow said admiringly. Of
course the bright colors would appeal to her.

Lois tossed it on the bed. Perhaps she would
wear it to a party in London, if she ever went
to another party. At the moment that just
didn't seem possible.

"Willow, do you think you could put
through that call now? It's getting late, and if
I'm to catch that train —"

She sat down on the edge of the bed, feeling suddenly dizzy. Willow looked at her with concern.

"Yes, miss. But do you think you're fit to
travel?"

"Of course I'm fit." She clenched her hands
fiercely. The idea of not leaving now was
intolerable. "I'll rest until it's time to go."

XV

There was still the letter to leave for Rodney. When Willow had gone she finished packing and sat down to write the brief note. There was nothing to put in it save that she would be waiting for him at Cass's apartment if he wanted her. He knew everything else. But it was difficult to write and when she had finished it she was crying. Dabbing angrily at her tears she looked around the room. There was nothing in it that didn't belong to the nightmare, even the fresh bowl of autumn crocuses brought up by Aunt Hester that morning, which were probably meant to constitute a peace offering. She went to the window and saw in the elms the black shadows of the crows fighting and screeching. If nothing else preyed on her mind, the constant noise of the crows would finally destroy her peace.

The stable clock struck four. She saw Dexter crossing the lawn with a rake over his shoulder.

There was another tap at the door and Willow's conspiratorial voice.

"I've arranged with Joe Higgins, miss. And the coast's clear now if you like to slip out. Miss Opal's lying down, Miss Hester's in the greenhouse and Miss Judith in her laboratory."

Lois slipped on her coat. She didn't think there were any traces of tears on her cheeks now.

"Thank you, Willow. You've done very well."

The girl said nothing. But her long golden eyes slid around the room as if she were taking stock of it, planning how one day it would be hers. As there was little doubt, if she expressed a wish for it, it would.

Lois snatched up her bag and hurried out of the room.

Halfway down the drive she had to sit and rest a few moments because of the annoying shakiness of her legs. But she reached the high main gates with the broken stone lions five minutes before Joe's taxi arrived.

Joe looked puzzled.

"Could have come right to the door, Mrs. Doc," he said.

"I thought I'd like the stroll down the drive," Lois answered, not worried about the weakness of her excuse. "I want to go to the station, please, Joe."

"You better again, Mrs. Doc?"

"Yes, thank you. I'm just taking a short holiday."

"Doc busy?"

"Very busy."

"Ah." That, to Joe, explained everything. He settled back and drove off without another word.

At the station, however, when Lois was paying him he lifted his heavy brows and said, "You take care of yourself, Mrs. Doc. You still look peekish to me."

"I'll be all right, Joe. Don't worry about me."

She had ten minutes to wait for the train. She began to stroll up and down the platform, but the effort of getting away from Crow Hollow had been more exhausting than she had realized. The unpleasant shakiness had returned to her legs. She would have to go and sit down in the tiny waiting room. She walked in its direction, but for all the miniature size of the station the waiting-room seemed a very long way off. The wall swayed. It seemed to be growing very dark. She was so tired, nothing could have been more wonderful than to lie down there on the dusty platform.

"I say, what on earth's wrong?"

The friendly voice cut through the fog that surrounded her. Lois felt an arm around her and she was half propelled, half carried to the waiting room.

It was the purest relief to lie back in one of the hard leather chairs and close her eyes.

Presently she heard the same voice saying, "Here's a glass of water."

With an effort she opened her eyes and took the glass. The cold water rapidly made her feel better. She began to be curious about her helper. She looked at the girl standing over her and saw that it was Diana Marcus.

"And where the devil do you think you're going?" Diana inquired.

"To London," Lois said. She sat up. "Is the train in?"

"It will be in a couple of minutes. But you're not traveling on it in that condition."

The thought of missing the train and returning to Crow Hollow after all filled Lois with a sensation much worse than faintness.

"I must," she said breathlessly. "It's important."

Diana looked at her curiously.

"There's another train in two hours. It's much slower, but it gets you there. Come along home with me and see if a couple of drinks will help."

Lois, realizing that in her present state she would be very likely to faint on the train, saw the wisdom of following Diana's suggestion.

"I've got the car outside," Diana said. "I just have to see a friend who's going through on this train."

"Anyway," she said later, when Lois was relaxing in one of the big armchairs in Diana's attractive sitting room, "I want to talk to you. I've been intending to have you and Rodney here for dinner, but you're such elusive people. Rodney's either up to his eyes, or you're away or ill. Are you going to be away long this time?"

"I – don't know."

Lois was feeling better now and her perception was acute enough to realize that Diana guessed at least part of her intention.

"I don't want to pry," Diana went on, "but mother always said she didn't envy the girl Rodney took to Crow Hollow, and really – don't mind my saying this – it looks as if she were right."

Lois sat up straight.

"Would you mind telling me exactly what your mother meant. I asked you once before but you — I don't think you told me everything you knew. Would it be anything to do with — odd accidents happening?"

"Look," said Diana, "I'll tell you all I can, which isn't a lot, and which I think is rather fantastic. Mother had the fixed idea ever since Rodney's aunts were so insistent about getting Willow, that they hoped Rodney would marry her. Don't ask me why she thought that — she probably had more reasons than she gave me — but that was why she guessed any other girl Rodney took home wouldn't have too good a time."

Lois, thinking rapidly, found the information difficult and yet not difficult to believe. As Armours the aunts had a great deal of family pride; they should have wanted Rodney to make a good match. Willow was only a maid. It would almost have caused a scandal to have young Doctor Armour marry one of the maids in his own house. But against that was the aunts' ridiculous and unreasonable infatuation for Willow, their desire to treat her like one of the family, their lavishness towards her. Lois had no doubt at all that had Rodney announced his intention of marrying Willow they would have overridden every possible objection made by grandfather or anyone else.

It must have been a great shock to them when they got Rodney's telegram to say he was married. To Willow it must have been an even greater shock — Willow, who was so attractive and yet had no boyfriends in the village, Willow who was always on hand to prepare Rodney's early coffee and perform small services for him.

Yes, whatever the aunts' resentment towards her as Rodney's wife it was Willow who suffered the death of her hopes and who had everything to gain by her removal. And she had just taken the girl into her confidence and given her a dress!

But this information of Diana's was no real surprise. It had been in her mind as a conjecture all along.

"I can just imagine how happy mother must have been to meet you," Diana was going on. "We've known Rodney for a long time. He was such a solitary boy. I suppose they were good enough to him at Crow Hollow, but something had made him reserved and shut in himself. I used to think he had been ill-treated as a child, but mother said it was probably a deeper reason than that, something that had caused him to hide his feelings, never letting you see anything but the quiet polite exterior of his."

She paused and offered Lois a cigarette. Lois shook her head and said in a low voice, "Go on about Rodney."

Diana lit her own cigarette and inhaled smoke.

"I remember one Christmas," she said. "Mother had a touch of bronchitis and old Doctor Armour was away somewhere, so Rodney came. It was just about his first case, I think, and he was scared stiff. My sister was home with her kids and we had a Christmas tree. Mother, who wasn't very ill anyway, shoved him off downstairs and one of the kids dragged him in to look at the tree. Well, I don't think he'd ever seen a tree before or had any sort of natural fun at Christmas. He ended up by being Father Christmas and taking the things off the tree, even the star on the very top — as if he couldn't have enough of the fun and the giving. He said afterwards he hadn't known Christmas like that existed outside books. He asked me if he could come again."

"And did he?"

"Oh, often. That's when mother began to talk about how important it was for him to marry the right girl. She used to say, 'If only Rodney would marry a nice girl who would understand him!' Then she said the girl would need to feel her way and not be frightened by his withdrawals or even his coldness. Being cold is the last thing about Rodney — he's got such an eager heart. But something had made him immensely distrustful. It would take a lot of love and care to give him confidence. But at that he didn't seem interested in girls at all. That was why mother got so nervous when the aunts put that lovely Willow into the house, right under his nose, so to speak. If he was human, he was going to fall."

Diana gave a short, slightly embarrassed laugh.

"This is funny, me analyzing your husband for you. How did it start, anyway?"

Lois said, "I think it started because you thought I was leaving Rodney." Her voice was perfectly calm and self-possessed. "I'm not, you know."

"I'm glad," Diana said sincerely. "I didn't think you were leaving him for good — I thought perhaps Crow Hollow had got a bit too much for you. Is it very heavy going?"

"Things happen," Lois said vaguely. "It's only Willow, you know. Now you've told me these things I realize it's just her jealousy and frustration. She's behaving very childishly. I couldn't let that drive me away, could I? Not when Rodney needs me."

Diana met her gaze with absolute sincerity.

"He does need you, Lois. Badly. Believe me."

"I do believe you. Thank you for telling me. I can't thank you enough."

"I'd like to have told you sooner, but one doesn't like to butt in. I thought you might have found it all out yourself, but I guess it's difficult." She reached for Lois's glass. "Have another drink."

"No, thanks very much. I ought to go. I – I don't think I feel up to catching that train tonight after all. I'd like to get back before Rodney gets home."

She didn't mention the letter on her dressing table, but she knew Diana was as aware of its existence as she was herself. Diana was a real friend. It was a pity she hadn't discovered that earlier.

There was the fact that by returning she might be placing her life in real danger. But she hadn't time to think of that now. She only knew she couldn't walk out on Rodney for a completely selfish reason like that. She had worried that he didn't love her enough. She hadn't realized that she herself had nearly been guilty of the same fault.

"I'll drive you," Diana offered.

"Thank you. I would like to get back quickly."

Because Rodney must not find that note. He must never know she had meant to leave him. Willow would tell him, perhaps. She would bribe Willow to be silent. Thank goodness Willow was susceptible to bribes.

On the way Diana said, "You lost your baby, didn't you?"

"Yes. I caught some kind of chill. It wasn't serious, but it was violent while it lasted." If Rodney didn't believe she had been poisoned she wasn't going to believe it either.

"It's plucky of you to go back after that."

Lois flashed her a glance. How much of what had happened at Crow Hollow was gossip in the village? Because it was Rodney's home she had to protect it.

"I won't get another baby unless I do."

Diana laughed.

"Mother was right. Although she only saw you for a few minutes, poor darling. She said, 'That girl will do.' They were just about her last words."

Tears stung Lois's eyes to think how nearly she had failed the old lady's expectations. She wouldn't fail again. This return to Crow Hollow was until the inevitable climax. She wouldn't speculate on what that might be.

At the gates she asked Diana to drop her.

"I'll just slip in quietly, if I can."

Diana nodded.

"All right. Take care of yourself. Ugh, those crows! Don't they give you the willies?"

Lois listened for a moment to the strident squabbling of the crows in the trees bordering the drive. Her raw nerves quivered.

"At first they did. But I'm getting used to them."

Diana recognized the lie. She gave a little gay salute.

"Good luck."

Lois hurried down the drive. She could scarcely expect to get up to her room unobserved at this hour, with dinner almost ready, but she would have to trust to her luck holding. Strangely enough, however, the house did seem deserted although the hall door stood wide open. There was no sound and no sign of anyone about. Rodney's car had not been at the door so he couldn't be home either.

Thankful for this good fortune, Lois went upstairs. She felt a great deal better since that drink at Diana's. It wasn't only the drink, of course, but her own sense of peace at having made her decision to stay at Rodney's side. All the same she was very tired and she wondered if she could make an excuse not to go down for dinner. The aunts would be understanding. They would make her lie down and get Willow to bring a tray to her room.

Willow! What would her reaction be to Lois's unexpected return?

Lois threw up her chin. It was fully time she coped with that lovely dangerous creature. They would have a showdown. If the aunts didn't like it that just couldn't be helped.

The door of her room was open. She thought she had left it closed, but in her haste to leave she couldn't really remember. She went in, taking off her hat, and then stopped dead.

For Willow, dressed in the green taffeta dress, was sitting on the stool before the dressing table. In a flash the thought went through Lois's mind that this was exactly what she had expected. The moment she had gone Willow had taken possession of her room.

But the odd thing was that the girl seemed to have gone to sleep. Her head was dropping over the dressing table, and her hair had come out of the pins securing it on top of her head and spread in a silvery shower.

"Willow!" Lois cried sharply, crossing the room. Vaguely she noticed that the gay little cocktail hat lay on the floor by the bed. Willow, of course, would have been trying that on, too.

Willow didn't stir. Lois grasped her lovely white shoulder and shook it. Willow gave a little sliding movement sideways.

Lois sprang back. Her breath was caught in her throat. She thought she would never breathe again.

For beneath Willow's left shoulder blade, partially hidden by the ruffle of the dress's neckline, its blade thrust deep, was the yellowed handle of a knife.

There was only one small trickle of blood. But Willow, drooping there with her eyes open beneath her tumbled hair, was dead.

XVI

Somehow she got downstairs and to the telephone. She dialed the number of Rodney's office and stood supporting herself against the wall while she waited for an answer. At last it came in Nurse Baxter's alert voice.

Lois couldn't say who was speaking. She just gasped, "Is the doctor in?"

Nurse Baxter said, "I'll put you on to him," and a moment later there was Rodney's brisk "Hello!"

"Rodney, could you come home quickly? It's Willow — Quickly!" That was all she could say.

"Hold it!" came Rodney's answer. "I'll be there in ten minutes."

Dimly she was grateful that he hadn't

stopped to ask questions. She collapsed into a chair in the hall and sat there unable to move. She found she was still clutching the hat that she had picked up in her hand from the bedroom floor. She put it on the table beside the telephone. She didn't know what she would say if one of the aunts appeared. The news would have to be broken gently, they would get such a shock, they were so fond of Willow.

Then why had one of them killed her?

Of course it was very clear what had happened, and the thought wasn't pleasant. Because, indirectly, it made her responsible for Willow's death. And little as she had liked the girl, she had never wished her any harm. Even when she had believed Willow had been the perpetrator of the attacks on her own life she had never consciously wished her a taste of her own medicine. It seemed now that Willow might not have been guilty at all. It must have been one of the aunts. Her intuitive uneasiness about them had been correct. But which one could it have been? Which one?

The stable clock struck the half hour. There was the sound of Kate, the new cook, distantly clattering dishes. Otherwise the house was quite still.

Where were the aunts? Why hadn't one of them found Willow? Why were they all so quiet when their cherished servant sat dead with a knife in her back?

Whoever had done it would need to have had a strong wrist and a very accurate idea of the most effective place to stab. Probably she had come in smiling and talking, and then, before Willow could turn and answer. . . .

"Steady now," came Rodney's voice from a long way off.

Lois tried to shake herself out of the dreadful nightmare that had closed around her like a fog.

"Rodney, Willow — in our room." She evaded his touch. "Don't worry about me. Go up quickly."

The breathless urgency in her voice sent him up the stairs two at a time. He vanished into the bedroom where the Chinese dragons sported on the walls and Willow, in the pretty green dress, sat dead.

It seemed only a minute before he was at her side again. She noticed that his face was shockingly gaunt. She clutched at his sleeve.

"Rodney! It was meant to be me."

He had the telephone receiver in his hand and was dialing a number. In a moment he said, "Constable Jenkins? Will you come up to Crow Hollow at once? It's urgent. I think you'd better get the inspector over from

Dalchester." He paused and then said, "Bring an ambulance, too."

He put down the receiver and looked at Lois. "When did you find her?"

"Just now. Just as I came in. She was — she was still warm."

Rodney nodded. There were two deep lines running from nostril to chin and his face was gray.

"I should say death took place within the last half hour. Do the aunts know?"

Then he stopped short and there was awareness in both their faces. One of the aunts must know!

"I had given her that dress," Lois said in a difficult voice. "She must have tried it on and sat there looking at herself."

"She had been making up her face," Rodney said. "Her fingers are smeared with face cream."

"She'd be trying my makeup. She loved to try my things. You remember the day she put my suit on? And then, tonight — someone came in and thought it was me. In a way, Rodney, I'm to blame for giving her that dress."

Rodney's fingers gripped her wrists.

"I'm responsible for refusing to believe the things you told me. But I saw there was no more nonsense in the kitchen by getting a woman I could trust. I gave her implicit instructions."

Someone was coming up the path to the front door, heavy footsteps rasping on the shingle. With a single instinctive movement Rodney pushed Lois behind him partially out of sight beneath the curve of the stairs. The hall door opened and Aunt Hester came in. She was dressed in gardening clothes, and her hair hung wispily around her hot face. She saw Rodney and exclaimed, "Am I going to be late for dinner? I was so anxious to finish staking the chrysanthemums. This gardening bug's quite got me, hasn't it? Killed my first rabbit today, too. I put the poison on carrots, you know. There he was, a fine big fellow, stretched out stiff, his nose still on the bit of nibbled carrot. Judith might like him for dissection."

She laughed, showing her large white teeth.

"I can't smell dinner. That cook of yours is efficient, Rodney, but she hasn't much imagination. We've had boiled turnip two days in succession."

It was impossible to think that Aunt Hester might be acting, that she might be fully aware of silly pretty Willow upstairs, paying for her vanity with her life. And yet she could be. She could have been upstairs within the last half hour, and then rushed down again and into the garden, using her gardening craze as an alibi. If Lois had come back a few minutes earlier she might have run into her on the stairs.

"Aunt Hester," Rodney began.

But that was as far as he got for at that moment there was the sound of a door opening upstairs.

"Willow!" they could hear Aunt Opal calling in her soft pretty voice. Rodney left Lois's side and bounded up the stairs. Aunt Hester stared after him and then began to follow him. Lois didn't know whether she had been noticed or not. She thought not. Aunt Hester was too puzzled by Rodney's strange behavior. Or was she puzzled?

"Oh, is that you, Rodney?" Lois heard Aunt Opal saying. "I don't know where Willow is. I've rung for her three times. She comes to put up my hair about this time."

Lois, moving out into the hall, saw Aunt Opal wearing a négligée with her white hair, brushed and loose, hanging to her shoulders. She looked very soft and feminine. She was moving towards Lois's bedroom.

"She surely can't still be with Lois. Lois was going to show her her clothes, you know."

Rodney seized Aunt Opal's arm.

"Don't go in there!"

Lois distinctly heard Aunt Opal's surprised gasp. Rodney said in a harsh voice, with no attempt at dissembling, "Willow's in there. I don't know which of you know, or if either of you do. Willow's in there, dead, with a knife in her back."

The words sounded brutal and unreal. They were followed by a complete silence. Lois moved to the foot of the stairs and began to walk slowly up them.

She heard Aunt Hester at last in an incredulous whisper ejaculating, "My God!"

Then came Aunt Opal's wail, "Not Willow! Willow can't be — Rodney, what a fantastic —"

Rodney sprang forward to catch her as she fell. Lois hurried upstairs then and bent with the others over Aunt Opal. Rodney loosened her clothing and then said he'd go downstairs for brandy. Aunt Hester stared at her prostrate sister, then she too straightened herself and with an air of determination went along the passage to Lois's room. The door was closed. She hesitated a moment, then firmly turned the knob and opening the door went in. She wasn't gone long. When she came back her high color had receded, leaving her face haggard and old.

"It is true," she said, but her voice was still incredulous. "She's got Lois's dress on."

Aunt Opal on the floor stirred and opened her eyes. She struggled to sit up.

"Don't move," Lois said, "Rodney's getting brandy."

Aunt Opal realized who was speaking. She winced away from Lois's touch.

"You —" She whispered. Her soft feminine face was transformed with fear and revulsion.

Lois felt sick. (Why, she thinks I've done it! I lured her precious Willow into my room and stabbed her in the back!)

"Now, Opal!" said Aunt Hester firmly. "Control yourself."

"Willow!" Aunt Opal moaned.

Rodney arrived with a glass in his hand. He knelt and held it against Aunt Opal's lips. Aunt Opal gulped and choked.

"Rodney — so strong!" But a little color had returned to her cheeks. She looked wan and pathetic with her soft loose hair, like Willow in there, with her hair falling over her face. . . .

"Pull yourself together!" Aunt Hester ordered sharply. "This is a terrible thing. We've got to get to the bottom of it. You won't help by fainting all over the place. Where's Judith? She must be told."

The moment she had spoken the words her glance became uneasy. It was so simple to read her thoughts. Did Judith know already? As

272

quickly as this the first terrible seeds of suspicion were commencing their growth.

Aunt Opal looked appealingly at Rodney.

"What do we do, Rodney? Do the police have to know?"

"The police are on their way now," Rodney answered.

"I should think so!" Aunt Hester said loudly. "So brutal! That old kitchen knife, Opal. The one Clara used for cutting meat."

Aunt Opal closed her eyes. Her face was paper-white again.

"It's no good being squeamish," Aunt Hester said. "That won't undo things. You'd better come downstairs and wait for the police. I'm going to find Judith."

Rodney looked at Lois.

"Go with her, Lois. I'll help Aunt Opal downstairs."

Lois realized what he meant. He wanted her to observe Aunt Judith's reactions when she saw that Lois was alive and well.

"You don't need to worry," Aunt Hester said. "Judith won't faint."

But she made no objection to Lois accompanying her. In silence they walked across the darkening garden. There was a glimmer of light showing through the windows of the summer house. Without ceremony Aunt

Hester pushed the door open and went in.

Aunt Judith, in her familiar overalls, was engaged in the peculiarly repulsive task of dissecting a frog. There was no electric light in the summer house and she worked by the light of an Aladdin lamp. The flaring jet cast a harsh unreal light so that it seemed that this scene, too, with Aunt Judith's engrossed face, the pale belly and angular green legs of the frog, and the knife in Aunt Judith's long strong fingers, was part of the nightmare. Aunt Judith was used to handling a knife, Lois found herself thinking. She most of the three sisters would know the fatal spot beneath the left shoulder blade.

"Judith," Aunt Hester said peremptorily.

Aunt Judith blinked her pale eyes. She looked as if she were being jolted out of a dream.

"Am I late for dinner? I'm sorry. I just have to wash."

She didn't appear to have noticed Lois at first. But her eyes moved from Aunt Hester to Lois then and it seemed, for a moment, that they held surprise.

"Lois shouldn't be out in the night air, Hester. You shouldn't have let her come. Or did you want to see my frog, dear? He's such a fine specimen. Dexter caught him in

274

the pool in the woods."

Lois clenched her hands to stop their trembling. If Aunt Judith enjoyed cutting up frogs, if she looked on life and death as biological events only, she would be able to remain calm after committing a murder. . . .

"Aunt Judith, Willow —"

Aunt Hester's loud blunt voice cut across her own uncertain one.

"Judith, you'd better come up to the house straight away. Willow's been murdered and the police will be arriving any minute."

If she didn't know anything about it she should have gasped or fainted, as Aunt Opal had done. But she just put down the knife she had been using and stared hard at Aunt Hester with her curious myopic eyes. Then she said briefly, "How?"

"Stabbed in the back with that old butcher's knife we use in the kitchen."

Aunt Judith began to shake her head in a slow shocked way.

"Dead, dear! How dreadful! What does Opal say?"

"Opal fainted, as you can imagine. It's not too nice knowing there's a murderer amongst us."

Again Lois felt that weight of suspicion, that terrible atmosphere in which they all must live until the guilty person was isolated.

Aunt Judith shook her head again.

"Ever since that queer business about my spider, and then my toadstool. . . . But not Willow! Why would it be Willow?"

"Heaven only knows!" Aunt Hester cried with her first touch of hysteria. "For goodness' sake wash that filthy mess off your hands and come up to the house."

Constable Jenkins on his bicycle was coming up the drive as they went back to the house. Rodney went to the door to let him in. He said something and the two of them went upstairs. Aunt Judith stepped into the hall and gaped after them. She looked half simple, her pale eyes prominent behind the thick glasses. There was no sign of Aunt Opal, but Aunt Hester found her in the morning room, and when Lois went in she saw that Aunt Opal had regained her outward composure, although she was still very pale. She had even put on a dress and done her hair up, and there were no signs of tears on her cheeks. But her knuckles showed white all the time.

"Come and sit down," she said to Lois. Her voice was faint, but it had all its old courtesy. That moment when Aunt Opal had looked at her with hatred and revulsion had probably meant merely her profound grief that Lois was living while Willow was dead.

"I've told Kate not to worry about the dinner," she went on. "I'm sure even you, Hester, won't feel like eating now."

"We can't starve," Aunt Hester said. But she sat down and said nothing about altering Kate's instructions.

"Where is the body?" Aunt Judith inquired.

Aunt Opal pressed her handkerchief to her eyes. But she wasn't weeping even then. When she removed the handkerchief her eyes had a new empty expression, as if she were deliberately making her mind a blank.

"In Lois's room," she said. "That's where Constable Jenkins has gone. Rodney says the police will want to question all of us. For my part, I have been lying down since tea. I think I fell asleep. I must have or I may have heard —" She paused and added on a note of anticlimax, "— something."

"I've been in the garden," said Aunt Hester. "I haven't even cleaned up. I was laying some poisoned carrots to see if I can catch more of those destructive rabbits. I was just coming in, thinking dinner would be ready —"

She automatically looked at Aunt Judith, waiting for her to make her explanation.

"The laboratory, of course," Aunt Judith said impatiently. "As you know very well. I've been working on that frog for the last two hours."

But none of them, Lois reflected, could get their alibis proved. Any one of them had had plenty of time to slip upstairs and into her room. . . . She realized that she was still in her hat and coat and that although none of the aunts had asked her where she had been three pairs of eyes were on her, waiting for what she had to say.

"I've been calling on Diana Marcus," she said. "She drove me home and dropped me at the main gate. I wanted to walk up the drive. I came in and went straight upstairs, and found —" She broke off, shuddering.

"Rodney said death could have occurred at any time within the last hour," Aunt Hester observed. "You understand what that means. It doesn't let any of us out." Her gaze rested particularly on Lois. "Wasn't this rather a strange time to go calling, Lois?"

(Could it be because you wanted a real alibi, not just unproved ones like ours? Lois could imagine her saying. What was to stop you killing Willow before you went, or immediately on returning, when you found her in your room with your dress on?)

"But I wouldn't go around carrying a butcher's knife," she heard herself saying.

She was aware that the aunts were looking

at her in surprise.

"I mean I wouldn't be likely to come home and take the knife from the kitchen because I knew I would find Willow in my room."

There was a silence. Then Aunt Opal said, "That's for the police to decide. The whole matter is in their hands now."

They might have been sitting at a tea party talking of something slightly scandalous. It was inconceivable that one of them had within the last hour committed a deliberate and audacious murder.

"I hope they solve the mystery of who took that spider of mine," Aunt Judith muttered.

"I shouldn't think that had any connection whatever with this," Aunt Opal said definitely.

Privately Lois thought she would let the police make up their own minds about that. But, to her surprise, they were inclined to agree with Aunt Opal when they heard the story, that the spider episode had been a malicious attempt to frighten Lois, and that the possibility of a toadstool being used to poison the soup was another similar attempt. The sergeant, who was up in country lore, said that the majority of toadstools were only deadly when taken in large quantities, and that it was extremely unlikely that Lois could unwittingly have taken enough to be fatal. As for grandfather's death, they made no comment at all on that. It seemed to make no impression on them.

Lois was the first to be interrogated. She sat in a chair in the cold dining room where, by this time, they should have been eating Kate's boiled turnips, and roast beef, and watched the sergeant taking down notes as she talked.

Inspector York, who had motored over from Dalchester, asked a great many questions, but he constantly came back to the same one.

"Had you observed anything significant between your husband and the deceased?"

He insisted on calling Willow "the deceased" so that she ceased to have any personality and was just a corpse to be buried. It was obvious the way his mind was working at present. The murder of a beautiful girl was clearly a crime motivated by jealousy. And the only person who could possibly be jealous was she herself.

"But I tell you," she persisted desperately, "that it wasn't Willow who was meant to be killed. It was me. And whoever did it mistook her for me because she was in my room, sitting at my mirror, and she had my dress on. Everyone knew particularly that that was my dress because it was the one I wore the night the spider crawled on me. I hated it and wouldn't wear it again."

The sergeant wrote busily. Inspector York looked at her with his brooding eyes.

"We find that difficult to believe, Mrs. Armour. For the reason that your hair is dark, almost black, isn't it, and the deceased was blonde. Platinum, I'd say."

"Ash, sir," the sergeant corrected solemnly.

"Thank you, sergeant. Ash, then. And particularly profuse. The sort of hair you'd notice in a moment when you walked into a room. I'd say it was quite impossible to mistake her for you, unless the assailant were color blind or extremely shortsighted."

There was something nagging in her mind, but Lois couldn't bring it to the surface. Was it something to do with the color of Willow's hair? Her brain was too numb to think. She supposed it was impossible for anyone to confuse her hair with Willow's. She hadn't thought of that before. She had just thought of the dress and how she and Willow were almost the same size.

"But why," she said, leaning across the table and trying to focus as keen a gaze on Inspector York as he focused on her, "would anyone want to kill Willow? She was valued a great deal here — and I wasn't. If you don't look at it from that angle you'll never solve it."

The sergeant wrote again. Inspector York

looked benevolent. She knew exactly what he was thinking — that she was pointing out that angle to remove suspicion from herself.

"I'm not here to surmise, Mrs. Armour," he added dryly. "I'm here to get the facts. Do you recognize this?"

He held out a gold locket.

Lois nodded without speaking.

"The deceased was wearing it. Do you know where she got it?"

"Yes. My husband gave it to her."

"Was your husband in the habit of giving her presents?"

It went on and on endlessly. When at last Lois came out of the room she was on the verge of collapse.

Rodney was waiting for her. In spite of the watching eyes of the impassive Constable Jenkins she tumbled into his arms.

"Rodney, they think I did it! How could I do a terrible thing like that?" She was trembling violently.

Rodney said, in a calm voice that belied the fierce grip of his arms. "They have to investigate every avenue. They're going to question the aunts now, and Kate and Dexter. Everyone has to go through it. You're done in, darling, you'd better go to bed."

Lois said breathlessly, "Not in our room!"

Nor in grandfather's either, she thought wildly. The whole house was becoming contaminated.

"We'll make up the bed in my old room," Rodney said smoothly. "You run up and get out some sheets. I'll bring you up a drink. I don't think the Inspector can have any objection to that."

He looked at Constable Jenkins for confirmation. The stout constable nodded heavily.

"That's all right, doc. So long as nobody leaves the house."

So after all Willow got the Chinese room. For Lois knew that she could never go in it again without seeing Willow's lovely tragic body.

Rodney brought her an eggnog laced with brandy and stood over her while she sat up in the narrow bed and drank it. She had on an old pair of Rodney's pajamas that she had found in a drawer. Even though Willow's body had been taken away now she couldn't bring herself to go back into that room and get her own night things.

Here, however, with the door shut, surrounded by Rodney's possessions and with Rodney beside her, she could almost delude herself that they were not at Crow Hollow at all and that none of the recent events had been real. Everything seemed so far away now, the delight on Willow's face when she got the green dress, waiting at the gate in the cool wind for Joe Higgins to come, Diana's story about Rodney and the Christmas tree, tiptoeing back up the stairs so no one would see her, and opening the door of the bedroom. . . . It was all a dream and she could relax now, if her aching body would allow her to.

When she had finished the contents of the glass Rodney took the glass and said, "Now lie down and go to sleep."

Lois leaned back against the pillows. With a last effort of will she shut out everything but the knowledge of Rodney's presence.

"Darling, can't you come to bed, too?"

He sat on the edge of the bed.

"Soon."

"Aren't you going to ask me why I was at Diana's?"

"I suppose you were tired of being shut up in the house."

"I was frightened. You wouldn't believe me about anything, and I got angry and hopeless. I thought if you didn't love me enough to at least try to believe me—"

"I know," Rodney said. He had his head in his hands. "You were going away."

"Did you know all the time?"

"Your letter was still on the dressing table. I destroyed it before the police came."

Of course. The letter she had come back to destroy and had forgotten about.

"But I came back, Rodney," she said.

"Why? You'd have been better to go. There was nothing I deserved more."

"No, darling. Diana told me things I hadn't understood before." She leaned forward to put her arms around him. "I came back to stay. I'll never leave you again as long as you want me. Truly. Do you want me?"

With a swift movement he had her in his arms. She could feel his tears on her cheeks.

"Want you? Oh, my darling! Want you!" He wasn't talking coherently, but it was all right. Everything lovely in the world wasn't dead. There were the two of them to work things out together. Now she could forget Willow and the miasma of horror and sleep.

A knock came at the door.

"Lois, are you in there?" It was Aunt Hester's voice.

Rodney released her.

"Come in," he called.

Aunt Hester opened the door and poked her long face in.

"There's someone downstairs asking for you.

She's just arrived. With bags. If she's staying, where are we going to put her to sleep?"

"Who is it?" Lois asked in bewilderment.

The door opened wider. Another figure appeared behind Aunt Hester.

"It's me," came Cass's cheerful voice. "And I don't mind where I sleep. I'll have to stay because although that burly policeman downstairs let me in I'm damned sure he isn't going to let me out!"

XVII

Lois opened her eyes to find that it was broad daylight and that Cass was standing at her bedside holding a tray. Cass wore an apron over her short sleeved print dress and she was grinning in her wide cheerful way. She was the most reassuring sight Lois had had in days.

"What happened to me last night?" Lois demanded. "What did Rodney put in that drink?"

"A knock-out pill, I should think," Cass said. "You certainly went right out. But you needed it. You look a whole heap better this morning."

Lois stretched tentatively. The ache had gone out of her limbs. Her head felt clear and, incredibly enough, she had a sensation that was almost happiness.

"I feel fine," she said.

"Good. When you've got this inside you you'll be on top of the world." Cass put down the tray which held toast, a boiled egg and coffee. "I prepared it with my own fair hands."

"Cass, you're an angel."

"Rubbish! I'm glad to take a weight off Rodney's mind by officiating in the kitchen. He's away off on an early call he got this morning now. Don't think he's been too casual, Lois. He's been as worried as the devil ever since you were ill."

Lois nodded.

"I know. I did misjudge him. But tell me, what ever made you come last night? Just at the psychological moment?"

"Because you never wrote to me. I knew there was something wrong. I knew you'd write if you could. So I thought, here goes, I barge in. Anyway, Alec and I have had a row. I just said, 'So long, pal. I might write, but don't expect me to.'"

"Oh, Cass!"

Cass grinned.

"It'll do him good. That's the way all men should be treated."

Lois slipped back among the pillows.

"It doesn't always work out right. If I hadn't —"

"Don't start these 'ifs,' kid. If I hadn't let you

come back here you wouldn't have lost your baby. Look at it that way."

"Cass, help us find out about Willow, because I'm quite sure the police aren't going to discover the truth. They won't believe my theory that it was me who was meant to be killed, and unless they do they'll never get anywhere."

"Whoever it was," said Cass, "had sense enough to wear gloves. There were no fingerprints on the knife handle. The only prints they've been able to pick up are yours and Willow's. At the moment, I gather, they favor the jealousy motive. That involves you. But they also toy with the idea that someone discovered Willow had been responsible for those practical jokes (the definition is the inspector's) played on you and decided to give her a fright — presuming, I imagine, that that very expertly placed knife was an accident. That theory, I believe, is Constable Jenkins'. He's so reluctant to believe that anything scandalous could happen at Crow Hollow. The third theory is that Willow had found out something about the old man's death."

"They think grandfather was murdered, then."

"They're considering the idea. The inspector maintains that most murders are carried out in order to silence the victim's tongue."

Willow's tongue was silenced now — not that it had ever talked a lot — all her beauty was wasted.

"So you see," Cass said cheerfully, "that the issue is very open."

Lois said feverishly, "We've got to discover the truth of this because if I hadn't decided to leave Crow Hollow and give Willow that dress she wouldn't have been in my room. And she certainly wouldn't have been sitting in front of my mirror using my face creams if she had known I was coming back — not after my catching her that first time. So I'm to blame."

"You're to blame for not being a corpse instead of Willow," said Cass ironically. "Well, you're not a corpse, my girl, so sit up and eat this egg before it congeals entirely. To my mind it looks as if Willow got what was coming to her. But for your sake I'll stay and try to help you get to the bottom of this."

"For my sake?"

"Don't you read your detective novels, girl? Because if you were meant to be killed instead of Willow do you think the murderer is going to stop at one large error?"

Lois felt a chill creeping over her flesh. Subconsciously she had been aware of that all the time, but she had been too tired and dazed to bring the knowledge to the surface.

"You were a damn fool to come back yesterday," Cass went on. "Some quixotic idea that your husband still loved you isn't sufficient reason to stick your head in a noose. Now you've got yourself in a nice hole by having the police think your visit to Diana Marcus was a clumsy attempt at an alibi, and by laying yourself wide open to danger."

"You don't believe in mincing words," Lois said rather faintly.

"Not I," said Cass. "Not in a situation like this. I've met those three witches from Macbeth —"

"Oh, Cass, they're not as bad as that."

"When you know that one of them is a particularly coldblooded murderer the witches might be prattling schoolgirls in comparison. Especially that one with the shortsighted look."

"Aunt Judith."

"Yes. Hasn't she some peculiar hobby?"

"She catches beetles and dissects frogs."

"Ah, ah! The zoological touch of those practical jokes make the thing look obvious. But it probably isn't in the least obvious. We're going to have fun and games. After you were asleep last night I went down and met the aunts. We all hated one another on sight.

Especially when I said I planned to sleep in late lamented Father's bed. But Rodney's okay, kid. You did right to stick by him."

When Lois went downstairs later she found the aunts in the morning room just as she had left them the previous night. She wondered vaguely if they had sat there all night. After Cass's remarks she couldn't help a feeling of revulsion as she walked into the room. Until she knew which one was guilty they must all be abhorrent to her.

Aunt Opal said kindly, "Good morning, Lois. I hope you managed to sleep a little."

"I never slept a wink," Aunt Hester immediately said in an outraged voice, as if nothing of sufficient enormity had ever happened before to deprive her of sleep.

Aunt Opal's face had a sunken look and her eyes were still wide and empty. Aunt Hester looked much as usual, but Aunt Judith was flushed and unhappy. Her pale eyes were red-rimmed. Clearly she had been crying. Was she the only one who grieved for Willow?

"The police have been searching my laboratory," she said. "One of those clumsy constables knocked over a slide of butterflies. Ruined them, of course. Utterly ruined them!"

"What a shame!" Lois murmured. So even Aunt Judith's grief was not for Willow.

"I'd spent twenty years making that collection and now some of the best specimens are gone. But what does that matter to a thick-headed policeman?"

"What were they searching for?" Aunt Hester asked coldly.

"I don't know. Really, I don't know."

"I should think it's obvious," Aunt Opal observed in her gentle voice. "They think you may have another poisonous spider, Judith, or something else dangerous."

"I didn't put that spider in Lois's flowers," Aunt Judith said shrilly. "Someone else did that. I know, because the box was shifted from the way I had left it."

"Never mind, dear, never mind," said Aunt Opal. "Lois, we're delighted to have your friend stay, but what a pity she's chosen to come at such a tragic time."

"Cass does unexpected things," Lois said. "She doesn't mind taking the consequences."

"There's no need for her to work in the kitchen," Aunt Hester said in an offended voice. It was clear there had been words between Cass and Aunt Hester. "We don't expect our guests to do that. If she doesn't consider the cook or Opal or myself fit to prepare her a meal there's a perfectly good hotel in Finchin where she could stay."

"Cass likes to do those things," Lois said. "Don't worry about her."

"Lois, dear!" That was Aunt Opal's faint gentle voice. "We're arranging flowers for Willow. I've ordered a wreath from you and Rodney."

Would they bury Willow in the green taffeta dress? Would her murderer send flowers to her funeral?

"Thank you, Aunt Opal."

"The funeral will be tomorrow, but Willow's parents are coming by car this morning from Dalchester. It's dreadful to think their daughter met her death in our house. I don't know how to face them." She squared her shoulders with pathetic courage. "But it must be done."

"And you needn't think of going on any jaunts today, Lois," Aunt Hester said, "because no one is to leave the place except Rodney, and he only on urgent calls."

"But Lois will have no need to go anywhere today," Aunt Judith said softly, her sly unreadable eyes on Lois.

The atmosphere of the house was intolerable. Lois went out into the garden, walking over the grass still drenched with dew, breathing deeply of the sharp fresh autumn air. The leaves were thinning in the elms and the black shapes of the crows constantly settling and departing were clearly visible. They were just noisy birds with nothing sinister about them. Nevertheless, their return and their harsh voices were bound up with the horror of the place.

She went down the rhododendron walk and stopped suddenly at the sight of a hawk lying on the path at her feet. Its hooded eyes were open. It was quite dead. She was going to pick it up, then couldn't bring herself to. She saw Dexter coming towards her. His face wore an interested look. He stopped and picked the bird up in his large hands. With a sensation of horror Lois saw that its head didn't droop but was completely stiff.

"What's wrong with it, Dexter? What made it die there?"

"I guessed I'd find it somewheres here," Dexter said. "The rabbit's just through the hedge and it had been mauled. That's mighty strong poison Miss Hester uses, stiffening up rabbit and hawk both."

"Is that what killed it?"

Dexter nodded. He fondled the bird's feathers.

"Well, I guess Miss Judith will be pleased. She ain't never had a hawk, so far as I know."

He went off in the direction of the summer

house, bearing the bird proudly.

Lois rubbed her hands together, trying to warm them. She couldn't go back into the house and she couldn't walk about the garden where one might stumble on death at every turn. She sat on the seat under the weeping elm and was still there half an hour later when Rodney came home.

He came over to her and said, "Where's Cass?"

"She was in the kitchen with Kate, planning lunch. I really believe she's enjoying herself."

"Darling, I won't be away more than I can help — it was Eliza Matthews' baby this morning — but when I am away, stick around Cass."

Lois turned edgily.

"It's perfectly safe out here in an open space in full view of the house — and with Constable Jenkins leaving his bicycle on the geraniums and prowling around."

"I know, but all the same —"

Lois clenched her hands. She laughed, not very successfully.

"It's a queer feeling to know that someone dislikes you enough to kill you. But *why*, Rodney?"

"We'll find out. I called on Diana Marcus this morning. There's something her mother knew."

"I know. That the aunts wanted you to marry Willow." Lois looked at him curiously. "Did you know that, Rodney?"

He looked disturbed and a little angry.

"Lately I'd wondered. But it seemed too fantastic. Just because she was a pretty kid and I'd fallen into the general habit of bringing her odd presents. She used to get such a kick out of something new — like a child. I didn't realize the significance that could be attached to that. I should have, of course. And I should never have let her get away with being impertinent to you. I thought she had the mentality of a child and should be treated accordingly. Now I realize she was either extremely clever, or subnormal."

Lois touched his hand.

"Never mind now, darling."

"But Diana thinks her mother knew something else as well as that crazy scheme. Probably something a good deal more important. She thinks it's possible her aunt in London might know. She's going up on the midday train."

"When will she be back?"

"She'll telephone tonight if she finds out anything."

"She's a good friend, Rodney."

"One of the best."

297

"She's a good deal wiser than I. You might have married her."

"There's only been one person I've ever wanted to marry."

For a moment the sun seemed warmer. Lois sighed deeply, relaxing.

"Me too," she said.

"Darling, I'll promise you something."

"Yes?"

"As soon as this business is cleared up we'll leave here."

"Truly, Rodney?"

"We'll go to London and I'll get a job in one of the big hospitals."

"You should, Rodney. It's important to you."

"I owed it to grandfather to stay here," he said. "But there are bigger things than debts to a dead man. One of them is having you safe and happy." He looked down at her. "Darling, stay looking like that."

"How am I looking?" She only knew how much she loved his thin eager face.

"As if there's hope in the future, after all. There is, my darling. There is."

Lois looked around, seeing the smooth yellow-tinged lawns, the garden beds with the last ragged dahlias and geraniums, the warm homely red of the stable roof and the shabby clock face in its little tower; then the house with its gray bones beginning to show beneath the thinning creepers. She should have loved this place. She should have been happy to bear Rodney's children here. For two centuries the Armours had lived on this land. It was right that they should have an intense pride in it. She could understand grandfather's desire for an heir. She had felt a thrill of family pride herself that first morning she had been here when she had got up early and looked out of the window at the garden in the growing light.

Remembering that, Lois suddenly remembered also the conversation she had overheard that morning, the voice in the passage saying, "I'll make it up to you, Willow!" The cold sharp deliberate voice that she hadn't been able to identify. She knew now what those words had meant, and if she could find out who had spoken them she felt she would have the identity of the murderer.

"Darling!" came Rodney's voice. "Stop worrying so hard."

"I was just thinking of the dead hawk I found — if we lived in the Middle Ages I'd say there were evil spirits about." She laughed and shivered. "Rodney, this is a beautiful place. Some day I'll be able to live in it — when this is all past and the crows have gone."

Willow's parents arrived just as everyone was sitting down to lunch. They were a stout middle-aged pair, completely unprepossessing. Their name was Briggs. Lois realized she had never known Willow's surname before, and the knowledge that it was a simple common name somehow reduced Willow from a mysterious beauty to an ordinary girl earning her living in the age-old way of penniless village girls.

Mr. Briggs had a red plain face, eyes of a washed out blue, and sandy hair. He also had a protuberant stomach. His wife, dressed in what was obviously her best black, had nondescript coloring, work-roughened hands, and an air of embarrassment. It was almost impossible to believe that those two very commonplace people were the parents of the exquisite Willow.

The odd thing about them, too, was that they showed little grief. Their chief emotions seemed to be awe and shock. But they were quite prepared to eat some lunch. Indeed, Mr. Briggs, once he had decided to feel at ease, ate with the heartiest enjoyment. Rodney plied him with ale, and as his inner comfort increased he became talkative.

"We had to go to the police station and the morgue first or we'd have been here earlier. I won't say it didn't give us a turn, seeing our

Willow dead in a place like that. The police asked a lot of questions, too. What had Willow told us at home about her place, was she happy there, did she get ill-treated?"

Mrs. Briggs looked up with embarrassment.

"Just as if any of you ladies would be hard on her. Why, she always said how you spoiled her. You did, too, and that's a fact."

"We were so fond of her," Aunt Opal whispered.

"That's what I say. We told the inspector, too, didn't we, Albert? I declare, I don't know how a dreadful thing like this could have happened."

Mrs. Briggs' tone said she was acutely ashamed that Willow should have got herself murdered in a nice place like this. But why wasn't she too grieved to feel shame? How could Mr. Briggs, having just viewed the murdered body of his daughter, so heartily enjoy his lunch?

Cass, Lois knew, was noticing everything without appearing to be noticing anything. Cass had always been curious about Willow's antecedents. Well, now she had Willow's parents before her. She would realize from their appearance that they wouldn't be the sort of parents a girl like Willow would confide in.

"I've been trying to pack poor Willow's

things," Aunt Opal said. She paused to press her handkerchief to her eyes, then she went on in her faint determined voice, "I haven't finished yet. It's so distressing —"

"Don't trouble yourself, Miss Armour," Mrs. Briggs said sympathetically. "Show me her room and I can do it."

And what would Willow's plain mother think of the charming room her daughter had had? It would be interesting to discover that. But there would be no opportunity, Lois guessed, and in a moment her guess was proved correct.

"No, indeed, Mrs. Briggs, that's the very least we can do," Aunt Opal said.

"I should think so," Aunt Hester boomed. "Judith and I will give you a hand, Opal."

"All we can say," Mr. Briggs declared, "is that you've treated our little girl like your own daughter."

(But one of them murdered her, Lois thought silently. Was everyone forgetting that?)

"We think," Mrs. Briggs said, "that Willow perhaps had an enemy she didn't tell anyone about. He could have climbed up that creeper and got through the window."

"First taking the old butcher's knife from the kitchen," Cass put in airily.

Everyone looked at her with indignation. What right had she, a stranger, to throw suspicion back on the inmates of the house when Mrs. Briggs was so chivalrously trying to protect them?

"There was that Clara," Mr. Briggs observed. "Willow never did like her. Said she was bad-tempered and hard to work with."

"Yes, Clara," said Aunt Opal eagerly. "No one has thought of her."

"The police are trying to get in touch with her," Rodney said. "If any of you has any clue as to her whereabouts you'd be wise to tell the inspector."

"Clara went like a thief in the night," Aunt Opal said sadly.

"*That* looks like a guilty conscience," Aunt Judith said, speaking for the first time. "Be sure to find out, Rodney, what she tells the police when they find her." Then she went on conversationally, "Dexter brought me a hawk this morning. Dead from eating your poisoned rabbits, Hester. It will be interesting to observe the effect of strychnine on its organs." She turned to the Briggs pair. "Would you people like to see my specimens before you go? I have some excellent ones, particularly among the insect family."

Mr. Briggs' pale eyes popped.

"Thank, you, Miss Armour. Thank you. But I'm just a plumber myself. Afraid insects aren't in my line."

"Thank you all the same," Mrs. Briggs added politely.

Lois helped Cass carry the dishes out to the kitchen. In the passage Cass whispered, "Something odd about those two."

"What do you mean?"

"Didn't you notice? They should be shattered with grief and they're not in the least. They just feel important. We've got to find out why. You go into the library and I'll tell Mrs. Briggs you want to have a few words with her. Then pump her."

Feeling nervous and uncertain — how did one pump a newly bereaved mother? — Lois went into the library and a few minutes later Cass showed Mrs. Briggs in. Cass went out, shutting the door.

Lois told Mrs. Briggs to sit down. She began, "I wanted to tell you how sorry I am that such a tragic thing happened to your daughter here."

"It fair staggers you, doesn't it?" Mrs. Briggs agreed. "All the way here Albert and I said we'd talked about something like this happening, but now it has it don't seem like real. It's knocked the wind out of us just as much."

"What do you mean, Mrs. Briggs, by saying you've talked about this happening? Surely —"

Mrs. Briggs looked at Lois earnestly.

"Don't think I'm not showing respect for the dead, Mrs. Armour. But Albert and I never did understand Willow. Just her looks set her apart from us, and as for her mind — well, she was a schemer, Mrs. Armour, and that's a fact."

"My husband's aunts thought a great deal of her," was all Lois could say. She had a sense of inner excitement that she had to hide. Cass had been right, she was going to find out something of importance.

"I know they did. Spoiled her shocking, if you don't mind me saying so. Encouraged her in her silly ideas."

"What ideas, Mrs. Briggs?"

Mrs. Briggs looked at Lois uncertainly. Her face was flushed. Clearly she was bursting to talk about a subject that must have rankled in her mind for a long time.

"Willow declared the Miss Armours wanted her to marry the young doctor. I used to talk my head off, thinking it was something she had made up and come to believe, but she swore it was true."

"And how did she feel about it herself?" Lois asked carefully.

"Why, she was wild for him. She was pretty

close, but I could read her. She used to come home weekends just so as he'd drive her to the train. That was the only reason. It wasn't to see us. When he married you — well, Mrs. Armour, I'm ashamed to say the way she was jealous. If queer things happened, as I've heard rumors, you could be sure Willow had a hand in them."

Mrs. Briggs drew a deep breath. Her indignant countenance bore no sign of grief. It was plain that she was reliving old grievances.

"All the same, Mrs. Armour, I will say Willow wasn't that bad until she came here and the three ladies encouraged her in her vain ways. When she was with Mrs. Marcus I had some hopes for her. But after she came to Crow Hollow she just got so as Albert and I dreaded her coming home. We told her time and again if she went on like that she'd come to a bad end. Her wicked vanity and her overriding ways must have been born in her, that's all we can think. It wasn't the way we brought her up. From the day she came to us she was taught to behave properly."

"The day she came to you, Mrs. Briggs. Do you mean — she wasn't your child?"

"Bless you, no. How would Albert and I come by a child like that? She never was our sort. We made a mistake in choosing her. It was Albert wanting a good-looking one. I told him the plain ones was nicer in the end."

"You adopted her?" Lois asked.

"Yes. We thought we wasn't going to have a family and we both wanted one. We made inquiries and then we heard of this baby. She was three months old then. She had been born in Italy, or some outlandish place. The wrong side of the blanket, I expect. But Albert and I thought a decent home would counteract that bad start. Anyway, you see, it didn't. Right from the start we couldn't understand her. And then when we had a baby of our own, after all, did she treat the poor little chap something shocking! Jealous! It was her nature, you see. Young Albert said when we got the news that he'd shed no tears for her. And I can't say I blame him."

Mrs. Briggs sat back.

"So that's how it is, Mrs. Armour. Poor Willow's had this shocking thing happen to her, but she's brought it on herself. You can rest assured of that."

When Mr. and Mrs. Briggs had gone Lois found Rodney and Cass and told them what she had learned.

Rodney said thoughtfully, "That might be what Mrs. Marcus knew. Diana might be able to throw more light on that. I don't know whether it's significant."

"It's significant insofar as it shows Willow's character," Cass declared. "This whole thing ties up with that scheming little hussy's ambitions."

"In that case," said Lois, "now she's dead there'll be no more reason to – to attack me."

Cass looked at Rodney. Her eyes were shrewd and hard.

"Do you agree with that, Rodney? Don't you think that this murderer has the kind of diseased mind that now beloved Willow has gone, by mistake, the right victim mustn't be allowed to live?"

Rodney's face had that gray strained look again.

"I don't know what to think. But I do know we don't dare to take the slightest risk."

"Right, boy! Because I think we'll find whoever did this is neither sane nor logical."

"How long does it have to go on?" Lois asked rather faintly.

"Oh, not long," Cass said cheerfully. "I should think, too, our murderer has the type of mind that can't brook delay. I'm not missing a thing those old women do. Pretty soon one of them is going to give herself away."

She looked at Rodney again.

"Sorry, doc. They are your aunts."

"They're my aunts," Rodney said harshly, "but one of them has tried to kill my wife. Go ahead. Let's have your views."

"Well, in the past all the methods of attack have been very simple and clumsy — spontaneous, sort of. The weapon has been in front of the attacker, and she has suddenly decided to use it. Their very clumsiness has prevented their success, except in grandfather's case, where the old man was probably so ill that he just needed a small shove over the brink. The spider was there, the toadstool was there, the butcher's knife was probably lying on the kitchen table when she was passing through. She has a haphazard mind — and that's where the danger lies. We can't anticipate the method. So we've got to have eyes all around our heads."

Lois could feel the color drained out of her cheeks.

"Why do you think grandfather was killed?"

"Obviously because he knew too much about the spider incident. Don't you agree?"

"I always did think that."

"And do you think Willow was responsible for these things?" Rodney asked.

"I think Willow put the spider in the flowers. I think that's what the old man knew. Didn't you say he made her cry the next morning? I think, too, that she may have been responsible for the toadstool poison. *But these things were done at the instigation of someone else.* That someone else is the person we're after."

"Yes," Rodney agreed heavily. Then he said, "Thanks a lot, Cass, for being here. It's a tremendous help. Lois and I —"

"You're a pair of babes," Cass broke in affectionately. "Don't know how to look after yourselves. Anyway, I like this place. And a separation will do Alec good." She looked self-conscious. "Though I did put a call through to the big goof this morning.

"The police are barking up the wrong tree," she went on presently. "Before they come to their senses, if they're not careful, another tragedy will have happened. So we've got to work this thing out among ourselves. We've got no clues. Lois was out of the house, Kate had spent the afternoon in the dairy making butter. She said she hadn't noticed the butcher's knife was missing. She hadn't been here long enough to know her way around, and said it could have been missing a day or an hour for all she would know. There were no fingerprints picked up beyond Lois's and Willow's. Dexter was about the yard and he knew Hester was working in the garden at the back of the house at one stage, but he wouldn't have noticed if she had gone inside. The same thing applies to Judith in the laboratory, and of course Opal was in her room. There's no clue at all. All we have to go by is the natures of the women themselves. Which one of them would be the most likely to act on the spur of the moment as the opportunity presented itself? Which one would have the necessary ruthlessness?"

"Aunt Hester," said Rodney, "has always known what she wanted and let nothing stand in the way. She'd have the courage and the purpose. She stood up to grandfather when he had the other two completely cowed. I don't know how she'd behave when she couldn't shift an obstacle in her path, because that's never happened to her before. I think if she wanted Lois out of the way badly enough —"

"And she'd have the strength," Cass said. "She's the biggest of the three. Also, she made the soup. That's Hester. How about Judith?"

"Aunt Judith has a peculiar mind. Sometimes I think she isn't quite human. She's more at home with her specimens than with people. She knows more about a frog, for instance, than a human being. But you never do quite understand Aunt Judith. She might just be starved for affection. Grandfather used to treat her as something of a joke, and her sisters are

311

ashamed of her. This craze for zoology might merely be an emotional outlet."

"But," said Cass, "if it weren't, if she counted human life comparatively lightly, if she thought death was no more serious than putting your finger on a fly, and she thought it would be better to have Lois out of the way. . . . And it was her spider and her toadstool," she added significantly. Then she went on briskly, "And Opal?"

Lois said quickly, before Rodney could speak, "But she's so gentle and easily distressed. She's the one who has been much the kinder to me. It's impossible to imagine her doing that to — to anybody."

"She's the one who pampered Willow the most," Rodney said.

"Because it's natural to her to pamper people. And besides, Rodney, Willow told me she used to hear the aunts quarreling over her. Apparently they were all jealous of each other."

"What a charming vicious circle!" Cass murmured.

"I wish I knew who had said that about making it up to Willow the first morning I was here," Lois said thoughtfully. "Willow had been crying. I didn't know why then, but I know now it was because she didn't like my being here as Rodney's wife. And someone was telling her they would make it up to her."

"Good God!" Rodney muttered.

"If I could hear that voice again and recognize whose it was," Lois said dreamily, "then it would be simple."

In the afternoon Inspector York was back. Now it was the night of grandfather's death that he was working on. Dexter was brought in and questioned at great length, then Aunt Opal, who had been the first person to go into grandfather's room, was called in. But in the middle of giving her evidence she fainted, and the inspector, with a mixture of apology and impatience, had to call for help.

Rodney and Cass assisted Aunt Opal out of the dining room. Lois was going to follow them, but the inspector called her back.

"Why did the old lady faint because I told her about this idea of yours that you were the one meant to be killed?" he asked.

"I don't know," Lois answered. "She's very distressed. She fainted yesterday, too. She was very fond of Willow. This is all a terrible strain for her."

The inspector tapped his teeth with his pencil, a habit that Lois found intensely irritating.

"I don't suppose it's exactly easy for any of

you. I can't agree with you, Mrs. Armour, about this idea of yours."

The inspector was baffled now, and couldn't hide it. He was willing to consider any theory, and eager to follow a good one. "That mass of hair. None of the women are color blind. I've tested them. And the shortsighted one isn't as shortsighted as that."

Again that elusive detail that she should remember nagged at Lois's mind. Her brain was numb. To think collectedly was utterly beyond her. She only knew that what Cass said was true, that by the time the police got around to her way of thinking it might be too late.

"My husband agrees with me," she said lamely.

There was skepticism in the inspector's eyes. Of course he was thinking that Rodney would shield her, for if her theory was true she must automatically be proved innocent of Willow's death.

Suddenly she became angry with the inspector for his obtuseness.

"Surely you don't think I could have done a thing like that?" she exclaimed.

"My God!" the inspector ejaculated. "Who could have done it? There's not one of you looks capable of murder, but that girl had a knife in her back. We didn't imagine that, did we? And she damn well didn't put it there herself!"

XVIII

After Aunt Opal had recovered and gone to her room to lie down Rodney wanted Lois to go and rest, too. But again, as in the morning, she found the house unbearable.

"Couldn't we go out?" she said wistfully. "You need some fresh air, too. Let's walk through the woods. Find out from Constable Jenkins if we can."

Constable Jenkins said heavily that there was no objection to their strolling a little way. His mild blue eyes rested on Lois and she knew by their kindness that he couldn't believe her in any way guilty.

"Thank you, constable," she said gratefully.

"That's all right. You take care of your lady, doc."

Rodney's arm tightened through hers.

"I'll do that, constable."

It was charming in the woods. A light cool mist was drifting among the tree trunks, and the reddening leaves shone like geraniums. It was very still with even the noisy squawking of the crows far off and intermittent. At one end of the woods lay Crow Hollow, with its deceptive air of peace, and at the other the cemetery where the latest generation of Armours lay — where she, save for one chance mistake, might have lain. But here it was fresh and quiet and beautiful and nothing existed but herself and Rodney stepping on the crackling leaves.

"We'll start all over again," Rodney was saying. "Do you think Cass will stand us another wedding?"

"We'll give Cass and Alec a wedding when we get our apartment in London."

"We certainly will. Whisky and champagne."

"And I'll buy carnations from our same man. He has them all the year round, I'm sure. By special dispensation."

"And our baby," said Rodney, "will arrive the day before Cass's and Alec's."

Lois laughed. She said in slow astonishment, "Rodney, I feel happy."

"So do I, oddly enough. Or is it oddly when

we're here together, alive?" He stopped to put his arms around her. She looked up to see the deep tenderness in his eyes. Then, before he could kiss her, a twig snapped behind them and the moment was gone.

Rodney turned sharply. But the intruder was only Dexter, coming along the path with his slow shuffling step, peering to left and right of him as if seeking something. When he saw them he gave his childlike grin and tipped his cap.

"Afternoon, sir. Afternoon, missus."

"Hello, Dexter," Rodney said. "What are you doing here? Isn't it past milking time?"

"It is that, sir, but Miss Judith, she said not to come home without one of these, and I've just found one this minute, sir."

In his grubby fingers he held a perfect specimen of a red-capped toadstool.

"It's like the one she lost, sir. She was that anxious to get another and they ain't easy to find."

"When did she ask you to find her another, Dexter?"

"This afternoon, sir. Right after lunch. She came down to the stable when I was grooming Jewel. She said she wanted it particular today."

"Rodney —" Lois began.

"Well, she'll be delighted with it," Rodney

said easily. "Hurry along home, Dexter, or you'll be working in the dark tonight."

"Yes, sir. That I will, sir."

The boy shambled off and Lois looked at Rodney in amazement.

"But Rodney, don't you see — she's up to her old tricks." Her voice was breathless with excitement and fear. "It *must* have been her. This proves it."

"Not entirely," said Rodney. "But this time we're one jump ahead. We know she's got the toadstool. We know she'll try to make use of it. The essential thing is to give her the opportunity."

"Because that way she'll be caught red-handed."

"Exactly." Rodney took her arm. "We'd better get back and warn Cass."

Aunt Hester was working over a fire of dead leaves in the back garden when they returned. Her large vigorous figure was partially obscured by the aromatic smoke. She called out to them, "Have a good walk, you two? There's nothing like outdoor work to take your mind off things. See all this rubbish I raked up today."

"It's hard work for you," Rodney said. "You ought to see about getting a gardener."

"Funny thing," Aunt Hester said, "I'm not

sentimental, but I feel I should try and respect father's wishes about gardeners. He always said they weren't to be trusted. Either they can't tell weeds from flowers or they dig up your good bulbs and sell them. Of course father was a bit over-prejudiced ever since that Jed Hawkins was here. You remember him, Rodney?"

"Yes, vaguely," Rodney said. "I must have been very small."

"Only a snippet. You'd remember his hair, though. It was such peculiar hair, almost white. You know the silky white some children's are. Well, his had never darkened. And his eyes were bright blue. Oh, he was an attractive brute. Maybe that was one reason father didn't trust him. Anyway, he dismissed him for pinching plants out of the greenhouse. Didn't he go to Mrs. Marcus after that?"

Rodney looked at her sharply.

"Is that so? I wouldn't remember."

"I seem to think that happened, though I don't think he stayed there long, either. He was a rolling stone. Anyway, he succeeded in completely putting father off gardeners. There hasn't been one on the place since, except an odd boy about Dexter's age."

She gathered up another pile of leaves and thrust them onto the fire as if she enjoyed seeing them burn. Her cheeks, hot and smudged, were almost the color of the flames.

"I got another rabbit this morning, Rodney. We'll soon have no more marauders." There was glee in her voice. She seemed to take a triumphant enjoyment in her work of destruction.

"Must you kill them?" Lois was forced to ask.

Aunt Hester eyed her with contempt for her soft-heartedness.

"They don't feel much. Just stiffen out where they were nibbling. Dexter will tell you that." In the same voice she said, "What time's dinner tonight? That friend of yours, Lois, seems to have taken charge in the kitchen and Opal and I don't know where we are."

"I asked Cass to do that," Rodney said. "I should think dinner's at the usual time, if the inspector has gone."

"Oh, he went off an hour ago. Damn busybody. Are we never going to have the place to ourselves again?" Her anger, Lois reflected, wasn't against the inspector but against the events that necessitated his presence. Was it guilty anger? "When's this thing going to be cleared up, Rodney?"

"When the murderer is discovered," Rodney said bluntly. "You should know that."

"I do," Aunt Hester muttered. Her previous

cheerful normality, which Lois realized had been nothing but bluff, had vanished. She seemed frightened. "I do, too damn well."

Cass met them in the hall and promptly took Lois's arm.

"Someone in the kitchen to see you," she said. "I've kept her out here so no one else would see her."

Lois followed her a little apprehensively, but when she reached the kitchen she saw that the visitor was only Clara. A rather scared looking Clara with none of her dourness left.

"Oh, Mrs. Armour," she cried when Lois came in, "I was in Dalchester and I heard about this terrible business, so I came straight back."

"That was very kind of you, Clara," Lois said. "But I really don't think there's anything you can do."

"It's not so much what I can do, mum, but what I can tell you," Clara said. "I debated telling you this when it happened, but I reckoned it wasn't any of my business and perhaps I was wrong, anyway."

"What is it, Clara?"

Rodney came in, too, and the three of them, Cass, Lois, and Rodney, stood waiting for the woman to speak.

"It was the night of the old doctor's death,

miss, after you and Doctor Rodney had gone to the ball. Somehow the old doctor found out Willow had had something to do with that spider in your flowers. He was terribly angry. He was in the drawing room and I'd been in the dining room tidying up so I heard quite plain across the hall. He was talking to one of the aunts, but I don't know which it was. He said it had been a wicked practical joke that might have had very serious consequences and after it Willow would have to be dismissed. He said she was to get her notice the next morning, and leave at the end of the week. And you know how the old doctor was. When he said a thing like that he meant it to be done."

Clara paused dramatically. Her dark somber eyes searched the faces of her listeners.

"Well, you all know what happened. The old doctor died that night and Willow didn't have to go after all. Mind you," she added, "I'm not saying Willow was responsible for the doctor's death. But I wouldn't like to put anything past her. She was a bad one."

"Why didn't you tell us this at the time, Clara?" Rodney asked.

"Well, sir, there was no suggestion then that the old doctor hadn't died a natural death. And I knew I wouldn't be very popular with the Miss Armours if I started telling tales about

Willow. But I'm sorry, sir. If any of what's happened since could have been stopped, I should have spoken."

"I don't think it would have been stopped," Lois said. "It was very good of you, Clara, to come especially to tell us now."

"She'd better tell the police that," Cass said. She was excited and her eyes were smoldering. "This'll make the scent much hotter."

"The police have been trying to locate you, Clara," Rodney said. "When you go back to the village will you call at the station? I'll telephone Inspector York."

"Certainly, sir," Clara said. "I'll answer any question they like, *including* the way that Willow could lie!"

"Where does that bring us?" Cass asked, when Clara had had a cup of tea and gone the way she had come on a bicycle borrowed from a friend in the village.

"It gives us the motive for grandfather's murder," Rodney said. "Apparently the idea of Willow being sacked was not to be tolerated at any cost whatever. It seems so simple now. My God, why didn't I work this out earlier?"

"You couldn't, Rodney," Lois said sympathetically. She hated to see the haggard despair in his face.

"But the old man was their father," Cass

pointed out. "Whichever one it was would need to have hated him. Probably for a reason apart altogether from Willow. That would make it easy to take a measure like that."

"I don't think any of them were overfond of him," Rodney said. "But to hate — no, I don't know they hated him. I don't know of anything he ever did to make them do that."

"What's happening out there?" came Aunt Hester's stentorian voice along the passage. "Aren't we ever getting any dinner tonight?"

"It's coming," Cass yelled back, matching with enjoyment, Aunt Hester's strident tones. "And you'd better mind your p's and q's," she added under her breath, "or you'll get toadstool soup."

"Oh, Cass —" Lois began.

"Aunt Judith has another toadstool of the same variety as the missing one," Rodney said quickly. "She especially asked Dexter to find one. So keep a weather eye open, Cass, will you?"

Cass's eyes opened wide.

"So it's Judith, is it? I can't say I'm surprised."

"We want final proof," Rodney said. "If she could perhaps be given an opportunity without her suspecting it was intentional —"

"Breakfast," said Cass, with relish. "I'll invite

her to help me. Kate can be sick. I'll hint I don't trust Hester and Opal." Her face sobered. "Leave it to me, kids."

Lois felt the weight on her mind easing. In a little while the horror and the uncertainty would be over, she and Rodney could get away, they'd have that second wedding breakfast. . . . Her excitement began to rise. She went forward and surprised Cass by kissing her vigorously.

"Hurry up and fix your wedding day, Cass. Rodney and I want to arrange the doings."

Rodney stayed in the kitchen and carved the meat while Cass and Kate, who had just come in from the dairy, dished up the vegetables.

"Anything to report since we've been out?" he asked.

"No. Hester's been playing with her bonfire, as you know. Judith rushed off to her laboratory as soon as the inspector let her go — he gave her a once over, believe me. All about her spiders and things, so far as I could hear through the keyhole." She grinned unashamedly. "And Opal hasn't stirred from her bedroom. If you ask me, Opal is taking this much the hardest."

"The other two won't show their feelings," Rodney said. "They never have."

Aunt Hester, with a scrubbed appearance,

her cheeks bright and her long nose shining, was first in the dining room. Presently Aunt Judith sidled in and sat down. She appeared to see nobody. Her eyes were vague and far-off. What was she thinking of? Lois wondered. The brew that she, like a witch, like one of Macbeth's witches as Cass had said, was going to make? Or had she made it already?

Aunt Opal came in last. She was carefully dressed in her silver gray and she held herself very upright, but she looked twenty years older. Within twenty-four hours she had become an old woman.

"Well, Opal," Aunt Hester said with characteristic callousness, "are you going to be able to sit through dinner? Because we don't want our meal upset through having to carry you out."

With dignity Aunt Opal replied, "I'm perfectly well, Hester. I was merely tired this afternoon. I suppose the inspector is doing his duty, but he pounces at one so with questions. I've had a little sleep since, and now I feel grand."

Aunt Hester looked at her sister's colorless face and sniffed unbelievingly. Cass sat down roast potatoes and carrots in front of her and her eyes gleamed.

"Ha!" she said. "This looks all right. Did you cook this yourself?"

"I did," Cass answered modestly. "Kate was making butter."

"Well, you'd better stay on here as cook. Eh? Kate could take Willow's job."

"Aunt Hester, Cass is a schoolteacher," Lois said.

"Schoolteacher! What's she wasting her time at that for when she can cook?" She turned again to Cass. "I might even let you into the secret of how I make some of my soups."

"Too dangerous," Cass answered blithely. "I wouldn't dare risk it." After that audacious remark had sunk in she added, "My fiancé would raise Cain."

"Goodness me," said Aunt Judith in mild astonishment. "Are you engaged?"

"Yes. Alec likes my cooking, too."

Lois caught Rodney's eye. She stifled a giggle. Thank heaven for Cass, dear audacious Cass with her ability to enliven and find humor in every situation.

"It's very good of you," said Aunt Opal, with her unfailing politeness, "to help us out here while we're in such trouble."

"Don't worry about me," said Cass. "I love it."

She sat down in her place beside Lois and beamed around the table. "Life must go on as usual, you know."

"Stop making hackneyed remarks," Lois murmured. "Eat your dinner."

Aunt Opal put a small piece of potato into her mouth, then laid her fork down as if to hold it were too much effort.

"Did I see a woman riding away on a bicycle just before dinner?" she asked. "I happened to look out of my window, but it was getting so dark I might have been mistaken."

Should she be told that Clara had been here? Hesitating as to what answer to make, Lois heard Rodney say, "That was Clara, Aunt Opal. She came with a rather important piece of information."

There was a general movement of interest from the three aunts. The tension, momentarily eased by Cass's nonsense, became very apparent.

"Well, what was it?" Aunt Hester demanded impatiently.

"It seems," Rodney said, making his words sharp and clear, "that the night of the trouble with the spider, grandfather insisted that Willow be dismissed."

"Willow!" said Aunt Hester.

"Dismissed!" echoed Aunt Judith.

"How extraordinary!" Aunt Opal exclaimed. "Why didn't I know anything of this?"

"One of you knew," Rodney said. "But since

grandfather died before morning his wishes were not carried out."

"He said nothing to me!" Aunt Hester declared. "I wouldn't have been afraid to stand up to him, but he said nothing to me. What was the reason, anyway? Did he find out that Willow had put the spider in the flowers?"

"I believe that was the reason."

"I knew it!" Aunt Judith cried triumphantly. Her face was flushed and excited. "I always did suspect Willow, but of course the way things were I knew I wouldn't be listened to."

"Rodney," Aunt Opal begged, "are you *sure* Willow did that? I just can't think how she could."

"The spider was in my room in its box when I went out and when I came back it was gone," Aunt Judith said conclusively.

"That proves nothing," Aunt Opal answered.

"We have no proof," Rodney said, "but it seems pretty clear Willow did put the spider in the flowers. On the other hand, Cass and Lois and I believe that she did it at the instigation of someone else. That person is the one who was told by grandfather to dismiss Willow. But she didn't. You all understand the implication of that?"

Rodney's voice was not accusing. It was simply impersonal. These were his aunts who had brought him up from a child. He had always treated them with courtesy and affection. But one of them had tried to kill his wife. Until that one was singled out he would treat them all as strangers.

Lois saw their three faces gaping at Rodney. Aunt Hester's a deeper shade of crimson, Aunt Judith's withdrawn and secret, Aunt Opal's white and blank, as if it could absorb no more horror.

But finally it was Aunt Opal who said, "Rodney, what a perfectly dreadful thing to suggest! That one of us might even have — brought about father's death."

"By deliberately not going to his aid when he was having a heart attack," Rodney elaborated. "That would amount to murder just as definitely as putting a knife in Willow's back."

Aunt Opal swayed forward a little.

"Look out!" Aunt Hester's voice rang out. "She's going to faint again."

Aunt Opal lifted her head.

"No, I'm not," she said faintly but clearly. "I'm quite all right."

"So none of you knows anything about grandfather's ultimatum?" Rodney persisted.

"That Clara!" Aunt Opal muttered. She was never going to forgive Clara for her unceremonious departure.

"Yes, I wouldn't take Clara's word as gospel," Aunt Hester said. "Her attitude towards Willow wasn't unbiased."

"Of course Willow was so pretty and Clara wasn't," Aunt Judith reflected. "There was bound to be jealousy."

"All right," said Rodney. His voice was still carefully impersonal. "We'll leave it to the police to see what they make of it. Clara should be at the station by now. By the way, Aunt Judith, I hope Dexter delivered your toadstool safely."

"Toadstool!" Aunt Hester exclaimed. "Not another!"

"Judith!" cried Aunt Opal. "Why do you keep the horrid things?"

Aunt Judith's face was a dark sullen color.

"I want to experiment with it," she said defiantly. Her voice rose angrily. "Leave me alone, will you? Don't interfere with my business."

"Your business!"Aunt Hester echoed. "When it comes to other people being accused of using the poisonous stuff to put in soup, it certainly becomes everyone's business."

Aunt Opal was visibly trembling.

"Judith, those dangerous things you have! Look what's already happened."

"And my word!" Aunt Hester exclaimed.

"Didn't grandfather order you the night before he died to get rid of all your specimens? And that, to you, was going to be worse than death."

Aunt Judith pushed her chair back. She stood up, and her little compact figure was quivering with angry indignation.

"I won't listen to another word! I'm perfectly innocent. You can do what you like and think what you like, but you'll never prove me guilty. Never!"

With that she flounced out of the room.

"Well!" breathed Aunt Hester, and even she seemed momentarily deflated. "Would you call that an exhibition of innocence — or guilt?"

"She hasn't eaten her dinner," Cass said mildly. "In fact, nobody has eaten much. What's wrong? There's no strychnine in the carrots!"

Nobody laughed at that joke. Lois said rather shakily, "Cass, that isn't in the best taste."

Aunt Hester wasn't listening. She had turned to Aunt Opal and was saying, "She can't be left to play around with poisonous things like that. Opal, do you think she's quite sane? I've wondered for years, but I always concluded she was harmless. Now I'm not so sure."

Aunt Opal had slumped back in her chair.

"Poor Willow!" she was whispering. "Poor,

poor Willow!" The first tears Lois had seen her shed were sliding down her cheeks.

Unable to bear it, Lois sprang up.

"Cass, let's make the coffee. I don't think any of us want to eat."

Cass followed her into the kitchen and in a little while Rodney came, too.

Cass turned to him.

"You handled it well, doc, but you put the pressure on, rather."

"It's the only way," Rodney said tiredly. "One of them will have to give herself away sometime."

"Well, Judith did, more or less, didn't she?"

"I don't know. I can't decide. Either she couldn't stick it any longer, or her indignation was genuine. We'll have to give her a bit of rope. Somehow I'm not too sure."

"Sure of what?" Lois asked.

"That Judith is the one. She might have wanted that toadstool to prove something to her own satisfaction."

"When will Diana telephone?" Lois asked.

"Any time. Soon, I hope. And I hope to God she's got something to tell us."

After dinner, as usual, Aunt Opal and Aunt Hester went into the chilly drawing room. The fire in the grate was laid but not lit.

Aunt Hester said impatiently, "How long are

we going to be without a maid? I suppose we won't be able to induce any girl to come to us now."

She went down on her knees and lit the fire herself, and Aunt Opal, without speaking, pulled a chair up and sat over the small blaze.

Lois went to the big windows and looked across the dark garden to the summer house where a light shone through the windows. Aunt Judith, of course, would have repaired to the place that was at once her refuge and her consolation. What was she doing there now? Working with her specimens or hatching further dark plans?

The telephone in the hall rang and everyone jumped.

Aunt Hester said, "It will be a call for Rodney. He hasn't had any all day except Mrs. Matthews. Nurse Baxter wasn't to put any through but urgent ones."

Lois heard Rodney answering the telephone. She hoped devoutly it wasn't a call. With the mounting tension in the house she couldn't bear to be left, even with Cass here.

Aunt Opal took up her knitting and began to work. Aunt Hester coaxed the fire, blowing into it vigorously and sending volumes of smoke into the room. All day, Lois realized, they had desperately been trying to behave normally because they knew that each one of them was suspect and any unusual action would arouse suspicion. In other circumstances it would have been pathetic. But one couldn't waste pity on any of them yet, because that one might be the guilty person.

What was Aunt Judith going to do with her precious toadstool?

Rodney stopped talking and Lois heard the click of the receiver.

"Come and get warm, Lois," Aunt Hester invited. "The nights are getting chilly now. But nothing, I might warn you, to what they will be."

Lois listened tensely for Rodney. He came into the room at last.

"Got to go out?" Aunt Hester asked.

"No. That wasn't a patient." He stopped to light a cigarette. His actions, too, were an attempt at absolute normality. "It was Diana Marcus."

"Oh! What did she want? News about the murder?"

Aunt Opal winced at Aunt Hester's bluntness.

"Hester!" she protested. Then she added, "I can't imagine what people must be saying about me. Was Diana very shocked, Rodney?"

"She's in London," Rodney said. "Gone up

to see her aunt."

"Her aunt," Aunt Opal mused. "Let me see, that would be Cora Lessing, I remembered meeting her once, years ago. She was very like Diana's mother. Rather an overbearing sort of person."

"What on earth does she want, ringing you from London?" Aunt Hester demanded.

Rodney, Lois realized, was going to follow his previous tactics of shocking someone into giving herself away.

"She thought her aunt might know something of importance associated with Willow. I suppose you two are aware Willow was an adopted child."

"Yes," Aunt Opal said quickly. "Poor darling. That's why we tried to be particularly kind to her. The Briggses are very worthy people, but not quite — well, you could see for yourselves that Willow was a great deal superior to them. She wasn't very well adjusted at home. One couldn't be surprised."

Did that, then, explain the absurd pampering that had gone on? But it was out of all proportion, considering that Willow was neither poor nor ill-treated.

"Did you know her parents?" Rodney asked.

"Wrong side of the blanket, wasn't it?" said Aunt Hester. "We wouldn't be likely to know

336

that. The Briggses didn't, either. Anyway, what can her parents possibly have to do with this business?"

"I don't know," said Rodney slowly. "Mrs. Lessing says her sister knew, but she isn't entirely sure. She thinks that Jed Hawkins may have been Willow's father."

"Jed Hawkins!" Aunt Hester exclaimed. "The gardener father sacked! Well, I never! He was a bad lot, sure enough. Good thing we got rid of him."

"I should think so!" Aunt Opal declared rather breathlessly. "Fancy that, Rodney. I suppose father found out and trumped up that excuse about the plants being stolen. We three were only girls then and father and mother were so careful what reached our ears."

"Just the sort of thing a handsome brute like that would do," Aunt Hester said. She was enjoying the scandal. "So that's where Willow got her looks."

"Do the Briggses know this?" Aunt Opal asked.

"Not yet."

"Then I hardly see any point in telling them. I think I heard some years ago that Jed had died."

"You heard, Opal? How could you possibly hear?"

"I don't remember. I think I read it in a newspaper. I really wasn't interested. It's so long ago."

"Jed Hawkins!" Aunt Hester was going to ruminate on this new and startling information all evening. "And we never even noticed how Willow resembled him. But of course now I can see the likeness. That hair!"

That beautiful silvery fair hair! Lois remembered the last time she had seen Willow alive when, from some whim, the girl had pinned her hair in too-elaborate curls on top of her head. On top of her head! So that when she had a hat on —

Lois gripped Rodney's arm. She was trembling with excitement.

"I know now," she gasped. "I know why Willow was mistaken for me."

She was conscious of everyone looking at her with startled interest.

"There was a hat I'd left on the bed," she went on. "A silly extravagant thing, all flowers, just the sort of thing Willow would want to try on — the way she always liked trying clothes on. It was on the floor beside her when I found her and I picked it up without thinking. But she had had it on! Of course she had had it on. It had hidden her hair. And when she was — attacked, it fell off and her

338

hair came down."

Rodney's eyes were narrowed to slits. He was looking beyond her at the two aunts. But Aunt Judith wasn't there. He couldn't see the effect of that information on her, also.

"That's it," he said. And now his voice was colder and harder than she had ever heard it. She hoped that never again would there be an occasion for him to speak like that. "Now we know where we are. We're not looking for Willow's murderer. We're looking for the person — in this house — who hoped to kill my wife!"

XIX

"That's done it," Cass said later. "Now someone will have to work fast."

"That's the idea," said Rodney. "We've got to force a showdown."

"Judith doesn't know yet."

"I gather she does. I saw Aunt Hester scuttling off down to the laboratory."

"Rodney, I can't follow it all," Lois said.

"I can't either, but soon enough we will."

"Did you telephone the inspector?" Cass asked.

"I did."

"What did he say?"

"He said, 'Ha!' He might have been Aunt Hester speaking. Then he said he'd be over first thing in the morning."

"Doesn't believe in hurrying," Cass remarked, and added with her devastating frankness, "Oh, well, I suppose because there isn't another body yet."

Aunt Opal had been left alone in the drawing room, but when Lois looked in there again she saw that the room was empty.

"She must have gone to bed," she said aloud.

Behind her Rodney said, "And that's where you belong, too. You've had a pretty strenuous day for someone who has just been ill."

All at once Lois realized her overpowering tiredness. But though her body was tired her brain was wide awake. She knew she wouldn't sleep.

"You come, too, darling."

"I will presently. I'll bring you up a hot drink."

"And put something in it again?"

"Weren't you glad to get a good sleep last night?"

"Yes, I was, but don't do that tonight. I might —" She didn't know why she was afraid, since she would not be alone; Rodney would be at her side. "I might need to wake up quickly."

Rodney nodded slowly.

"All right, darling. You'll sleep without it, anyway. I'll bring you hot milk."

It was as she was passing Aunt Opal's room

on the way to the bathroom that she heard Aunt Opal call.

"Is that you, Lois?"

"Yes, Aunt Opal."

"Come in a minute, dear. I want to talk to you."

From the little window at the end of the landing she could see across the garden the light shining from the summer house. Aunt Judith was still there concocting her potions. As long as she stayed that far away, it was all right.

Unhesitatingly she went into Aunt Opal's room.

Aunt Opal was in bed. She had on a lacy soft-looking bed jacket and her hair hung in plaits on either side of her face. She looked wan and tired and completely harmless. It was impossible to think that she had any knowledge of or any part in the recent events.

Looking at her Lois could feel nothing but sympathy for her. Poor Aunt Opal, who had lavished all the affection of her starved heart on pretty Willow and now was left with nothing.

"Sit down for a few minutes, dear," she said to Lois. "I felt tired so I came to bed. Bed is such a refuge, isn't it? It's so difficult to keep going normally, and then when I'm stupid enough to faint Hester gets so cross. Hester

342

isn't the sensitive kind. But she can't help that, so I mustn't criticize her."

All Aunt Opal wanted, Lois realized, was to ease her mind by prattling a little. She was a natural prattler, and the atmosphere downstairs for the last two days must have been a terrific weight on her.

"I wanted to tell you," Aunt Opal went on, "how sorry I am that you have had this tragic beginning to your married life."

"Don't worry about it now, Aunt Opal," Lois said uneasily.

"But I do worry about it. All the time. Particularly since you think someone meant to kill you. Oh, my poor dear child!"

"Don't you think so, too?" Lois asked, borrowing Cass's bluntness.

"My dear, I don't know what to think. I'm afraid to think. I'm only so sorry you've had this dreadful time."

The queer thing was, Lois was convinced of Aunt Opal's absolute sincerity. She was shocked and grieved that Rodney's wife should have had those things happen to her.

"It hasn't been easy for anyone, Aunt Opal."

"You're Rodney's wife," Aunt Opal went on in her crooning, caressing voice. "You're such a pretty thing, too. Your soft dark hair. No wonder Rodney lost his head for once. We had thought, my sisters and I, that he was so serious he would never lose his head. Then he sent us that telegram that he was married and we got so excited. I, at least, could scarcely wait for him to bring you home."

Was she going to reminisce all night? Lois moved restlessly. But politeness and pity for the tired sad woman in the bed kept her there.

"I wanted you to be so happy here. Rodney's wife. I've dreamed about what she would be like ever since that day father brought Rodney here. And Marguerite, too, of course."

Lois forgot her impatience.

"What was Marguerite like?" she asked eagerly.

"Oh, quite a good-looking young woman. Rather tired-looking. Those hot countries spoil a woman's looks. And she hadn't much spirit, we thought. Of course, she had lost her husband and was still in mourning. And her health wasn't very good. She was ailing off and on all the time until she died."

Poor Marguerite. What had they done to her here to break her spirit, to make her ill? And *why?*

"But Rodney!" Aunt Opal went on fondly. "He was such a stand-offish little boy. Summed everybody up from a distance and wouldn't be touched."

So he had been untouchable even then, Lois reflected, thinking of the small shy proud boy standing his ground.

"But we soon became great friends," Aunt Opal went on. "Father wouldn't have him spoiled; he didn't understand small boys, not small lonely boys, but I used to make it up to him in little ways."

What about his mother? Lois wanted to ask. Didn't she love and comfort him? Or had they taken her child from her as surely as they had destroyed Lois's own baby?

"How old was he when his mother died, Aunt Opal?"

"About seven, if I remember rightly. Poor girl, she had never really settled down here. She was always so low-spirited. Sometimes I think it was a blessing she was taken."

"If she wasn't happy why did she stay here?"

"She had no relatives and nowhere else to go. And father was very good to her, unnecessarily generous, I and my sisters used to think, considering how our brother had behaved. But she just didn't seem to settle down. Now you, my dear, must be different. You must be very happy here. We want you to be happy."

Her voice was almost pleading. Did she know that yesterday Lois had planned to leave and never come back? Was she growing afraid, like grandfather, that there would be no heirs? That was the logical conclusion, but again Lois had the unreasoning feeling that Aunt Opal was genuinely desirous for her own happiness, as an individual, excluding altogether the fact that she was now an Armour with a duty to her husband and the Armour family.

"So far it hasn't been very easy to be happy here," she said in a hard voice.

"I know, child, I know. But this will pass." She smiled vaguely and tenderly. "Kiss me good night, dear. I mustn't keep you up any longer. You look worn out."

With the briefest feeling of repulsion Lois stooped and kissed the lined forehead. As she stood up again she noticed, for the first time, the beautiful antique design of the lamp on the table beside Aunt Opal's pillow.

"That's a nice thing," she said. "Where did you get it?"

"The lamp, dear? In Switzerland. In a little shop in a mountain village."

"I didn't know you'd ever been abroad."

"Oh, yes. Years ago. I did what was once known as the Grand Tour. France, Spain, Italy, Switzerland. It was very enjoyable. In those days I was more adventurous."

She smiled placidly.

"And in all those countries you never once

fell in love!" Lois joked. "Not even with a handsome Swiss mountaineer!"

Was it her fancy that a shadow crossed Aunt Opal's face, destroying briefly its placidity? Was it? It must have been, for the next moment Aunt Opal was patting her hand and saying, "You young things! You think of nothing but love. Don't think I haven't had my broken hearts, too! Now off to bed with you. And sleep well, Lois dear. Everything will be all right."

Rodney was waiting for her when she returned to the bedroom.

"Your milk's getting cold," he said. "Where have you been?"

"Just saying good night to Aunt Opal. She's garrulous tonight. Do you know, I have the feeling she's recovering from Willow's death and she's going to transfer her affections to me."

"These starved women with their surplus of emotions!" Rodney groaned.

"Rodney, we really ought to be sorry for her. She was so determined to be cheerful, but I expect the moment I went out she was crying for Willow."

"I'm not wasting my sympathy on anyone," Rodney said in his hard aloof voice, "until I know who's guilty."

Now he was the small wary boy withholding his affections until he knew surely where to bestow them. Because if you bestowed them on the wrong person you got very hurt. Was that what had happened to Rodney in his childhood? He had been so hurt that he had shut his innermost person away?

Lois, wearily, began to undress.

"Has Aunt Judith come in yet?"

"Yes. She's gone to her room. She said she wasn't feeling well."

"Did she say anything else?"

"Not a word. She seemed deep in thought."

"About her horrid toadstool, I expect."

"Darling, don't worry about the toadstool. We won't be caught that way again, and I doubt if anyone would be foolish enough to try it."

"They do such childish things, Rodney, that you don't know what to expect next. Where's Cass?"

"Finishing up downstairs. And Aunt Hester's fixing some carrots for those poor devils of rabbits. Then she's coming to bed."

"She likes killing them," Lois murmured. "It's a game to her."

She gave herself a little shake, determined to put those thoughts out of her head.

"Then you come to bed, too, Rodney.

Nothing more can happen tonight."

The talk with Aunt Opal had done her good, she reflected. She felt more normal, less afraid. She could even shut her eyes without seeing Willow's lovely graceful body slumped across the dressing table. And Rodney was beside her, warm and reassuring and safe.

On the edge of sleep she said drowsily, "Rodney, was there any significance about Jed Hawkins being Willow's father?"

"I don't know. There might be. I'll find out."

"In the morning, Rodney. Everything can wait until the morning."

Then again, after she had drifted off to sleep and half wakened, she thought she heard footsteps going down the passage, the stairs creaking. But that was part of her dream.

XX

It was past midnight, however, when she and Rodney were really awakened, and then it was in a sudden and terrifying manner, by someone screaming.

The screams came from the direction of one of the aunts' rooms. They sounded three times in quick succession, then there was silence. The silence was more terrifying than the screams.

Rodney leaped out of bed and switched on the light.

"Who is it?" Lois whispered.

"I don't know. You'd better stay there."

Lois hastily got out of bed.

"No, don't leave me alone. I'll come."

She followed Rodney into the dark passage.

There was still utter silence. But a shaft of light shone from the open door of Aunt Opal's room. Rodney made towards it. At the same time Cass appeared in the passage.

"Thank God it's not you!" she exclaimed on seeing Lois. "Who is it? Opal? I suppose she's seen a mouse." Her derisive voice didn't succeed entirely in hiding her apprehension. She pressed after Rodney into Aunt Opal's room, and Lois followed.

The scene there was completely unexpected. Aunt Opal, apparently unhurt, was sitting on the edge of the bed. Lois noticed ludicrously her little pale blue veined feet and thin ankles sticking out beneath her nightgown. She noticed next her wrung hands and her face crumpled and pallid with fear.

"What's wrong, Aunt Opal?" Rodney was asking. "What made you scream?"

"There was someone in here," Aunt Opal quavered. "I woke and heard someone."

"Who was it?"

"I couldn't see, it was too dark."

"What were they doing?"

"They were going through my bureau. I heard a drawer shut. That's what woke me. And I could see a figure and a ray of light, from a flashlight, I expect. I was so frightened I screamed. I should have put the light on, of

351

course." Her attempt at apology for her lack of presence of mind was pathetic. "But I just lost my head and screamed. And whoever it was went out."

"What would they be looking for in your bureau?" Rodney asked.

"I haven't the faintest notion. There's nothing there that could interest anyone — only my personal belongings. Why would they be interfering with my things?"

Rodney said in the impersonal voice that he now used all the time when he spoke to the aunts, "Get back into bed, Aunt Opal."

Aunt Opal did so, shakily, and Lois helped to straighten the blankets over her.

"Thank you, dear," Aunt Opal said, looking up at Lois with her large dilated eyes. "I suppose I gave you all a fright."

Cass was shutting one of the bureau drawers that had been left half open. It held handkerchiefs and gloves and odd ribbons and lace. One glove lay on the floor where it had fallen when the intruder had hastily scrabbled in the contents of the drawer.

"You must have some idea who this person was," Rodney was continuing.

"It may have been a burglar," Aunt Opal said faintly.

"Nonsense. A burglar isn't interested in the

odds and ends a woman keeps in her bureau. It was someone in the house, Aunt Opal."

Aunt Opal's mouth quivered again with helpless fear.

"You mean – it must have been Hester or Judith."

Rodney nodded.

"But what would – they want –"

"You know that better than I do. What do you keep in your drawers?"

"Only my personal clothing – a little jewelry – one or two sentimental things of our mother's." Her voice grew stronger. "Nothing Hester or Judith could possibly want, that is, if one of my own sisters is going to rob me."

"Hester and Judith are very different in appearance," Rodney said. "Even in the dark – it wasn't entirely dark if they had a flashlight – you must have noticed something that would indicate which one it was. Please try to remember. It may be very important."

Aunt Opal's fingers opened and closed on the blankets. Her knuckles were bone white, as if no skin at all covered them.

"That heavy way Hester breathes when she's absorbed in something," she said reluctantly. "I thought I noticed that." Then she started up in alarm. "Please don't go and accuse her!

Please don't! I'd rather nothing were said."

"Why?" Rodney asked bluntly. "If Hester has been messing around with your personal belongings why should she escape scot-free?"

"In any case," Cass said suddenly, "where are your charming sisters? Are they deaf at nights?"

"Aunt Judith's room is around the turn in the passage at the east end," Lois said. "She might not have heard anything."

"But Aunt Hester must have," Rodney added. He looked down at Aunt Opal. "You'll be all right now. No one's likely to worry you again and obviously no harm was intended to you yourself. Try to get some sleep."

"Yes, Rodney," Aunt Opal said meekly. "But don't bother Hester or Judith tonight. It isn't necessary. I'm just all on edge, the things that have been happening." She smiled pathetically. "But I'm feeling better now. I think I shall sleep. So sorry to have been such a bother."

Out in the passage, with the door into Aunt Opal's room shut, Cass said in a low voice, "That woman knows something and she's scared to death we'll find it out. She's kicking herself that she was such a fool as to scream. Well, what do we do now? See Hester?"

"Definitely," Rodney answered. "We've got to know whether she found what she wanted."

354

Aunt Hester's room was in darkness, and a sleepy voice answered Rodney's knock.

"What is it?"

Rodney unceremoniously switched on the light and went in. Aunt Hester sat up in bed. Her attempt at drowsiness was a little too obvious.

"What the devil do you all want?" she asked irritably. "Has anyone else been murdered?"

"What did you find in Aunt Opal's bureau?" Rodney asked.

"I? Find?"

"None of that innocent stuff," Rodney said impatiently. "You're not deaf and you're too close to Aunt Opal's room, not to hear her scream. If it wasn't you in there why didn't you get up to find out what was wrong?"

He picked up a flashlight that lay on the table by Aunt Hester's bed and handled it ostentatiously.

Aunt Hester said sullenly, "Oh, Opal and her hysterics. If she hadn't woken up I might have found something. But I didn't."

"What were you looking for?"

"Nothing," she began. Then she thought better of it and said, "If you must know, it was only a guess on my part, but Opal's the kind of person to hoard sentimental things. I thought there might have been some old letters."

"Such as?" Rodney prodded.

"Well, I had an idea Opal was soft on that white-haired gardener, that scoundrel Jed Hawkins. When you said tonight that Willow was his kid I thought Opal might have known that all along, and that's why she was so stuck on the girl. A transference of affections, do you see what I mean?"

"To the illegitimate daughter of a man you loved," Cass said skeptically. Then she added, "Could be, with a bundle of perverted emotions like Opal."

"Well, that's all," Aunt Hester said ungraciously. "And it's caused a lot of rumpus about nothing. Now, if you'll all get out, I might get some sleep."

Cass went back with Lois and Rodney to their bedroom.

"Does that stuff of Hester's sound plausible?" she asked.

"I think it may," Rodney said reflectively. "Certainly Aunt Opal is the type of person to hoard old letters."

"She was in love with someone once," Lois said suddenly. "I remember her telling me. She was very secretive about it, just making enigmatic remarks about broken hearts." Then she added, "But we've no right to pry into poor Aunt Opal's love affairs unless they have any bearing on this business. And I don't really see how they can have. Jed Hawkins sounds to have been a most inconstant person for a nice girl to break her heart over."

"It could be why grandfather sacked him," Rodney said. "He'd found out he was flirting with Aunt Opal as well as getting one of the village girls into trouble. Well, Cass, there's a job for you."

"I know," Cass said briefly. "Search Aunt Opal's bureau. And I hope a little more skillfully than Hester did. But not tonight. I'll watch my opportunity. We can't have any more of that screeching."

"No, go back to bed and get some sleep," Lois said. "If you can."

"Trust me to sleep," said Cass. She yawned widely "Good night, children. Pleasant dreams."

How could one's dreams be pleasant in a place that was alive with suspicion, fear and hatred? In spite of Rodney's reassuring arm around her Lois felt she would never sleep again under this roof. She kept seeing Aunt Opal's quivering face, her stricken eyes and her little clenched hands; then Aunt Hester sitting up in bed, full of bravado that only half concealed her fear; and Aunt Judith the way she had been at the dinner table, darting her sly glances at her sisters, provoking them with her secrecy and then growing defiant and hostile.

Whatever affection there had been between the three sisters was now destroyed. One of them was guilty and the other two were, perforce, filled with suspicion and fear. Which was the one who, knowing all, felt neither suspicion nor fear? Judith, sly amusement at her sister's antics, or because she genuinely had heard nothing? Hester, who may have been searching for something, or who may have planned to attack Opal in the dark? Opal, who had cherished a foolish and hopeless romance for a good-for-nothing gardener?

Lois, with her brain whirling, thought there was no more sleep for her that night. But the next thing she was aware of was a faint gray daylight on the window pane and someone tapping gently but insistently at the door.

"Who's there," she called. Her voice woke Rodney and he rolled over sleepily.

"It's for Rodney, dear," came Aunt Opal's voice. "The telephone. Rodney's wanted."

Rodney raised himself on his elbow.

"The devil!" he muttered. He raised his voice, "Who is it?"

"Mr. Matthews, dear. The baby you delivered yesterday."

"What's wrong with it? It was a fine healthy baby."

"Not the baby, Rodney. The mother. She's running a high temperature."

Rodney swung his legs out of bed. He reached for his trousers.

"I'll have coffee ready for you," Aunt Opal called. "I'm just going down."

No Willow to make the early morning coffee, Lois thought. She was aware of a peculiar feeling of fear, different from anything she had yet experienced. Hitherto she had had sensations of danger and panic, but not this cold infiltration of utter terror. She could feel her mouth dry and the palms of her hands damp. She was shivering with cold.

"Rodney!" she pleaded. "Must you go?"

He was already in his trousers and putting on his shirt.

"I'll have to. But I'll be as quick as I can. Go in to Cass. Wake her and stay with her all the time I'm away. Promise."

Lois nodded miserably.

"I promise, but —"

"But what?"

"Nothing. I just feel — I can't explain it, Rodney." Her voice was rising in sheer hysteria.

"It's this ungodly hour, darling. And you've

had a disturbed night."

"Rodney, you said all the attempts had been made in a haphazard way with whatever weapon came to hand."

"Yes."

"Then how can we possibly be prepared? I might just be walking downstairs, or – or taking a bath."

Rodney sat on the edge of the bed and took her hands between his.

"You're trembling," he said. "Your hands feel like sparrows – cold and scared to death. Darling, I'll be back as soon as I possibly can. Before you and Cass have awakened again. Come, and I'll take you in to Cass."

Lois got out of bed and let him put on her wrap.

"I'm sorry," she said. "I've got the jitters. I guess it is the early morning."

Cass was just waking.

"You've got to go out?" she said to Rodney. "Too bad. Who answered the telephone?"

"Aunt Opal. She's downstairs making me coffee."

Cass sat bolt upright.

"What a wonderful opportunity to get into that bureau of hers. Come along, Lois. Here we go."

"Then watch your step," Rodney cautioned.

"I'll slam the hall door when I'm leaving, so you'll know she'll be on her way up. And Cass —"

"Sure," Cass nodded, looking at Lois. "I won't let her out of my sight."

Lois felt shame and contrition at going into Aunt Opal's room and deliberately prying into her private possessions. No such qualms affected Cass, however. She was at the bureau and delving into the drawers without wasting a moment.

"My guess is," she said, "that there's a false bottom to one of these drawers. Or maybe a locked jewel box, and the key hidden in the toe of a stocking. There'll be a bunch of love letters tied with faded blue ribbon, all right. And maybe a lock of hair. Or I haven't read our Opal correctly."

"Cass!" Lois said urgently.

"What's the matter, kid? If we don't do this, the police will. Better us than that long-nosed inspector."

"It's not that, Cass. I'm just thinking about the telephone."

"What about it?" Cass looked up. "Gosh, child, you look as if you'd seen your own ghost. What's wrong?"

"I don't know." Lois tried to rid herself of that cold creeping fear that was keeping her trembling. "I was just wondering how, if

Rodney couldn't hear the telephone, Aunt Opal could."

"Rodney was sound asleep and Aunt Opal was awake. That's the answer."

"But, Cass, if it's audible at all Rodney hears it. He hears it in his sleep. He's trained himself to do it. And our room is nearer the stairs than Aunt Opal's."

"He could have slept particularly heavily," Cass reflected. "Who has usually called him in the past?"

"Willow or Clara. They were both downstairs and couldn't fail to hear a ring."

"Then Kate will have heard it this morning."

"Of course," Lois said eagerly. "I'll go down and ask her."

"Good idea," Cass agreed. "And you might detain Opal downstairs a while, also. Give me some scope."

The house was completely still as Lois went downstairs. It was lighter now, objects in the hall were clearly visible, and outside there was the first intermittent cawing from the crows.

Lois hurried across the hall and down the passage towards the kitchen. Kate's room, which had been Clara's, was the first on the left. The door was slightly ajar, so that Kate must have heard the telephone ringing. Why, then, hadn't she answered it instead of waiting for Aunt Opal to come downstairs?

Lois tapped and put her head around the door. Kate was still in bed, but awake. On seeing Lois she started up guiltily.

"Why, Mrs. Armour! It isn't that late, is it?"

"No, Kate. It's early still. I just wanted to ask you whether you heard the telephone ring in the last ten minutes."

"No ma'am. It hasn't rung. I'd have heard it all right if it had because those blinking birds woke me half an hour ago. Anything wrong, ma'am?"

"No, Kate. At least I don't think so. You'd better get up, I think."

She closed the door again and stood in the passage trying to control the violent beating of her heart. They wanted to get Rodney out of the house so that when he had gone she would be there at their mercy. Cass – but no doubt Cass could be disposed of in some way, too.

This murderer was haphazard, doing the thing that entered her head first, like faking up a telephone message to get rid of Rodney. It needn't necessarily be Aunt Opal. She could be the go-between, the one who innocently carried the message, as gullible as Rodney and herself. . . . Hester or Judith could be up and concealed somewhere. . . .

Somehow Lois pulled herself together and

forced herself to walk steadily to the kitchen. She had to stop Rodney before he left. Thank heaven she had had that premonition upstairs, that chilly sensation of intense fear.

She pushed open the kitchen door and saw Rodney standing in his overcoat, about to pick up the cup of steaming coffee Aunt Opal had placed in front of him. Aunt Opal herself, in her soft warm dressing gown, looked cherubic and kind.

"Drink that," she was saying in her crooning voice. "It's chilly these mornings, quite frosty. It'll keep the cold out on your drive."

"Thanks, Aunt Opal," Rodney said, lifting the cup.

"Rodney!" Lois cried from the doorway. "It's a trick. The telephone didn't ring! You mustn't go!"

"A trick!" Rodney glanced sharply from Lois to Aunt Opal.

"It's a ruse to get you out of the way so while you're gone they can kill me!" Lois insisted breathlessly.

"Lois, what an extraordinary thing to say!" Aunt Opal exclaimed, her eyes wide.

"Is it true?" Rodney demanded harshly.

"I'll find out, Rodney. It was Judith who answered the telephone. She was up early and on her way to her laboratory — she's making some experiment with that nasty toadstool – and she called out to me that you were wanted urgently. But perhaps I misunderstood. I'll go and ask her. First, though, let me pour Lois a cup of coffee. She looks frozen. And drink yours, Rodney, before it gets cold."

"Rodney, don't believe it!" Lois whispered. "They want to kill me!"

Rodney put his arm around her.

"Sit down and have some coffee, like Aunt Opal says. There!" Aunt Opal, with her gentle smile, put a brimming cup in front of Lois. "We'll get to the bottom of this in a moment."

Reassured by his calmness – nothing *could* happen to her while Rodney stayed in the house – Lois pulled the cup towards her.

"Silly child," said Aunt Opal in her soft voice. "Who wants to kill you now?"

Now! Why *now?* What had altered the situation? What did Aunt Opal . . . Her thoughts breaking off as she lifted her eyes, Lois saw Aunt Opal's face. She was watching Rodney lifting his cup to his lips and for one unguarded moment . . .

"Don't drink it!" Lois shrieked. "Rodney! Don't!"

Then she hid her eyes from the expression on Aunt Opal's face, the expression of frustration, of madness, of bitter black hate.

"Are you going to listen to an hysterical girl?" she heard the cold deliberate remorseless voice that had spoken to Willow in the passage that morning say, a voice so removed in tone from Aunt Opal's gentle croon that it was impossible to believe it came from the same person.

"Certainly I am," said Rodney quietly. "Lois's intuitions are pretty sound. I should have taken notice of them long ago." He put down the cup, careful to spill none of the liquid.

"Don't be such a fool, Rodney! What do you think is in the coffee? Toadstool poison? Judith —"

"You can't put this on Judith, Aunt Opal. It was Judith's spider, Hester's soup — you thought you were so clever — but this is your coffee. Entirely yours." He paused and asked, almost with curiosity, "Why should you want to kill me, Aunt Opal?"

Aunt Opal took a step backward. Her eyes were dilated and terrifying. There was no other change in her round soft face, only those dilated eyes. But she was breathing rapidly. And she had given up dissembling.

"Why shouldn't I?" she demanded harshly. "Why should you live when Willow is dead? Why should you have everything, you who aren't even an Armour? I know, you see. I've known for years, ever since your mother, your adopted mother, told me in her delirium." She clenched her hands so that Lois thought the bones would break through the flesh. "Why didn't you marry Willow, you fool? Then everything would have been all right. But since you didn't —" she met Rodney's gaze with a long hard bitter stare. Then, abruptly, her face crumpled. Lois saw despair, hopelessness, again that frightening madness. "I did it," she muttered. "I killed Willow. I thought she was Lois. I stuck the knife in her back — hard. . . ."

With a trembling hand she reached for Rodney's coffee cup.

"If you don't want this," she said heavily, "I'll tip it out."

Rodney made a quick movement to follow her to the sink. Then he stopped. He stood rigid.

"Don't let her!" Lois moaned.

The perspiration was standing out on Rodney's forehead. His face was gray. As Aunt Opal swayed and the cup fell from her hands he leaped forward and caught her.

"It was the only way," he said desperately. "Don't you see? It was the only way."

Lois looked at Aunt Opal's contorted body.

"What — was it?" she got out between her

stiff lips.

"Strychnine, I should think. Probably enough to kill a man ten times over. Poor crazy creature! Call Cass, darling. And then telephone the police."

XXI

Long after, although in time it was less than an hour, for the sun was scarcely above the treetops and the birds were still busy with their early morning frenzy, Cass said in her practical, comforting, matter-of-fact voice, "I suppose you've all guessed that Willow was her child!"

They were all in the cheerful morning room, with its honey-colored wallpaper, its bright cushions, its little low chair at the window where Aunt Opal had used to sit. Aunt Judith was dressed, but her hair hadn't been combed and she looked strange and fierce beneath the untidy locks. Aunt Hester's mouth was set in a grim line – to stop its treacherous trembling, Lois guessed. Aunt Hester's façade of bravado

369

was always so frail. At first it had scarcely hidden her fear and now her shocked grief was showing through.

"No!" Aunt Judith gasped. "I never once guessed that."

"That's because you were always so wrapped up in your old specimens," Aunt Hester said impatiently, but with an undertone of tolerance and kindness. "I've known all along there was some reason above simply being fond of the girl that made Opal pamper Willow so ridiculously. The quarrels we three have had about that — Judith and I trying either to get rid of Willow or bring Opal to her senses. But no, she must go on and completely ruin a girl who might otherwise have been a good maid."

"The way they fight about me," Willow had said smugly. But it wasn't in the way Lois had interpreted, after all. If only she had known Hester and Judith shared her dislike of Willow — it might have made a difference; they might all have behaved differently. But nothing could be changed now.

"Father disliked her, too," Aunt Hester went on. "But I'm sure he never guessed the truth. He just wanted an excuse to get her out of the house. And apparently he got that when he found she'd had something to do with the spider."

"And did — did Opal really kill father?" Aunt Judith asked Rodney in a shocked voice.

"It seems probable," Rodney admitted. "But I don't think that was premeditated. She was worrying about grandfather saying Willow had to go — she knew he didn't say things idly — and in the night, when she found him ill, it must have flashed into her head how simple it would be just to turn him sideways and hold his head in the pillow. He would be too weak to struggle. Besides the trouble about Willow, she must have hated him for years, ever since he sacked Jed Hawkins."

Lois slipped her arm through Rodney's. She hated to see his face so gaunt.

"It's over darling," she whispered. "It's over and we couldn't have stopped it."

"The spider and the toadstool," Aunt Judith reflected, "wouldn't have been meant to really kill Lois, but to frighten her away. If they did kill, well and good, it would be more like an accident than ever. But the spider didn't bite her and the toadstool wasn't really deadly enough. I know, because I experimented with it last night. I ate a small piece and it merely made me uncomfortable. So the amount Lois got wouldn't be fatal, although it could make her very ill."

"You deliberately did that to try to solve

things!" Lois exclaimed.

"The true scientist," Rodney said. His voice held both affection and admiration. "Good for you, Aunt Judith."

Aunt Judith flushed and looked embarrassed. Her eyes no longer seemed sly to Lois. They were both shy and observant.

"Someone had to do something," she said. "I had a pretty good idea Opal took that toadstool, but I wanted to be sure it was that that had upset Lois."

"And all this," Aunt Hester said incredulously, "was so that Opal could marry off her illegitimate daughter to Rodney!"

"Not illegitimate," Cass interrupted surprisingly. She had a folded paper in her hand. "I found what you couldn't last night, Hester. Your dear sister's marriage lines. Opal was married to Jed Hawkins in a register office, apparently at the time she went on that tour abroad."

"She married him!" Hester exclaimed. "I remember that time. She was ailing and father said she had better have a complete change. I remember suspecting it was something to do with being too fond of Jed Hawkins, but of course you couldn't talk about that sort of thing to father."

"Mrs. Briggs said Willow had been born in

Italy," Lois observed. The whole tragic story was like a jigsaw puzzle, fitting together piece by piece.

"So Jed went with her!" said Aunt Judith. "As her husband! Opal, the deceitful creature!"

"Then why didn't she bring him back with her?" Rodney asked.

Cass said, "It wasn't pleasant reading someone else's private correspondence – but apparently Jed walked out on her in Rome. He left a note. She's got it up there with her marriage license. It's the most heartless thing I've ever read, especially when she was expecting a baby. I should say Willow was a chip off the old block." She looked around the room. "I've worked it out this way. Opal knew if she came back to Crow Hollow as Mrs. Jed Hawkins the old man would toss her out – then, I suspect, was when her mind first showed signs of growing unsound. Anyway, she decided to wait until the baby was born, get it adopted where she could keep an eye on it, and come back as she had gone, a single woman. Then she would bide her time. Well, as you all know, she bided her time. . . ."

"She got the idea that Willow should marry Rodney and get her rightful place that way," said Aunt Hester.

"With no questions asked," Cass added.

"But Rodney married Lois instead," Aunt Judith said. "And without warning. What a panic Opal must have been in. She never showed it. I'll say that for her. She could keep her own counsel."

"Mrs. Marcus must have known this," Lois said suddenly. "She warned me."

"She knew Opal was keen on Jed," Aunt Hester said. "She probably guessed the rest. She must have seen Willow's likeness to her father where we didn't."

"Opal still hoped to retrieve matters by frightening Lois away," Cass said. "When that failed she got serious — with the butcher's knife, and with that dangerous strychnine of yours, Hester, that I'd get rid of right off, if I were you. But she made a mistake and killed the wrong person. When Willow died she decided that not Lois, who was no longer of importance, but Rodney, could not live. However, Lois stepped in in time there. I must say that in some ways Opal was a great woman. She took that shock of discovering that she had mistakenly killed her own daughter right on the chin. Poor Opal. Events caught up with her." She looked at Rodney. "Well, that seems to be all. Shall we hand it all over to the inspector?"

"Not quite all," Rodney said. He had Lois's

hand in his and she could feel the hard clenching and unclenching of his fingers. "Aunt Opal seems to have known something about me that none of the rest of you know. Apparently by accident Marguerite told her, and she kept the secret for future use. First of all, you ought to know, Aunt Hester and Aunt Judith, that I'm not your brother's son. You all know your father's obsession about having an heir, particularly when his own son failed him and then died. Well, he got the idea of locating your brother's wife, whom he guessed would be in poor circumstances, and making her an offer. She was to be provided with an income and a permanent home at Crow Hollow if she adopted a child, a male child, and told nobody it was not her own."

Rodney drew a deep breath.

"Marguerite made the bargain, and I was that child. Grandfather never knew she hadn't kept the secret. Apparently it was only when she was very weak, almost dying — she wasn't happy here, Lois, but she died from natural causes — when it slipped out. I was brought up as an Armour. The price I had to pay was in my promise to live here, marry here and have my children here. Grandfather's passion for prolonging the Armour line was the greatest in his life. It was all right," he added, "until Aunt

Opal discovered that I was an impostor."

"How old were you then, Rodney?" Lois asked.

"About eight."

"And she made you feel you weren't wanted, you didn't belong."

"In little ways. She was very subtle."

"And so you —" Lois's voice caught. Now she understood so much, the shy lonely child who had never had a Christmas tree, the reserved boy living in himself. . . .

The doorbell rang long and violently.

"That'll be the inspector," Cass said. She looked at Lois and Rodney. "Why don't you two nip out the back way. Get some fresh air. I'll handle the inspector for half an hour."

Outside the air was like cold water, the lawns sparkled with dew. The top of the summer house caught the sun and shone like a gilded top. The crows flew back and forth, tossed black rags across the blue sky. The place was lovely but unreal, like something seen in a dream. Lois realized now why she had never felt at home here from the very first minute. It was because neither she nor Rodney belonged.

"Rodney," she said, "you don't owe anything to grandfather. He tried to buy you, and you can't buy people." She added under her breath, "You can only love them."

"Are you glad it's like this?" Rodney asked. She sighed.

"So glad. Now we're two people together, individuals, belonging to nobody but each other." Her face glowed. She was vividly conscious of him at her side, aware now that she knew all of him, there were no more withdrawals. . . .

Dexter, whistling, crossed the lawn in front of them. He had a crimson carnation in his buttonhole.

"Morning, miss. Morning, sir," he called cheerfully. "I'm late milking this morning."

"Come here, Dexter," Rodney called. "How much for the carnation?"

Dexter grinned. He took the flower out of his buttonhole and handed it to Rodney.

"I knocked it off with the mower. Guess you can have it, sir."

"You come to London," said Rodney, "and we'll buy flowers from you every morning."

He tucked the heavily scented bloom into the neck of Lois's dress. His eyes were bright, laughing, alert. He seized her hand.

"How do you like the city today, darling?"

"Wonderful! And the flowers are so cheap."

"And the air suits your complexion. And I love you very much."

He bent to kiss her. Dexter across the lawn

stopped to look and grin.

"But the damn place is too crowded," he complained. "Can't we ever be alone?"

THORNDIKE PRESS HOPES you have enjoyed this Large Print book. All our Large Print titles are designed for the easiest reading, and all our books are made to last. Other Thorndike Press Large Print books are available at your library, through selected bookstores, or directly from the publisher. For more information about our current and upcoming Large Print titles, please send your name and address to:

THORNDIKE PRESS
ONE MILE ROAD
P.O. Box 157
THORNDIKE, MAINE 04986

There is no obligation, of course.